SLAUGHTER
OF EAGLES

SLAUGHTER OF EAGLES

WILLIAM W. JOHNSTONE
with J. A. Johnstone

PINNACLE BOOKS
Kensington Publishing Corp.
www.kensingtonbooks.com

PINNACLE BOOKS are published by

Kensington Publishing Corp.
119 West 40th Street
New York, NY 10018

PUBLISHER'S NOTE
Following the death of William W. Johnstone, the Johnstone family is working with a carefully selected writer to organize and complete Mr. Johnstone's outlines and many unfinished manuscripts to create additional novels in all of his series like The Last Gunfighter, Mountain Man, and Eagles, among others. This novel was inspired by Mr. Johnstone's superb storytelling.

All Kensington titles, imprints, and distributed lines are available at special quantity discounts for bulk purchases for sales promotions, premiums, fund-raising, educational, or institutional use. Special book excerpts or customized printings can also be created to fit specific needs. For details, write or phone the office of the Kensington special sales manager: Kensington Publishing Corp., 119 West 40th Street, New York, NY 10018, attn: Special Sales Department; phone 1-800-221-2647.

PINNACLE BOOKS and the Pinnacle logo are Reg. U.S. Pat. & TM Off.
The WWJ steer head logo is a trademark of Kensington Publishing Corp.

ISBN-13: 978-0-7860-1870-3
ISBN-10: 0-7860-1870-4

First printing: August 2010

10 9 8 7 6 5 4 3 2 1

Printed in the United States of America

Chapter One

From the *MacCallister Eagle*:

Statue of Jamie Ian MacCallister
To Be Dedicated July 4th

The noted artist and sculptor Frederic Remington has, for some time now, been busy creating a life-size bronze statue of our founder, the late Colonel James Ian MacCallister. The work was commissioned by the MacCallister City Council and will be paid for by the city of MacCallister and the state of Colorado.

Governor Frederick Pitkin will be present for the dedication, and will be the featured speaker. Colonel MacCallister's children will be guests for the occasion, and will occupy positions of honor upon the stage with the governor. It is not mere coincidence that the dedication is to be held on the Fourth of July, for Colonel Jamie Ian MacCallister embodied all that was noble about our country and our

country's founders. Festivities for the event
are now being planned.

Falcon MacCallister read the article as he waited
for his lunch to be served at City Pig Restaurant.
The youngest son of the legendary Jamie Ian Mac-
Callister, Falcon was the biggest of all his siblings.
He had his father's size, with wide shoulders, full
chest, and powerful arms. And, of all his siblings,
he had come the closest to matching his father in
reputation.

However, he did have two siblings, the twins
Andrew and Rosanna who, in their own field, were
just as well known. Andrew and Rosanna MacCallister were, according to a recent article in the *New
York Times,* the "Toast of New York Theater." They
had performed for every president from U. S. Grant
to Chester Arthur, missing only James Garfield because assassination had limited his term to seven
months. They had also performed for the Queen of
England and the King of Sweden.

But they would not be present for the dedication
of their father's statue.

That very morning, Falcon had a letter from
Andrew and Rosanna, explaining they would be
unable to attend because they would be closing one
play on the fourth, and opening a new play one week
later. Falcon had visited them in New York a few
times, had gotten a glimpse of their world, and
though he wished they could come for the dedication, he understood why they couldn't. He was going
to have to explain it to his other siblings, and he
knew they would not be quite as understanding.

"Hello, Falcon, it's good to see you."

Falcon looked up from his paper and saw the Reverend and Mrs. Powell. He stood.

"Brother Charles, Sister Claudia," Falcon said, greeting his old friends with a smile. "How good to see you."

"Please, please, keep your seat," Reverend Powell said. "It's a wonderful thing, isn't it? I mean our town getting a statue of your father."

"Yes," Falcon said. "When I learned what the city council had in mind, I have to admit, I was very pleased."

"I have been asked to give the invocation," Reverend Powell said. He chuckled. "I told them, I'm retired now. They would be better off asking young Reverend Pyron."

"I asked that you give the convocation," Falcon said.

Reverend Powell smiled. "I thought, perhaps, you did. Though I'm sure there are others who are imminently more qualified."

"Nonsense," Falcon said. "Who better than you? You and my father were very close friends, and, like my father, you were one of the founders of the valley."

"I confess, Falcon, that I am both honored and pleased to have been asked to do the invocation. I am very much looking forward to it."

"Won't you join me for lunch?" Falcon invited.

"Claudia?" the reverend deferred to his wife.

"We would be pleased to join you," she said.

Falcon called the waiter over to take their order. "Delay my order until theirs is ready," he said.

"Yes, sir, Mr. MacCallister."

"Now," Falcon said as the waiter left. "Tell me what is going on in your life."

"We are about to be great-grandparents," Claudia said. "Any day now."

"Think of it, Falcon. That makes four generations of Powells. What have we loosed on this unsuspecting world," the Reverend teased.

The Dumey ranch, Jackson County, Missouri

As Falcon and the Reverend and Mrs. Powell enjoyed their lunch, 750 miles east, at a small ranch in Jackson County, Missouri, young Christine Dumey had come out to the barn to summon her brother, Donnie, to lunch.

"Hey, Christine, look at me!" young Donnie shouted at his sister. "I'm going to swing from this loft over to the other one."

"Donnie, don't you do that! You'll fall!" Christine warned, but, laughing at his older sister's concern, Donnie grabbed hold of a hanging rope, then took several running steps before leaping off into space. The rope carried him across and he landed on a pile of loose hay.

"Ha!" Donnie said as he got up and brushed away several bits of straw. "You thought I couldn't do it."

"You are lucky you didn't break your neck," Christine scolded.

"Ah, you are always such a 'fraidy cat," Donnie said.

"Mama said we need to wash up for dinner," Christine called up to him. Donnie was eleven, towheaded and freckle-faced. At thirteen, Christine was beginning to look more like a young woman than a little girl.

"I'll be right down," Donnie said. He walked over to the edge of the loft and looked out the big window, toward the main house. He saw three horses tied up at the hitching post. "Hey, Christine, who's here?" he asked. He grabbed onto another rope, then slid easily down to the ground.

"What do you mean, who is here?"

"There are three strange horses tied up at the hitching rail."

"I don't know. There was nobody here when I came out to get you. Maybe it's somebody wantin' to buy some livestock."

Donnie shook his head. "We ain't got nothin' to sell right now," he said. "Papa just sold off all the pigs. Got good money for them too."

"You look a mess. Come over to the pump. I'll pump water while you wash your face and hands. I wouldn't be surprised if you didn't have pig doo on you, somewhere."

"It's on my hands," Donnie said. Laughing, he ran his hands through Christine's hair. "And now it's in your hair."

"Donnie, stop it!" Christine shouted in alarm.

"Oh, don't get so excited, I didn't really put pig shit in your hair," Donnie said.

"Don't be using words like that."

"Words like what?"

"You know."

"How am I going to know, unless you tell me?" Donnie teased.

"You know exactly what I'm talking about. Hold your hands under the pump."

Donnie stuck his hands under the mouth of the pump and Christine worked the handle until a solid stream of water poured out. Then, wringing his hands to get rid of the water, Donnie and Christine walked into the house. As soon as they got inside they sensed something was wrong. Three men were standing in the kitchen, while Donnie's mother and father were sitting in chairs against the wall. Donnie's mother had cooked pork chops for dinner and one of the men was holding a pork chop in his hand. He had just taken a bite and a bit of it was hanging from his moustache. He was, by far, the biggest of the three. The other two men were not much taller than Donnie.

"Mama, Papa, what's going on?" Christine asked, the tone of her voice reflecting her concern.

"Children, these gentlemen are Egan Drumm, and Clete and Luke Mueller," Chris Dumey said.

"The Mueller brothers!" Donnie said.

One of the two small men smiled at Donnie, though the smile did nothing to ease the tension in the room.

"So, you've heard of us, have you?"

"I've heard you rob banks and trains," Donnie said.

"What do you think, Luke? We're famous."

"Shut up, Clete, you damn fool." Luke said.

"Where at's the money?" Egan Drumm asked. Using his teeth, he tore the last bit of meat from the pork chop bone, then tossed the bone onto the floor.

"What money?" Chris Dumey asked.

"Tell him what money, Luke," Drumm said.

Luke's pistol was in his holster, but he drew it and fired in the blink of an eye. The bullet hit Lillian Dumey in her left leg, and blood began to ooze down over her foot. She screamed out in pain, then doubled forward to grab the wound.

"Mama!" Christine shouted, and she ran to her mother.

"You son of a bitch!" Chris Dumey yelled angrily.

"I know you got a lot of money from selling your hogs yesterday," Drumm said. "So don't be playing dumb with me. I'm going to ask you one more time, where is the money, and if you don't answer, I'll put a bullet in her other leg."

"No, please! All right, all right, I'll tell you! Just don't hurt her anymore! The money is over there, in that vase, under the flowers.

Drumm nodded at Clete Mueller, and he walked over to the vase, picked it up, then threw it on the floor, smashing it. In the shards of broken glass, was a packet of bills, tied together with a string into one neat bundle.

"Ha!" Clete said, holding up the money. "Here it is!"

"How much is there?" Drumm asked.

Clete began to count. "Six hunnert dollars," he said after a moment.

Drumm smiled. "That's a pretty good haul," he said. "Two hunnert dollars apiece."

"That's an entire year's work," Dumey protested. "If you take that, how will I feed my family?"

"You won't have to worry about feedin' 'em," Drumm said.

"What do you mean?"

"I mean you'll all be dead." He shot Dumey down, and, laughing, Luke and Clete began shooting as well.

Some time later, Chris Dumey came to. For a moment, he wondered why he was lying on the kitchen floor, then remembered what had happened. Looking around he saw his wife, and both his children, lying lifeless on the floor with him.

There was blood everywhere. Dipping his finger into it, he began to write on the kitchen floor:

WE WAS KILT BY DRUM
AND MUELLER BR . . .

From there the letters trailed off and that was as far as he got before he died.

Egan Drumm and the Muellers rode hard, away from Dumey ranch, each with two hundred dollars in their pocket. They had ridden for a little better than an hour, when Clete spoke up.

"What do you boys say the next town we come to we get us a couple drinks and maybe a woman?"

"A woman, Clete?" Luke replied, laughing. "You want us to all share the same woman?"

"Well, why not? It'll be cheaper if we share one."

"I ain't sharin' a woman with nobody," Luke said. "What about you, Egan?"

"I ain't sharin' 'cause I ain't goin' into town," Drumm replied.

"Why not? We're far enough away, there ain't likely to be nobody aroun' here to know nothin' about what we just done. Fac' is, I doubt there's anyone here 'bout who has ever even heard of the Dumeys."

"That ain't it," Drumm said.

"Then what is?"

"I aim to go out on my own, now."

"Damn, Egan, you don't like us no more?" Clete asked.

"No, it ain't that," Drumm said. "It's just—well, think about it. We just kilt four people back there, and what did we get for it? Two hunnert dollars apiece. Two hunnert dollars, that's all."

"Two hunnert dollars ain't nothin' to sneeze at," Luke said. "Hell, if you was ridin' for twenty and found, it'd take you damn near a year to earn that much money."

"I know, I know, that's why I don't ride for twenty and found," Drumm said. "But I think I want to go out on my own, none the less. No hard feelin's."

"No hard feelin's," Luke replied.

As Luke and Clete turned their horses in the direction of the small town, Drumm continued to ride on in the same direction they had been going.

"Where do you reckon he's a'goin?" Clete asked.

"Who knows? He's got a burr in his saddle over somethin'," Luke replied. "Ahh, we don't need him. We'll find someone else to work with the next time we do a job, and when we do, it'll be a lot bigger than this one we just pulled."

"Yeah," Clete said. "We don't need him no more, no how."

Brownville, Colorado, one month later

In the Gold Digs Saloon Clete Mueller was talking with one of the bar girls. Talking was all he could do because he had already spent nearly all of the money he had gotten from the Dumeys.

Luke Mueller was playing cards with three others. Ollie Terrell was dealing the cards. He had only three fingers on his left hand. Bo Caldwell had a patch over his right eye, though a few minutes earlier he had removed the patch to scratch his eyebrow, and Luke saw there was no eye there at all, just a puff of scar tissue. The third man was Clarence Poole.

The Muellers had never met Terrell or Caldwell, but they knew Poole. They had served a little time with him in the Missouri State Penitentiary in Jefferson City.

"What the hell you dealin' for, Terrell?" Caldwell asked. "Hell, you can't even hold the cards proper."

"What do you care whether or not I can hold them proper? Hell, you got only one eye so you can't see 'em anyway," Terrell replied, and the others laughed.

"I like it when he deals. With no more fingers than he's got on that hand, that means he can't deal off the bottom of the deck," Poole said.

"You can tell he ain't a' doin' that," Caldwell said. "The onliest one of us winnin' is Luke Mueller. If I don't win somethin' soon, I'm goin' to have to get me a job some'eres."

"I've got a job for you," Luke said as he picked up the cards Terrell had just dealt.

"What kind of a job?" Caldwell asked. "'Cause I tell you true, I don't want to be shovelin' no shit out of a stall or nothin' like that."

"Believe me, it is nothin' like that," Luke answered. "It's quick, easy, and there's a lot of money in it."

"Ha!" Terrell said. "Where are you goin' to find somethin' that is quick, easy, and has a lot of money? Unless you're plannin' on robbin' a bank."

Luke looked at Terrell, but made no comment.

"What?" Terrell asked. "I'll be damned, that's it, ain't it? You're a' plannin' on robbin' a bank, ain't you?"

"Why don't you just go out into the street and shout it?" Luke asked.

Caldwell looked over at Poole. "You know this feller, Poole. Me'n Terrell don't. Is he serious?"

"You recruitin' people to ride with you?" Poole asked Luke, without responding to Caldwell's question.

"I might be," Luke replied. "That is, if I can find a few good men I can depend on."

A broad smile spread across Poole's face. "You know you can depend on me. I'm in," he said.

"What?" Caldwell asked. "You really are serious, ain't you?"

"Are you in, or out?" Luke asked.

"I'm in, hell yes," Caldwell replied.

"Me too," Terrell added, excitedly.

"What about Egan Drumm?" Poole asked.

"What about him?" Luke replied.

"Don't he ride with you and Clete? Where's he at?"

"I don't have no idea where he is," Luke said.

"So, what you're a' sayin' is that he ain't a' goin' to be a part of this," Poole said.

"That's what I'm sayin'."

"Good. I never liked that son of a bitch anyway. Don't know why you and Clete ever took to runnin' with him."

"When do we hold up this here bank?" Terrell asked.

Luke fixed a stare at Terrell, then he looked back at Poole. "Does this dumb bastard not know when to keep his mouth shut?"

"Who are you callin' a dumb bastard?" Terrell asked angrily.

"I'm callin' you a dumb bastard," Luke said coldly.

"Ollie," Caldwell said, reaching over to put his hand on Terrell's shoulder. "Don't get carried away here. You know damn well you don't want to get into a pissin' contest with Luke Mueller."

Suddenly Terrell realized how close he was getting to making a very foolish mistake, and he forced a smile. "Come to think of it," he said. "I guess I can be a dumb bastard from time to time."

Caldwell laughed to ease the tension, then the others laughed as well.

"To answer your question," Luke said. "It'll be tomorrow, over in a place called MacCallister."

MacCallister, Colorado, the next day

The Reverend Charles Powell and his wife, Claudia, were standing outside the bank when the teller, Clyde Barnes, opened the door to let them in.

"Good morning, Brother Powell, good morning, Mrs. Powell," the teller greeted. "You're here awfully early today. You must have some important business to attend to."

"More pleasure than business," Powell said. "We're going to Denver to see our new great-granddaughter, and I thought we might need a little walking around money."

"Walking around money? You mean you are going to walk to Denver? You aren't taking the train?" Barnes teased.

For a moment Powell didn't get it, then when he did, he laughed out loud.

"No train for us. I figured Claudia and I would just walk along the track 'til we got there," Powell said. "No, sir, who needs an old, loud, smelly train?" He laughed again.

"You aren't going to miss the dedication of Colonel MacCallister's statue, are you?" Barnes asked.

"Oh, goodness no. I wouldn't miss that for the world," Reverend Powell said. "But that's some time away, yet. We'll be back in plenty of time for that."

"I didn't think you would want to miss it. I've heard you are giving the invocation."

"I will be giving it, and mighty proud to do so," Reverend Powell said.

"Come on up to the window, Reverend, and I'll give you your money. Have you drawn the draft yet?"

"Yes, I have it right here," Reverend Powell said, pulling the draft from his pocket.

"Well then, we'll have you out of here in no time."

Suddenly the front door burst open and five men came charging into the bank. All five had their guns drawn, and they were so sure of themselves, that none of them were wearing masks. One of them had only one eye, and Mrs. Powell had to turn her head away in revulsion, rather than look directly at him.

"Everybody, get your hands up!" one of the men shouted. He was a small man, but the gun in his hand made him look big enough. "This is a bank robbery. Teller, get behind the cage and give us all the money you got!"

Barnes stepped around behind the counter, opened his drawer, and pulled out a couple hundred dollars. He handed it through the window to the robbers.

"What is this?" the small man asked. "Are you tellin' me this is all the money you've got in this bank?"

"There is more money in the safe, but it's locked and I don't have the combination," Barnes said. "Mr. Dempster only lets me have what he thinks I'll need durin' the day."

The leader of the group, the one who had given the teller his orders, turned his pistol on Claudia Powell and pulled the trigger. The woman let out a cry of pain, then fell.

"Now, you open that safe or someone else dies," the little man with the big gun said.

"What have you done?" Reverend Powell shouted. Even though he was unarmed, he started toward the shooter.

Calmly, and without changing the expression on his face, the little man fired again, and the good reverend went down, collapsing on the floor next to his wife. At that moment a young woman came into the bank, and the little man pointed his pistol toward her.

"No!" Barnes shouted. "Please, don't shoot her! That's my wife! I'll get the money for you!"

The small, evil man smiled. "So, you've suddenly remembered the combination to the safe, have you?"

"Yes, Mr. Mueller. Please, no more shooting."

"Luke, the son of a bitch knows us," one of the other men said. He was only a little taller than Luke.

Luke smiled. "What can I tell you, Clete? When you get as good at something as we are, people learn your name."

"That ain't good, is it?"

"It ain't all bad. If the law in this one horse town knows that it was the Mueller brothers who held up the bank, they'll be too scared to come after us."

Barnes returned from the safe, carrying a sack.

"This is it," he said. "This is all the money the bank has."

"Open the top. Let me look down inside," Luke Mueller said.

Barnes opened the top, disclosing several bound packets of twenty dollar bills.

"Now, that's more like it," Mueller said. He smiled, then took the bag. "It's been a real pleasure doing business with you," he said.

Chapter Two

The metal bit jangled against the horse's teeth. The horse's hooves clattered on the hard rock and the leather saddle creaked beneath the weight of its rider.

When Falcon MacCallister rode into town just before noon, he knew something had happened. It wasn't due to some sort of psychic perception, though the clues were so subtle that there are many who would not have picked up on them.

Nobody was pitching horseshoes alongside Sikes's Hardware Store.

No one was playing checkers in front of Boots and Saddles.

There were no clusters of women shoppers, standing on the corners, laughing and talking.

In fact there was a pall hanging over the town that was palpable. Wondering what was going on, Falcon stopped in front of the sheriff's office, swung down from his horse, tied it off, and stepped inside. The sheriff and two of his deputies were looking at a map they had spread out on a table.

"Good morning, Amos," Falcon said, greeting the newly elected sheriff, Amos Cody.

"Ah, Mr. MacCallister, am I glad to see you," the young sheriff said.

"I keep telling you, Amos, to call me Falcon."

"Yes, sir, I know you do, but it's just that I grew up hearin' about your pa's exploits, then yours. Well, it just seems hard."

"You are making me feel very old, Amos," Falcon said. He glanced out the window and saw a little cluster of people engaged in an intense conversation. The somber expressions on their faces reinforced his feeling that something bad had happened.

"What's going on, Sheriff?"

"You mean you haven't heard?"

"No, I haven't."

"The bank was robbed this morning," Amos said.

"And the Reverend Powell and his wife was murdered," Deputy Bates added. Bates was a lot older than the young sheriff, and had been a deputy for many years.

"What?" Falcon said in surprise and anger. "Brother Charles and Sister Claudia have been killed?"

"Yes, they were in the bank when it was robbed."

"But I don't understand. Why were they killed?"

Sheriff Cody shook his head. "Who knows?"

"It was Luke and Clete Mueller," Deputy Bates said. "From all I've heard about them two, they don't really need no reason. Accordin' to Clyde Barnes, the Powells were just standing there in the bank when the robbers came in. Next thing you know, Luke Mueller shot them. Then they got away, clean as a whistle."

"The Mueller brothers, you say?"

"Yes. And three others," Sheriff Cody said.

"Have you ever run across the Mueller brothers?" Bates asked.

"No."

Bates smiled. "I didn't reckon you had. 'Cause if you had, both them bastards would be dead by now."

"Who were the other three?" Falcon asked.

Sheriff Cody shook his head. "We don't know. Barnes recognized the Muellers, but he had never seen any of the others."

"Are you going after them?"

"By now, they have more than likely left the county," Sheriff Cody said. "Even if I found them, I would have to work with the sheriff of that county. But you hold a special deputy's commission from the governor, which gives you authority all over the state. I was hoping you might take a personal interest in this. Reverend Powell was a friend of yours, wasn't he?"

"Yes, he was a close friend. He did the funeral for my mother and my father, and he baptized nearly every one of my nieces and nephews. I guess I've known the Reverend and Mrs. Powell for just about all my life. They were among the earliest settlers of the valley, and they were good people."

"He had already retired when I came here," Sheriff Cody said. "But I knew him, of course, and from what I knew of him, he was a good person. I heard that he could give one stem-winder of a sermon."

"Yes, he could," Falcon said. He remembered, as a young boy, sometimes getting very impatient with the length of the good parson's sermons. Falcon was usually anxious to get to a fishing pond or some such place, and he would squirm until his mother or one of his older sisters would fix him with a steely glare.

"Did anyone see them leave? Do we know which way they were going?" Falcon asked.

"Yes, we had quite a few people who saw them ride out of town. The only thing we know for sure is they were headin' east when they left here. Bates and I went out lookin' for 'em, but didn't see anything.

"I know you probably have other things to do, but I was hopin' you'd take a look around for us, see what you could come up with."

"Sheriff, they killed two people who were as close as family to me. I would go after those men whether you asked me to or not. Yes, I will find them."

It did not escape Sheriff Cody's attention that Falcon said I "will find" them, rather than I "will go after" them.

"Thanks," Sheriff Cody said.

"I told you he would," Bates said with a smile of smug satisfaction on his face.

"Good, good. So, what do we do next? What can I do to help you?"

"The teller was the only witness?" Falcon asked.

"Clyde Barnes was the only witness to the actual hold up, though several saw them riding out of town."

"Let's start with Barnes," Falcon suggested.

* * *

For the next half hour, Falcon gathered as much information as he could about the robbers.

"Well, you know what the Muellers look like, don't you?" Barnes said. "I guess just about ever' one knows what they look like. They're little short, dried up, evil looking men. As for the others, one of them has only one eye. That's his left eye. There is nothing but a big old ugly mass of purple flesh where the right eye was. And another one had only three fingers on his left hand. Don't know as I saw anything particular about the third man, I mean, he was pretty ordinary as men go."

"What about their horses?" Falcon asked.

Barnes shook his head. "I didn't see them. I'm sorry."

"That's all right," Falcon said. "You've given me a good description of the men. It will be very helpful."

At least half a dozen citizens who had seen the bank robbers ride out of town at breakneck speed reported two were riding roans, one was riding a black horse, one a white horse, and one was riding a paint. Falcon examined the ground where the horses had been tied up outside the bank and saw something that made him smile. One of the horses had a tie-bar shoe on his right forefoot.

Riding out to the east end of town, he looked around until he found that same tie-bar. He chuckled. They may as well have left behind a series of arrow shaped signs reading, WE WENT THIS WAY.

* * *

Somewhat farther into the trail, Falcon realized the Mueller brothers weren't going to make it as easy as he first thought. They had been on the run for nearly all their adult life, so they knew how to confuse and disorient anyone who might be tracking them. They took great pains to cover their true trail, while leaving false trails for anyone to follow. To that end they rode through streams and over hard rock, trying every trick in the book to throw off anyone who might be following them. But Falcon hung on doggedly.

In trying to shake off anyone who might be following them, the Mueller brothers and their cohorts were actually helping Falcon. Since it was always the same five horses who broke the trail, he had a way of identifying each of them, not just the one with the tie-bar shoe. One of the horses had a slight turn-in of its right rear hoof. Two of the horses had noticeable nicks in their shoes, one on the left rear and the other on both rear shoes. Only one horse had no noticeable features and that, in itself, became a way of identifying it. In addition, all the horses had grazed together for the last few days, because their droppings were filled with the same kind of wild, mountain meadow grass.

"Whoever that feller is that's a'doggin' us is still on our trail," Terrell said.

Luke twisted around in his saddle. "Are you sure?"

"Hell yes, I'm sure. I just got me a glimpse of 'im on the other side of that far ridge."

"That makes 'im a little more'n a mile back."

"Ain't they no way we can shake 'im?" Caldwell asked.

"You got 'ny ideas that we ain't tried?" Luke replied. "We done ever'thing I can think of, an' it ain't even slowed 'im down none."

"Whoever the hell he is, I swear, he could track a fish through water," Poole said.

"I tell you what we ought to do," Clete said.

"All right, brother, let me hear your idea."

"We ought to just wait behind a couple rocks and shoot him, soon as he comes up on us."

"If I thought for certain we would get 'im, I'd be all for it," Luke said. "But we're not likely to get a clean shot at 'im out here."

The five men had stopped for a few minutes, not only to discuss the situation of the man on their trail, but also to give their horses a breather. All five were looking back, trying to get a glimpse of the man who was following them. When Luke turned back around, he chuckled.

"I got me an idea," he said.

"What's that?"

Luke pointed to a narrow draw in front of them. "If we can get through that draw, he'll have to follow through."

"So?"

"Look at them rocks up on the top there, on the right hand side. Do you see 'em?"

"I see 'em."

"If we push the rocks down, it'll block the draw and he can't get through," Luke said.

"Hell, why don't we just wait until he gets into

the draw, then push them rocks down on him?" Clete asked.

"Yeah, all right, we can try it," Luke said. "Come on, let's hurry through the draw."

Fifteen minutes later, Falcon reached the spot where the five men had halted. He could tell by the tracks they had stopped there for a few minutes, and he could also tell they had left the spot at a gallop.

Why?

What would cause them, out there in the middle of nowhere, to suddenly break into a gallop?

Looking ahead, he saw the trail led to a very narrow draw. Slapping his legs against the side of his horse, he urged the animal on.

"Here he comes," Luke said. "Get ready.

Clete and the others got in position behind the rocks and waited.

"Now!" Luke shouted. "Now!"

The word rolled down from the top of the rock wall, amplified by the narrow confines of the wall. The word itself got Falcon's attention, and he jerked his horse to a stop. Then, he heard the scrape and clatter of rocks, followed by the thunder of a rockslide. Glancing up, it looked as if the entire wall was collapsing right on him.

* * *

"Ha!" Luke shouted. "We got him! There ain't no way he got out of that!"

Clete, Terrell, Caldwell, and Poole stepped up alongside Luke to look down into the draw. They saw nothing but a large pile of rocks on the floor below.

"Who was it, do you reckon?" Poole asked.

Luke shook his head. "I don't have no idée," he said. "Prob'ly some deputy or somethin'. Whoever it was, it don't make no never mind now, 'cause he's deader than a doornail."

"Ha!" Poole said. "And we've got away clean as a whistle."

"Yeah, what say we divide up our money now, and each one of us go on our different way?" Caldwell said.

"Not yet," Luke replied.

"What do you mean, not yet? Why not?"

"If they was one deputy comin' after us, there's just as likely to be another one. Or maybe two or three more. We'd be better off all stickin' together 'til we're sure."

From the moment he heard the word *Now*, Falcon was on the alert. Jerking his horse around, he was at a full gallop by the time the rocks began falling, and well clear of the draw by the time the rocks started piling up on the floor below. Turning back toward the draw, he watched the dust rise as the rocks closed the passage.

Fortunately he had been there many times, and he knew another way around. Coming out on the other side no more than half an hour later, he picked up their tracks immediately. Thinking they were in the clear, they no longer made an effort to hide their trail. They were heading in a straight line for the little town of Black Hawk.

The sun went behind the clouds just before noon, and the clouds thickened and darkened.

"Purty soon it's goin' to commence to rainin' here like pourin' piss out of a boot. And we're goin' to be right in the middle of it," Terrell said.

"What if it does rain? You ain't made of sugar," Clete said. "You ain't goin' to melt."

Poole laughed. "You ain't made of sugar," he repeated. "I like that."

"I ain't goin' to melt, that's true," Terrell said. "But it ain't goin' to be none too comfortable bein' out here in it, neither."

"Let the rain come," Luke said. "The more rain the better."

"What do you mean?"

"Think about it, Terrell. If anybody else is on our trail, why this rain will wash out all the tracks," Luke said.

Terrell was quiet for a moment, then he nodded. "Yeah," he said. He laughed. "Yeah, that's right, ain't it? It would wash out all our tracks. Hell, I say, let the rain come."

"Not yet," Luke said.

"What do you mean, not yet? You just said the rain would wash out all our tracks, didn't you?"

"Yes, I did, and it will. But if it will just hold off for another half hour or so, we'll be to Black Hawk."

"Black Hawk? What's Black Hawk?"

"It's a town me and Clete have already scouted out. No railroad comes to it, there's no telegraph wires, and even if they have heard of us, there ain't likely no one there who has ever seen us. We'll be safe inside, and the rain will wash away the tracks. We can hole up there for a while until they quit lookin' for us."

"And spend some of our money?" Terrell asked, hopefully.

"Yeah," Luke replied with a grin. "We can spend a little of our money there."

"I ain't never been to Black Hawk," Caldwell said. "What's it like?"

"It's got beer, whiskey, food, and women," Poole said. "What else do you need to know about it?"

Terrell chuckled. "Don't need to know nothin' more about it a'tall, I don't reckon."

It took the better part of a quarter hour to reach the town after they first saw it, and they rode in slowly, sizing it up with wary eyes. It was a town with only one street. The unpainted wood of the few ramshackle buildings was turning gray and splitting. There was no railroad, but there was a stagecoach station with a schedule board announcing the arrival and departure of four stagecoaches per week. The first few drops of rain started to fall, and the few people out on the street ran to get inside before the rain started in earnest.

"There's where we're headed," Luke said, pointing to a saloon. Painted in red, outlined in gold on the false front of the saloon were the words *Lucky Nugget*.

The five rode up to the front of the saloon, dismounted, and tied off their horses. Luke reached for the little cloth bag that was tied to his saddle horn.

"You takin' the money in with you?" Terrell asked.

"You don't think I'm goin' to leave it out here, do you?"

"I reckon not. Just think it might be a little strange for you to be carryin' all that money."

"Don't worry about it," Luke said as they stepped onto the porch. Almost as if on cue, the clouds opened up and the rain fell in torrents.

"Ha!," Clete Mueller said, a few minutes later. "I'll just bet you that ol' Egan Drumm is a' wishin' he was with us now, after all the money we just stoled. He got to thinkin' he could do better goin' out on his own, so he left. But now here we are. We got us all this money, and he ain't got nothin'."

"We don't know that he ain't got nothin'," Luke said. "We don't know nothin' about him, not even where he's at."

"Yeah, but I'd be willin' to bet he ain't got nothin'," Clete said.

"Speakin' o' goin' out on our own, I think maybe we ought to divide up the money now, and go our own ways," Ollie Terrell said, bringing up the subject again.

"We'll divide the money when I say we divide it," Luke Mueller said. "Anyway, what are you worried about? We got plenty of money to spend now, ain't we? Order whatever you want, we can afford it."

"Yeah," Clete added with a cackle. "We can afford it."

"What about women?" Terrell asked. "What if I'm a' wantin' me a woman?"

"Don't you be worryin' none about gettin' yourself a woman," Luke said. "They's plenty of women around, and once we start spendin' the money, the women will be comin' out of the woodwork."

Terrell laughed. "Women comin' out of the woodwork. I like that. I ain't never heard nothin' like that before."

"How bout we start spendin' some of that money now?" Caldwell asked. "I'm hungry. And I got me a thirst worked up, too."

"Barkeep!" Mueller called. "Bring us a couple bottles of whiskey, some glasses, and some food. Lots of food."

"And some women!" Terrell added. "Let's get some women over here."

Three of the bar girls who had been wandering around the saloon, flitting from table to table like bees around flowers, answered the call and within a moment the five bank robbers and three women were having themselves a party.

Though Luke Mueller was the smallest of the men, he turned all his attention to the biggest of the women.

"Ain't that there'n a little big for you, Luke?" Terrell teased, laughing out loud.

As quick as a thought, a pistol appeared in Luke's

hand, and he pointed it at Terrell, pulling back the hammer.

"You have somethin' to say about what woman I pick?" Luke asked.

The laughter died on Terrell's lips, his pupils dilated with fear, and he held his hand out as if by that action he could ward Luke off. "'Course, you know I didn't mean nothin' by that, Luke. I was just a' funnin' you is all."

There was a long moment of high tension and absolute silence as everyone watched the tableau. Then, suddenly, a smile spread across Luke's face, and he eased the hammer down and put the pistol back in his holster.

"I didn't mean nothin' neither. I was just funnin' you, too," he said.

The burst of laughter that followed was precipitated more by the release of tension, than humor.

"What's your name?" Luke asked the big woman.

"Patsy," the woman answered. A moment earlier she had been enjoying her flirtation with the little man, but now he frightened her.

"Tell me, Patsy, what will you charge for me and you to go upstairs?"

"A dollar for one hour," Patsy said. "Three dollars for the rest of the day."

"Here's five dollars. I might want to stay longer than the rest of the day."

Smiling, Patsy took the money and stuck it inside the top of her dress, between her very large breasts. "Oh, honey, we're goin' to have us a real good time," she said. The money had changed her attitude about him.

Luke reached under the table and picked up a cloth bag.

"What's that, darlin', your laundry?" Patsy asked. "Honey, for five dollars I'll give you a very good time, but I ain't a' goin' to be doin' no laundry."

The other soiled doves laughed.

"You can leave your—uh—laundry here, if you want," Clete said.

"That's all right, I'll take care of it," Luke said. "This way, we'll all know where it is, won't we?"

"This way, darlin'," Patsy said, leading Luke away from the table. The others in the saloon watched them go up the stairs.

"Looks like a mouse following an elephant," someone said on the far side of the room. Having seen the lightning draw of the "mouse," he made the observation quietly, and his friend's resultant laughter was just as quiet.

Chapter Three

Two hours later

From the moment he left MacCallister, Falcon had been on the trail of the band of outlaws. Though the tracks were gone, washed out by the steady downpour, before he lost them they had been leading directly and inexorably toward Black Hawk. The cold, driving rain that had started up in the higher elevations then moved down the slopes of the Front Range Mountains had turned the single street of Black Hawk into a rushing river.

Falcon knew if he couldn't find his quarry in Black Hawk he would have to give up. But he was also reasonably certain the men, confident they had gotten away cleanly after the rock slide, would be there somewhere, taking shelter from the rain. Shivering in the cold downpour, Falcon perused both sides of the street as he rode into town. He rode past the buildings, subconsciously enumerating them as he passed. There was a rooming house, a livery, a smithy, and a general store that had

DRUGS, MEATS, GOODS painted on its high, false front. There was a hotel, a restaurant, and of course, the ubiquitous saloon.

It was not exactly a bolt from the blue when he saw the horses he had been tracking—two roans, a black, a white, and a paint—tied up outside the Lucky Nugget Saloon.

"Well, boys," he said aloud. "I'll just bet you thought you were home free. Looks like you are in for a little surprise."

He steered his horse toward the saloon, the hooves splashing up water from the flooded road as he crossed the street. Stopping in front of the saloon, Falcon slid down from the saddle then walked over to examine the right forefoot of each horse. He struck pay dirt on the third horse he checked. The paint had a tie-bar shoe, the same shoe he had been following for the last two days.

Falcon stepped up onto the porch and used the edge of the wide, weathered planks to scrape mud from his boots. He could hear the discordant pounding of an out of tune piano, and the loud guffaw of a man laughing, followed by the higher trill of a woman's cackle.

Falcon slipped out of his poncho and hung it on a nail sticking out of the front wall. Taking his hat off, he poured water from the top of the crown, then put it back on his head. Finally, he eased his pistol from the holster and spun the cylinder to check the loads, satisfying himself he was ready for any contingency. Squaring his shoulders, he pushed through the swinging bat wing doors and stepped just far enough inside to be out of the rain blowing in.

The inside of the saloon was a golden bubble of light. A dozen lanterns hung from a couple wagon wheel chandeliers. A large cloud of drifting tobacco smoke spread throughout the room, dimming the light and creating an artificial fog sufficient to becloud the view. The features of people standing no more than a few feet away looked as if they were being viewed through a film of gauze cloth.

The wood burning stove put off enough heat to remove the chill from the damp, dreary day, and the room was redolent with the smell of burning wood, tobacco, stale beer, and wet clothing. It was noisy, with a dozen or more conversations, periodic outbreaks of laughter, and music—if the cacophonous result of a piano player banging away at the old, scarred, upright piano could be called music. The saloon was crowded. After a brief perusal, Falcon's attention was drawn to a table in the far corner, where four men and two bar girls were laughing and engaged in loud, animated conversation.

"Honey, if you are going to put your hand there, you are going to have to pay for it," one of the girls said with a loud squeal, her laughter joined by that of the others.

"Darlin' I'll be happy to pay for it," the man replied. "Me'n my pards here done got us a lucky streak in a big poker game." The speaker had only three fingers on his left hand.

"Yeah," one of the other men said. "That's what it was. It was a poker game." He was wearing an eye patch over his right eye.

The others laughed, as if sharing some sort of inside joke.

"With all the money you boys are spendin', that must have been quite a game," the bar girl said.

"It was, darlin', it was."

Falcon moved a little closer so he could get a clearer look at the men.

He had been looking for five men, but there were only four. However, with one of them wearing an eye patch, another with only three fingers on his left hand, and a third noticeably shorter than the other three, he was convinced they were the men he had been following. The fourth man, as described, was unremarkable in any way. Those four men, as well the horses that were tied up outside, perfectly fit the descriptions of the men he had been following; the ones who had held up the bank in MacCallister.

Falcon had never seen the Mueller brothers, but he was well aware of them. Not since Frank and Jesse James had a pair of brothers become so notorious, and not even the James brothers had a reputation for killing to match the Muellers. Luke Mueller, particularly, was known to be a deadly gunfighter—deadly because he was both quick with a gun, and willing to use it. The one with the loud mouth was clearly the dominating figure among the four, in spite of being the smallest. Falcon was certain he was one of the Muellers—though which one he didn't know. He had no idea where the other Mueller was.

"Tell you what, darlin'," the little man said to one

of the bar girls. "Why don't me'n you go on up and join my brother and that big ol' gal he is with?"

"What? In the same room?" the bar girl gasped. She shook her head. "No, sir, I couldn't do anything like that."

"Don't get yourself all in a tither," the little man said. "I didn't mean join 'em in the same room. I just meant go upstairs like they did. We'll find our own room."

"Oh, well, that's more like it," the soiled dove replied. "I thought you'd never ask. I was beginnin' to think you didn't like me."

"Oh, I like you, darlin'. I like you just fine. How 'bout gettin' a bottle to take up with us?"

"All right."

"Never mind the bottle, miss, he won't be needing it," Falcon called out. "None of them will."

The four men sitting at the table looked at him in surprise, wondering who had the audacity to make such a confrontational declaration.

"Mister, what do you mean I'll not be needin' me a bottle of whiskey?" the little man asked.

"You won't be needing it, because you will either be going back to MacCallister with me to stand trial for bank robbery and murder, or you'll be dead."

Falcon's voice was loud and sharp, drawing the attention of everyone in the room. All conversation halted. The piano playing came to a ragged end, save for the last discordant note that hung in the air as everyone in the room turned to look at the man whose words had been so challenging.

The little man stared incredulously at Falcon for a moment, then he started laughing. The other three men who were sitting around the table with him laughed as well.

"You're a funny man, mister. You've give me a good laugh. But tell me, what makes you think we held up a bank in MacCallister? Where is MacCallister, anyway? They ain't none of us ever even been there."

"Oh, you've been there all right," Falcon said. "I know that, because I trailed the five of you from there to here."

"You trailed us?" the little man asked in surprise. "Wait a minute. That was you?"

"It was me," Falcon said.

"But I thought—"

"That you had got me with a rock slide. Yeah, that was close."

"Who the hell are you, anyway? What's your name?"

"The name is Falcon MacCallister."

"Falcon MacCallister?" Terrell gasped. "You and your brother said takin' that bank would be real easy. Jesus. Now we got Falcon MacCallister after us!"

"Shut up, Terrell, you damn fool! Don't you realize you just confessed to murder in front of a dozen witnesses!" Mueller said.

"What the hell you talkin' about? I didn't kill nobody!" Terrell shouted. "Your crazy brother Luke is the one that done the killin'."

"I told you to keep your mouth shut," Mueller said angrily.

The bar girls standing near the table moved away quickly, while all the others in the saloon, sensing something was about to happen, moved back against the walls, opening up the center of the saloon. Falcon and the four men were at center stage in the unfolding drama.

Mueller smiled. Rather than softening his features, the smile twisted his face into a macabre, harlequin mask.

"You seem to have put yourself into a bit of a pickle here, Mr. MacCallister," Mueller said. "There's only one of you, and there's four of us. 'Pears to me like you would've been a heap better off, just stayin' out of this. I'm goin' to enjoy this."

"Take your guns out of your holsters and put them on the floor," Falcon ordered.

Mueller shook his head, quietly. "Huh," he said. "You want us to take our guns out of the holsters and put them on the floor, do you?" Mueller laughed. "Well now, MacCallister, I would call that bold talk for someone who's not only outnumbered four to one, but who ain't even holdin' a pistol. I'll tell you right now, the only way my gun is comin' out of my holster is when I pull it to kill you."

The grin that appeared on Falcon's face, though not as broad, nor as forced as Mueller's had been, was more frightening because it was cold, calculated, and confident.

The warmth of the stove felt hotter, and the smells seemed stronger. With everyone rooted in position, the scene could have been a Matthew Brady photograph taken from real life—a piece of time snatched from the present and eternally frozen in sepia tone.

What was different from just a heartbeat earlier was the sound, or more accurately, the lack of it. All music, all conversation, the clinking of glasses, and the scrape of boots on the floor were gone. Only the steady ticktock of the great regulator grandfather clock standing at the wall just under the stairs, interrupted the deadly quiet. More than one person in the room, sensing fortune had chosen them to witness an event that, one day they would speak of with their grandchildren, glanced at the clock in order to have it well memorized. In their telling of the day they saw the famous Falcon MacCallister killed, they wanted to be accurate in every detail, down to the exact time.

There was not the slightest doubt in anyone's mind as to what would be the outcome of the dance of death they were about to witness. Falcon MacCallister was facing four armed and desperate men, and though MacCallister was wearing a pistol, it was still in his holster.

Outside a sudden, brilliant flash of lightning struck so close it was concurrent with an explosively loud peal of thunder. A couple of men shouted out in alarm, and one of the bar girls screamed.

Perceiving it provided him with the best opportunity to make his play, Mueller jumped up, his gun in his hand.

"Now boys!" he shouted, as the chair he had been sitting in tumbled over behind him.

The other three matched Mueller, jumping up and pulling their guns.

Falcon fired four times, the shots coming so close together it sounded like one sustained roar. Mueller got off one shot, but it was wide of its mark, crashing into the mirror behind the bar. Two of

Mueller's compatriots also managed to get off shots, one going into the floor, the other into the ceiling. All four men fell with fatal gunshot wounds.

"Did you see that?"

"I seen it, but I ain't a' believin' it."

"Ain't no man alive can do that!"

"They sure as hell is, and we just seen it done!"

Falcon held his pistol at the ready, a little stream of smoke still curling up from the end of the barrel. Added to the other smells in the room, was the distinctive odor of burnt gunpowder.

One of the saloon patrons started toward the four bodies, lying where they fell. He stopped and held his hand out toward Falcon. "I just aim to check 'em is all, to see if they're all dead."

"They are dead," Falcon answered as he put his pistol back in his holster.

"How do you know they're all dead?"

"Because I didn't have time not to kill them," Falcon replied.

Everyone's attention was drawn to the four dead men, so nobody noticed the piano player go up the stairs. Once upstairs, he tapped lightly on the door of one of the rooms. The door opened and a woman's face appeared in the crack.

"What is it, Arnie? This feller paid me for the whole night."

"Let me in, Patsy. I got somethin' to say that he's goin' to want to hear," Arnie said.

"I just heard somethin' sounded like gunshots. Does it have somethin' to do with that?"

Arnie nodded his head.

"All right, come on in."

Patsy was naked from the waist up, but she had no sense of modesty toward Arnie with whom she had often shared her favors. Her breasts were large and flabby, laced with blue veins. On one of her breasts was a lump of scar tissue—the result of having had her nipple bitten off by a drunken customer. She led him over to the bed where slept the little man who had paid almost twice her normal fee.

"You say you heard the gunshots?"

"Yes. They woke me up."

"Don't know how they didn't wake him up," Arnie said, nodding toward the figure on the bed.

"He's been drinkin' all day," Patsy said. "He was so drunk he couldn't even do nothin'."

Arnie chuckled. "You ain't goin' to give him his money back, are you?"

"No, are you crazy? I'll just tell him how wonderful he was. He'll never know the difference."

Arnie started over to wake him up, then, remembering the incident downstairs when Luke had drawn his pistol against one of his own friends, Arnie hesitated. He pointed toward the bed.

"Maybe you had better wake him up," he suggested.

Patsy smiled. "Are you afraid of him?"

"Yeah, a little," Arnie admitted.

Patsy put her hand on the sleeper's shoulder and shook him slightly. "Wake up, mister. Wake up."

Chapter Four

When Luke Mueller opened his eyes he saw Patsy sitting on the side of the bed looking down at him. At least she had told him her name was Patsy, though he knew whores seldom gave their right name. He was surprised to see a man standing over the bed.

"Who the hell are you?" he asked, sitting up quickly. Almost as quickly, a gun appeared in his hand.

The man gasped, and held his hands out before him. "Easy, mister, easy. My name is Arnie Cates. I'm the piano player here."

"Oh, yeah, I remember you. What are you wakin' me up for? I ain't had me a bed sleep in a week of Sundays."

"Them four men you come in with?"

Luke lay back down and scrunched up his pillow. "Yeah," he replied, sleepily. "What about 'em?"

"They just got themselves kilt."

Luke's eyes popped open, and he sat up again. "What did you say?"

"They just got themselves kilt. All four of 'em," Cates said.

"What the hell? What happened?"

"They was a feller come in here by the name of Falcon MacCallister," Cates said. "You ever heard tell of him?"

"Yeah, I've heard of him."

"Well, he come in, said somethin' about goin' to take 'em all in for bank robbin' and murder. Next thing you know they was all a' shootin' at each other and this man MacCallister, he kilt 'em all."

"All of 'em? My brother too?"

Cates nodded. "Yes, sir. I'm sorry to have to tell you this, but he was the first one to get hisself kilt."

"Are you saying that Falcon MacCallister, one man, kilt them all?"

"Yes, by himself. I tell you, I ain't never seen nothin' like it."

"If you was there watchin' it, how come you didn't you come up here and get me?"

"I come up here as soon as I could, but it all happened too fast for me to come get you," Cates said. "Besides which, if you had been there, you would more'n likely have been kilt too."

"Is MacCallister still here?"

"Yes, he's still here. He's downstairs now with the sheriff and a couple deputies."

"That's good to know," Luke said. He reached for his pants and began to pull them on. "I'm going to go down and take care of this right now."

"Mister, I don't think you really want to do this," Patsy said.

"Why not?" Luke picked up his pistol and spun the cylinder to check the loads.

"Didn't you hear what Arnie said? The sheriff and all his deputies are downstairs now."

"Besides which, now ever'one knows you five robbed a bank and kilt a couple people over in MacCallister," Cates added.

"What? How do they know that?"

"Your brother purt' near confessed to it," Cates said. "And what with the sheriff and all his deputies down there, you wouldn't stand a chance."

"He kilt my brother," Luke said.

Patsy nodded. "That's right, he did. Even if you manage to kill MacCallister, your brother will still be dead. What's more than likely though, especially with the sheriff and his deputies there, is you'll wind up gettin' yourself kilt."

Luke lowered his pistol and sat there for a moment, then he sighed. "You're right," he said. "I can wait a while. I do plan to kill the son of a bitch, I just won't do it tonight."

Luke had finished dressing and was reaching under the bed where he had put the money sack, when there was a loud knock on the door.

"Miss Patsy? It's Sheriff Gibbons, Miss Patsy. Anyone in there with you?"

Without a word, Luke fired through the door. There was a grunt and moan from the other side, then the sound of a body falling.

Patsy screamed. "What have you done?"

Luke reached again under the bed for the sack, when he heard a loud crash against the door. Abandoning the sack, he moved across the room to the window, raised it, then crawled through it, onto the mansard roof. At that moment a brilliant flash of lightning illuminated him. He jumped, just as the sheriff's deputies and Falcon burst into the room.

"Where is he?" one of the deputies shouted.

"He went out through the window!" Cates shouted.

The deputies looked outside, but there was only a small space between the hotel and the building next door, so they saw nothing.

Falcon turned and ran to the end of the hall, which had a window that looked onto the street. Even though he had a view of the road, he could see nothing in the dark and the rain.

Hurrying back to the room he saw the sheriff sitting up, holding his hand over a wound in his shoulder.

"Did you see the son of a bitch?" the sheriff asked, his voice strained with pain.

"No," Falcon answered.

"He got away."

"For now," Falcon said.

Falcon went into the room where he saw an overweight, naked woman, trying to hide something under the bed quilt.

"I'll take that, miss," Falcon said, holding his hand out.

"It's nothing but laundry," the woman said.

"Really?" Falcon took the sack from her, and opened it.

"I'll be," the whore said, feigning surprise. "There is money there. Who would have thought that?"

Falcon chuckled. "Yeah," he said. "Who would have thought it?"

* * *

Luke Mueller managed to make it to the far end of town without getting shot, but his horse was still tied up in front of the saloon. He stole a horse to make good his escape, and rode through the downpour, cursing Falcon MacCallister, and swearing revenge on him. Though in truth, he was more angry over the loss of the money than he was over the fact that his brother had been killed.

He began planning ways to kill MacCallister. He wouldn't get his money back, but somehow, he would get revenge.

Downstairs in the Lucky Nugget Saloon, the bodies of the four men Falcon had shot were lying in a neat row alongside the wall, next to the piano. Manuel, the fourteen year old boy who worked at the saloon, had a bucket of water and a mop, and was cleaning up the blood from the floor.

Most of the regular customers of the saloon had already satisfied their curiosity, but Hodge Deckert, the barkeep, was doing a brisk business as people from the town kept coming in to get a look. Of the four bodies stretched out on the floor, Caldwell garnered the most attention. The eyes of the other three were shut, but Caldwell's one eye was open and appeared to be glaring. It gave him a macabre look, juxtaposed as it was alongside the puff of flesh where his other eye should have been.

Patsy had come back downstairs and was sitting

at a table with two other women. They were talking quietly among themselves.

Sheriff Gibbons was sitting in a chair by the stove, with his shirt off, while Dr. Urban treated the wound in his shoulder. Falcon stood close by, with his arms folded across his chest.

"Did you count the money?" Sheriff Gibbons asked.

"Yes. Except for twenty dollars, it is all here," Falcon said.

"You probably ran them so hard they didn't have a chance to spend any of it, and Hodge says twenty dollars is just about what they spent here. I imagine the bank back in MacCallister will be pretty pleased to get—damn! What are you doing, Doc? That burns!"

"I've poured alcohol on your wound," Dr. Urban replied. "You don't want it to mortify on you, do you?"

"No, I reckon not. But I didn't plan on you settin' me on fire, neither."

"Don't be such a baby," Dr. Urban growled as he began applying the bandage.

"You goin' after Luke Mueller?" the sheriff asked Falcon.

Falcon shook his head. "Not right away. First thing I need to do is get this money back to the bank in MacCallister. Folks back there will be needing it."

"You starting back tonight? In this weather?"

"No, I thought I would get a room tonight, start back first thing tomorrow."

"You can spend the night in one of the jail cells

if you'd like," Sheriff Gibbons said. He chuckled. "Believe me, you'll be as comfortable there as you would be in anything that passes for a hotel here."

Luke Mueller found a rock shelf that enabled him to get out of the rain, but it was a cold, wet, miserable night and he spent every waking moment of it, thinking about Falcon MacCallister. He had never met MacCallister. But everything changed from the moment MacCallister came onto the scene. By rights, Luke thought, he should be waking up in a whore's bed, having a breakfast he didn't cook, and spend the day drinking and planning on how to spend his money. Money that he no longer had—money that Falcon MacCallister took from him.

Oh, how he hated that son of a bitch.

From the *MacCallister Eagle*:

JUSTICE DISPENSED:
Falcon MacCallister the Dispenser

Readers of this newspaper are well aware of the dastardly murder, last week, of Reverend Charles Powell, and his wife, Mrs. Claudia Powell. There are few men to whom the town of MacCallister owes more gratitude than it owes to Reverend Powell. He had been specially selected to offer the convocation to the Lord in the dedication of the statue of Colonel Jamie Ian MacCallister. The good reverend was one of Colonel MacCallister's contemporaries in time, and his peer in service to his friends, neighbors, and indeed, the whole valley.

This newspaper is pleased to report nearly all the perpetrators of the appalling murders of this saintly man and his good and loving wife have been brought to justice.

Clete Mueller, Ollie Terrell, Bo Caldwell, and Clarence Poole, four of the five brigands who underhandedly murdered the Reverend and Mrs. Powell, have been sent to appear before their maker for final judgment. The instrument of their demise was Falcon MacCallister who was so moved by the most foul bank robbery and murder committed by the villains, he tracked them down and brought them to justice. Confronting them at the Lucky Nugget Saloon in Black Hawk, it was reliably reported by witnesses that Colonel MacCallister gave the thieves and murderers ample opportunity to surrender and present themselves for a fair trial. The outlaws refused to avail themselves of this prospect so graciously offered, choosing instead to test their mettle against Falcon MacCallister, believing their superior numbers to be to their advantage.

Their supposition was wrong, and in the resultant gunplay, described by witnesses to the event as "quicker than thought," all four desperados were killed. Luke Mueller, the fifth member of the gang, was not present at the time of the aforementioned confrontation and, as of this writing, is still at large.

New York, New York

A young woman sat in the front of the hansom cab holding her baby under the blankets and against her body to protect it from the cold night air of early spring. Though her part of the cab was partially enclosed, the driver sat outside the enclosure, on a high seat above and behind her. Janelle Wellington was a strikingly pretty woman with dark hair, deep blue eyes, high cheekbones, and a smooth, olive complexion.

When the cab stopped, Janelle spoke to the driver through the hole in the roof.

"Please wait for me," she said. "I'll only be here for a few minutes."

"Yes, ma'am," the driver answered, calling back down to her. Tying the reins off, he pulled his scarf up around his neck all the way to his ears, stuck his hands into his pockets, then hunkered down into his heavy coat to wait for his fare.

The young woman carried the baby to the front door of the brownstone, then up one flight of stairs. She knocked on the door and when it was answered, stepped inside.

"Janelle? What are you doing here? And out on a cold night like this with that baby?"

"Sue, I need to leave the baby with you for a while."

"Over night?"

"For a while longer."

"What is this about? What is going on?"

"You know what is going on. You know the disgrace I have brought to the family. I can't stay here anymore, and I can't take the baby where I'm going."

"Janelle, what do you mean? What are you talking about? Where are you going?"

"I don't know. I mean, I'm not quite sure yet where I'm going. I guess I'll know when I get there."

"No, don't do this. Don't do this to yourself, don't do it to the family."

"The family," the young woman said with a derisive laugh. "After all that I have done, do you really think I could do anything more to this family? I have disgraced myself, I have disgraced Mother and Father, and I have disgraced you."

"Don't be silly. You haven't disgraced me."

Janelle's smile became more sardonic.

"I haven't disgraced you," she said. "See, even you realize that I have disgraced our parents."

"I didn't mean that and you know it. They were upset and disappointed, yes," her older sister agreed. "But I think it was more over what happened to you, than they were with you. They love you. We all love you, and I don't want to see you throw your life away like this."

Janelle sighed. "Please, just tell me you will take care of the baby. At least for a while. I need some more time, is all."

"Of course, you know I will take care of the baby. But what about Mother and Father? Do they know you are leaving?"

"No. And please, say nothing to them until after I have left."

"You don't know what you are asking of me."

"I do know. Believe me, I do know. And I know I couldn't ask this of any other person in the world."

"I will say nothing until after you have gone, on one condition."

"What condition is that?"

"You must let us know where you are, and that you are safe."

"I promise I will let you know."

"No, not just me. You must let Mother and Father know as well. We must be assured that you are all right."

"I will, I promise. Thank you for loving me, even after all this."

The two embraced, then the younger woman, kissing her baby on the forehead, handed him over to her older sister. Her eyes bedimmed by tears, Janelle didn't look back, She hurried down the stairs, then outside where she climbed into the cab.

"Where to now, miss?" the driver asked.

"Grand Central Station," she said, barely able to get the words out.

The driver nodded, then slapped the reins against the backs of the horses. The team plodded on, the clip-clop of the hoofbeats echoing off the three- and four-story brownstone houses that fronted the street from each side.

Janelle wept silently.

Chapter Five

Idaho Springs, Colorado

"Mister, if you think you're goin' to get someone to go up agin' Falcon MacCallister for a thousand dollars, you're crazy," Jerry Kelly said. "I heerd what he done agin' your brother and three other men."

"Clete and the others tried to take him face on," Luke Mueller said. "I ain't askin' you to do nothin' like that. I got it all planned out."

"You got it all planned out, do you?" Toby Collins asked.

"Yes, absolutely."

"All right, let me hear your plan," Kelly said.

"We're goin' to ambush him. He'll be ridin' right down through the middle of the street without no idea of anything about to happen. We'll all be hid out and we'll shoot him down before he even knows we are there. How hard can that be?"

"You're talkin' about Falcon MacCallister," Kelly said. "It can be damn hard."

"Too hard for you to do it for your share of a thousand dollars?"

"There's three of us here," Kelly said. "Me, Collins, and Tucker. Four, countin' you. So how many will there be to divide this money?"

"Just what you see here," Mueller answered.

"So you're talkin' two hundred fifty dollars?"

Mueller shook his head. "No, you misunderstand. It will only be the three of you sharing the money. So you'll each get three hunnert thirty-three dollars," he said. "I'm the one goin' to give the money, remember? I won't be takin' none of it for myself. All I want is for the son of a bitch to be kilt."

"But there's goin' to be four of us doin' the shootin?" Collins asked.

"Four of us, yes."

"That's kind of funny when you think about it, ain't it?" Kelly said.

"Funny? How?"

"When your brother went up agin' MacCallister, they was four of 'em tryin' to kill him. But MacCallister not only kilt your brother, he kilt all four of 'em. Four, just like we are four."

"I done told you, this ain't goin' to be like that. It ain't goin' to be nothin' at all like that. Clete and the others tried to face him head-on, and all four of 'em got themselves kilt. We ain't goin' to give him no chance a'tall. We'll have him kilt afore he even knows we're anywhere around."

"I got a question," Tucker said.

"What's that?"

"How are we goin' to get him into a spot where we'll all be a' hidin' out and he'll be in the open?"

Mueller smiled. "You don't need to be worryin' nothin' about that," he said. "Just leave that to me. I done got that all set up."

It was the letter that brought Falcon to Idaho Springs. He had received it two days ago.

Dere Mr. Macalster
  I heer that you are lookin for Luke Mueller and if you are willing to pay me some mony come to Idaho Springs and I will tell you where he is at. I will be at the hotel. Don't tell nobody I tode you where at to find him.

Yurs truly
Bill Jones

Falcon MacCallister should have seen it coming. Normally he was much more observant, more aware of his surroundings, but he had no reason to sense danger. He was in Idaho Springs, Colorado which wasn't too far from MacCallister Valley, and therefore was almost like a second hometown to him.

He had just ridden into town when he felt the impact of the bullet as it plunged into his horse's neck. He saw a stream of blood gush out as his mount went down, even as he heard the sound of the shot. He leaped from the saddle to avoid being fallen on by the horse, and as he did so he saw a

white puff of smoke drifting up from just behind a
sign that read J.C. BEALE'S HARDWARE.

Snaking his rifle from its saddle sheath and holding it low in one hand, Falcon darted out of the
center of the road, then dived for cover behind the
watering trough. A bullet plowed into the dirt just
behind him, and another plunked into the trough,
kicking up water and causing it to gurgle out. He
saw several people running for cover, screaming
and shouting in alarm, though they weren't the
target.

Crawling on his belly, Falcon reached the end of
the trough, then looked up toward the hardware
store where he had seen the gun smoke. Jacking a
shell into the chamber he sighted down the barrel
and waited. The shooter on the roof lifted his head
above the false front, just far enough to take a look.
He saw the muzzle flash of Falcon's rifle, but before
he could assimilate it, he was dead, with a bullet in
his brain.

Falcon determined there were two more adversaries in the loft of the livery stable, and another
one standing behind the corner of Murchison's
Gun and Ammunition shop. He turned his attention toward the livery loft, but couldn't see anything through the opening because of the darkness
inside. He knew the shooters had the advantage—
they could see him quite clearly as he was outside
in the sunlight.

Another bullet plunged into the watering
trough, and the water began running out more
swiftly. Falcon threw a shot toward the livery
where he had seen the muzzle flash, not with any

real expectation of hitting anything, but to drive them back. He turned his attention to the corner of the gun and ammunition shop where, earlier, he had seen another man firing at him. Falcon perused the alley opening next to the shop, but saw nothing. While his attention was directed toward the shooters on top of the hardware store and in the loft of the livery, the gunman behind the corner of Murchison's had apparently gotten away.

Turning his head he saw Tom Murchison standing just inside the window of his store, waving fiercely. Succeeding in getting Falcon's attention, he pointed toward a stack of salt blocks in front of McGill Feed and Seed.

Looking in that direction Falcon saw a shadow cast against the feed store wall. He watched the shadow move toward the edge of the stack of salt blocks, then cocking his rifle he aimed at the extreme corner of the stack of blocks, and pulled the trigger. The bullet cut through the corner, sending out a spray of salt before hitting the would-be shooter. The shooter fell heavily to the wood plank porch.

Falcon turned his attention to the two men in the loft of the livery. Getting up from his position behind the watering trough, he left his rifle on the ground and, with pistol in hand, ran toward the door of the stable. Two shots rang out—one so close Falcon felt the breeze of it as the bullet whizzed by. He darted through the wide, double door into the barn before another shot could be fired and moved under the loft so his adversaries above had no shot at him.

"Mueller! Do you see him?" someone called. "Where is he?"

"Collins, you damn fool! Don't be a' shoutin' my name out like that."

"I'm goin' to get over here and see if I can see him," Collins said.

Falcon heard the sound of footfalls on the loft above, and looking up, saw bits of straw fluttering down through the cracks between the boards. He followed the falling straw, then raising his pistol, fired three quick shots.

"Ahhh!" the man yelled, and Falcon saw him pitch over the edge of the loft, catching his foot in the rope and tackle used to lift bales of hay into the loft. The man fell, headfirst, ensnared by his ankle, both arms extended. Hanging down, like the pendulum on a grandfather clock, he swung back and forth across the open front door.

Even as Falcon looked toward the swinging body, he heard the sound of a horse behind him. Running through the barn to the back door, he saw a rider leaning over the horse's neck, slapping the reins from one side to the other as he urged the animal into a fast gallop. Falcon fired at him, and saw the rider slap his hand to the side of his head.

He raised his pistol to take another shot but, realizing that the rider was already out of range, he eased the hammer down, then lowered his weapon. He watched as the rider continued on, sitting strong in his saddle. He must not have hit him.

By the time Falcon left the barn the citizens of the town were spilling back into the street. Most were gathered around the two bodies, one lying in the dirt in front of the hardware store, the other on the porch in front of the feed store. Some were looking at the body hanging upside down from the hay-lift rope.

Falcon went to check on his horse and, though the horse was still alive, there was a lot of blood bubbling from his mouth. "Damn. I'm sorry," he said as he pointed his pistol at the horse's head and pulled back on the hammer. "I'm really sorry."

The expression in the horse's eyes was one of acceptance, as if he knew what Falcon was about to do, and welcomed it.

Falcon pulled the trigger, and the horse died instantly.

Falcon stood there for a moment longer, holding the pistol pointing straight down by his leg, feeling a profound sense of sadness over having had to end the life of the noble animal.

"I know it hurts, Falcon, but it had to be done," a voice said, and turning, Falcon saw a man, wearing a badge, coming toward him.

"I know," Falcon said.

"Are you all right?" Sheriff Ferrell asked, solicitously.

"Yeah, I'm fine, thanks, Billy," Falcon replied, returning the pistol to his holster. He motioned toward the horse. "He was a good one."

"It's a shame when animals get caught up in the doin's of man. They wind up sufferin' through no fault of their own," the sheriff said.

"Yeah. The others dead? The one by the hardware and the one by the feed store?"

"They are, and so is the one hanging from the livery. Tell me, Falcon, you got 'ny idea who these fellers are, or why they tried to ambush you?" Ferrell asked.

"I didn't have any idea when the shooting started, but when I came into the barn, I heard a couple names. One was Collins, and the other was Mueller. I'm thinking it is probably Luke Mueller."

"Yeah, that fits," the sheriff said.

"Fits what?"

"It fits with what I'm thinkin', because I know what it was about."

"Do you now? How do you know?"

"You're a wanted man, Falcon."

"What? Impossible! There's no paper out on me."

"There is now," the sheriff replied. "I took this off the feller lyin' over there in front of the feed store," the sheriff said, handing a circular to Falcon. "You're wanted all right, but not by the law. Take a look at this."

Sheriff Ferrell gave Falcon a poster. It was exactly like the reward dodgers the law put out for wanted men. In every way, shape, and form, this was a wanted poster. Only, as Sheriff Ferrell pointed out, it had not been put out by the law.

REWARD

to anyone who kills

Falcon MacCallister

$1,000.00 *will be paid*,
when Proof of Death is furnished to
Luke Mueller.

"You know this here Mueller feller, do you?" Sheriff Ferrell asked.

"Sort of," Falcon answered.

"What do you mean, sort of?"

"I killed his brother a few weeks ago."

"Oh, yes, I read about it in the paper. The Muellers held up a bank and murdered a couple folks over in MacCallister, if memory serves."

"Memory serves you right," Falcon replied. "I reckon what Luke Mueller is trying to do now, is get even with me."

"Do you think one of these men was Luke Mueller?"

"That was the name I heard called out," Falcon said. "But he isn't one of the ones I killed."

"He got away, did he?"

"Yes."

"That feller seems to make habit of that, doesn't he?" Ferrell asked. "Getting away, I mean."

"Yeah," Falcon said. "But it won't be forever. It would appear that I've got a trap set for him now and sooner or later, he's going to step into it."

"You have a trap set?"

Falcon laughed, a low, mordant chuckle. "Yeah," he said. He held up the reward poster the sheriff had given him. "I just realized this is the trap set for him. He set it himself, and I am the bait."

Sheriff Ferrell chuckled. "I reckon I see what you mean," he said. "You ever run a trap line, Falcon?"

"Oh, yes, I have."

"Well, if you have, you'll notice somethin', I'm sure."

"What's that?"

"Even though you trap your prey, the bait purt' near always gets took. So do me a favor and be careful, will you?"

"I'm always careful," Falcon said.

It hurt to touch his ear, but Luke Mueller wanted to know how badly he had been hit. From what he could determine, his earlobe had been shot off, leaving a bloody piece of mangled flesh. It could have been a lot worse. One more inch to the left, and the bullet would have plowed into the back of his head.

He stopped by a stream, then jumped down from the horse to check out his ear in the reflection of the water. The current was running too swiftly to provide an image, but allowed him to clean his ear. And the cold water eased the pain a little.

Chapter Six

Superstition Mountain

Had someone been on top of Superstition Mountain looking down on the reddish brown canyon floor, they would have seen one man, walking slowly and with a slight limp, leading a mule. The man was walking with a definite purpose, for earlier he had picked out the exact spot where he intended to make camp for the night.

Although he had not been keeping an exact count, it would be the three hundred and fifteenth consecutive night spent in the desert. The old prospector's name was Ben Hanlon. Not knowing the exact date or year he wasn't sure how old he was—in his late fifties or early sixties he believed. He could pretty much estimate the month by the position of the sun, and he was fairly certain he could come within a year or two of the correct year, though he wouldn't bet on it.

He made his camp at the foot of Weaver's Needle—a tall rock obelisk so precisely formed it looked almost as if it had been made by the hand of man. Weaver's Needle guarded Superstition Mountain and as Hanlon settled in for the evening, he looked up at the mountain. "Well, Mr. Mountain, you have beaten a lot of men," he said. "And you may beat me as well, but I plan to give you one hell of a battle before I cross over that canyon."

He was tired from a full day of digging into crevices and breaking open rocks. It was all part of his ceaseless quest for the gold treasure of Superstition Mountain, known by everyone as the Peralta Vein.

A kangaroo rat scampered out from under a mesquite tree, then waited quietly for a long moment to get its bearings. Ben saw the rat, but the rat did not see Ben. Very slowly, Ben reached for his short handle pickax. With one quick, practiced move, he brought the pick down on the rat's head, killing it instantly.

"Well, little feller, you dropped in just in time," Ben said to the rat's carcass. He pulled his knife from its scabbard, and started to work. "I was beginning to wonder what I was going to have for supper."

Working quickly, and expertly, Ben skinned, cleaned, and spitted the rat. He cooked it over an open fire, watching it brown as his stomach growled with hunger. The rat was barely cooked before he took it off the skewer and began to eat it ravenously, not waiting for it to cool. When all the meat was gone he broke open the bones and sucked out the marrow.

After his meal, he allowed himself a smoke, filling

his pipe three fourths with dried sweetgrass and one fourth with tobacco, in order to conserve his tobacco. Finally, with his hunger satisfied, he stretched out on the ground, more hospitable in the cool of evening. Listening to the quiet, almost melodious hoots of a great horned owl, he drifted off to sleep.

Somewhere in Kansas

Janelle had read about it, of course, but she had no idea how large America was until she started her journey two days ago. All day long, except for the occasional stops at places so tiny she wondered how they could call themselves towns, there had been nothing to see through the windows but open space.

Earlier she had asked the conductor if he could supply a board so she could write a letter and he had obliged her with one. As it grew too dark for her to see anything outside, she used the light of the wall mounted kerosene lantern to write a letter.

> *My Dearest Sister Sue,*
>
> *My heart is heavy with sadness over being separated from my baby, but I know that what I am doing now is the right thing. With every mile of distance I place between myself and New York, I am removing myself from the scandal and shame I brought on myself. Not until I am well clear of that scandal and shame, will I be able to recover some sense of dignity and self-worth.*
>
> *I will try and describe for you some of the sights I*

have seen on this trip. First, I had no idea of the size of this country. From New York we can easily travel to Boston, or Philadelphia, or Baltimore within a day and, for the entire trip be well aware of the civilization which surrounds us. And, though the distance was long, such was the case as far as St. Louis, which likes to call itself the Gateway to the West. It is modern and civilized in every way. As we crossed the Mississippi River, I counted almost forty great riverboats tied up on the banks of the river. The city itself is filled with big buildings and teeming with masses of people. Except for the rather peculiar, flat sounding accents, one could almost believe they were in New York.

But the farther west I go, the less of civilization I see. For this entire day, we could have been at sea, so flat and featureless is the land. Often the horizon is so far away, and so clearly delineated, that one gets the impression of seeing all the way to the outer edge of Earth itself. I find it all exciting and rather strangely magnificent, and were my heart not heavy with sorrow over the conditions which have placed me here, I rather think I might enjoy it.

Please take care of my baby, and tell Mother and Father that I love them dearly. I do this so as to bring them no more sorrow. And, Sue, my dearest, dearest darling sister, know that my love for you exceeds all bounds.

> *Your sister,*
> *Janelle*

Finishing the letter, Janelle put it in an envelope, sealed it, and affixed to it a gray blue Franklin, one-cent postage stamp. When the conductor walked by a short while later, she called out to him.

"Yes, ma'am?"

"Here is your writing board, and I thank you for allowing me to use it. I wonder if you could tell me the best way to mail my letter?"

"Why, I can take the letter for you, miss," the conductor said. "We have a mail car attached to this very train. I shall just take it to the clerks there."

"But we are going west, and this letter is for New York."

The conductor smiled. "Not to worry, miss. They will simply set it off with the mail at the next stop, and an east bound train will pick it up."

"Oh, yes, I suppose that is how it would be done. Thank you," Janelle said, handing him the letter. "Thank you very much."

"You are quite welcome, miss. I notice that some of the other passengers have had their beds made. Shall I send the porter to turn down your bed?"

"Yes, thank you. I would appreciate that."

Half an hour later, Janelle was in the lower bunk, which she preferred over the upper because she could look through the window. A full and very bright moon painted the barren landscape in stark shades of black and silver. Seen at night, the landscape seemed softer, and less harsh than it did by day, under the blows of a midday sun.

At such quiet, introspective moments, Janelle wondered if she had made a huge mistake in leaving New York to come to a land that she had never seen before. She thought of her baby. She missed him terribly, and wished he had been old enough to understand why she felt it was necessary that she leave.

She wept for a while. Then, listening to the clack of the wheels on the track joints, and gently rocked by the sway of the car in motion, she drifted off to sleep.

Superstition Mountain

At dawn the notches of the Mazatzal Mountains, which lay to Ben Hanlon's east, were touched with the dove-gray of early morning. Shortly thereafter, a golden fire pushed over the mountain tops, filling the sky with light and color, waking all the creatures below.

Hanlon woke up, checked his mule, then walked away to make water. He craved some coffee, but in truth he couldn't remember the last time he'd had a cup. He had some sassafras root, so he could make sassafras tea, though it was a poor substitute. He was able to have a morning smoke, but even with his strict conservation of tobacco, he was quickly running out. Soon he would have to cut down to only one smoke per day, and the time would come when he couldn't smoke at all.

He would have enjoyed a biscuit with his tea, but he had no flour. He wished he had preserved a little of his supper so he could have some breakfast, but he didn't, so he started work without eating. He could always eat later.

Thinking he saw some "color" in the dirt under a small, spiny tree, Ben reached for his short handled pickax, then moved over to the mesquite bush. On his knees he worked the ground beneath it until he heard a scurrying noise. He jumped back, afraid he might have stirred up a rattlesnake. Seeing that it was only a kangaroo rat, he chuckled.

"Damn, you little critter!" he said aloud. "You ought to know better'n to scare a feller like that. What are doin', lookin' for your brother? Well, I got news for you. He's gone. I had him for supper last night. And if I could sneak up on you, I'd have you for breakfast."

The rat scurried away and Ben went back to striking the hard packed dirt around the mesquite bush, pulling up clods and breaking them into smaller pieces, looking for ore bearing rock, working with the patience and skill developed by more than twenty years of desert prospecting.

Born in South Carolina, Hanlon was twenty-five years old when he boarded a ship in Charleston Harbor to be a part of the California gold rush. That was in 1849, and for several years he panned enough gold from the rivers and creeks to keep himself going, though he never made the big strike. Finally, hearing rumors of a gold mine discovered and lost on Superstition Mountain of Arizona— *"It's got a vein of pure gold, ten feet high, fifteen feet deep, and near 'bout one mile long,"*—he left California.

Since coming to Arizona Ben had very little interaction with people, though from time to time he ventured in from the wilderness to take some sort of job, staying just long enough to earn sufficient money to allow him to go back out to continue his quest. He didn't need much money to survive.

Not too long after arriving in Arizona, he married an Apache woman. She taught him a lot about desert survival. As a result he was adept at trapping animals for his food, he knew enough edible plants to consider the desert his own private garden, he knew the location of every source of water for miles, and he knew where to find salt. After a few years of isolation she had had enough and returned to her people.

As Hanlon knelt under the mesquite tree, working the hot, rocky dirt with his pickax, he heard his mule moving around behind him. "Now, Rhoda, you just stay put," he said. "If you wander off you're on your own, 'cause I don't plan to be a' comin' after you. And remember, I'm the one knows where to find water."

Rhoda whickered, and scratched at the ground with her hoof.

"What 'n tarnation do you want? Can't you see I'm a' workin' over here?"

Rhoda whickered again and, with a sigh, Hanlon put his pickax down and got up.

"All right, all right," he said as he walked over to his mule. "Tell me what's wrong."

Again, the mule raked her hoof along the ground.

"What? You got a thorn in your foot? All right, I know how them things can hurt. Lift up your foot and let me—"

He stopped in midsentence, then dropped to his knees to look where Rhoda had been scratching.

There, on the ground at Rhoda's front two hooves, was a small pile of color bearing rocks.

"What in the world?" Hanlon asked. Dropping on his knees, he began moving the rocks around. "Rhoda, is this real?" he asked in excitement.

Pulling his knife from its leather scabbard, he scraped away the dirt, then poked the knife into the color. The knife punched easily into the color. "Gold!" he shouted. "Rhoda, these here rocks is all gold nuggets. Ever' damn one of 'em and lookie here! They got more gold than rock!"

How did they get there? Why were they just lying here? Where did they come from?

"Rhoda, ol' girl! You know what you've just done? You've found what we been lookin' for all these years! The next time we go into town I'm a' goin' to buy you the biggest sack of oats you've ever seen!"

Rhoda whickered and nodded her head as Ben began gathering up the nuggets.

Denver

Janelle found a seat in the middle of the car. It was the fourth time she had changed trains since leaving New York, and the first train that had only day cars. Fortunately, she had only one more night to spend on the train. Though it was bound to be uncomfortable for her she was certain she would be able to handle it.

She was told they would be going through the Rocky Mountains, and the flyer she had picked up in the Denver depot, promised *wonderful vistas of canyons, lakes, crags, and streams in the Colorado Rocky Mountains. You never saw, nor have you ever dreamed such wondrous sights as will greet you along every mile of track.*

She thought about writing another letter to her sister, describing some of the scenery to her, but the very act of writing would take her eyes away, so she simply stared through the window, soaking up memories she could access later.

She still felt some remorse over having left her baby behind, as well as sadness for isolating herself from the rest of her family. But, given the grandeur of the marvelous country she was passing through, that sadness was temporarily set aside and she found herself looking forward to the excitement before her.

Chapter Seven

Idaho Springs

Because he was without a horse, Falcon had to take a train back to MacCallister.

"Do you have any baggage, Mr. MacCallister?" the station agent asked.

"My saddle and saddlebags," he said.

"What about your rifle?"

Falcon considered checking his rifle through, but decided against it. "No, thanks, I guess I'll just keep it with me. I'm only going a few stops, so it won't be that much of an inconvenience for me—if it doesn't violate any of the railroad rules."

"No sir, no problem at all. However, we do have a rule that no game shall be shot from the train."

"What would be the sense of shooting game from the train, if you can't get off to get it?" Falcon asked.

"Precisely, sir," the station agent said. He wrote out the ticket and handed it to Falcon. "The train should be here within the hour."

Falcon thanked him, then took a seat in the waiting room. True to the station agent's promise, it was just under an hour when he heard the whistle of the approaching train. He walked out onto the platform to wait for it.

The train swept into the station with belches of steam and smoke, and the squealing sound of steel on steel as it drew to a stop. Falcon waited until the arriving passengers on the train, two young men, stepped down. Once all arriving passengers had detrained, the conductor looked out over the platform then, with all the dignity and authority of his office shouted out, "'Board!"

Having issued the call, he moved toward the boarding step to greet those who were climbing onto the train. Falcon was the last of six passengers to board, and as he approached the step the conductor smiled broadly and said, "Mr. MacCallister, it's good to see you, sir. It's been a while since you rode with us."

"Hello, Andy. Yes it has, hasn't it?" He left unstated the explanation as to why he was riding the train. Carrying his rifle low in his left hand, Falcon passed from the front to the rear of the car. Midway to the back, he saw a very pretty woman sitting next to a window. She noticed him looking at her and returned his gaze with a smile.

"Ma'am," he said, touching the brim of his hat and nodding as he continued toward the back of the car.

Falcon chose a seat that was unoccupied so he could spread out a bit. It wasn't that he was too big to sit in one half of the seat, it was just that he found it more relaxing if he could have the entire seat to himself. Putting his rifle butt down on the floor between his knee and the wall of the car, he settled back to get comfortable for the ride.

Janelle had almost blushed under the tall, handsome man's scrutiny. He was handsome, courteous, and possessed all the qualities vile Boyd Zucker lacked. Why couldn't she have found someone like that?

Wait a minute, she scolded herself. What on earth was she thinking? She didn't know that man. She had less than a three second encounter with him, a brief exchange of glances, and she was extolling him with virtues that, though they may have been correct, were certainly not in evidence from the brief meeting. With nothing more than his looks and polite greeting to validate her hasty assessment of him, she was lamenting the fact that she had not met him before she met Zucker.

Besides, the man was armed to the teeth. He had a big pistol strapped to one side, a knife on the other, and was carrying a rifle. Did he expect to get into a war? No, she would be better off not getting such silly romantic notions in her head as to start fantasizing over a well armed, albeit tall and very handsome, stranger on the train.

Once the train pulled out of the station Janelle again turned her attention to the magnificent scenery outside. The long trip from New York had been exhausting, and the first part of the trip, through the farmlands of the Midwest, had been boring. But since coming farther West the vistas were becoming more and more magnificent and she found that she was actually enjoying the trip, tiring though it might be.

Two stops later a young man dressed all in black, got onto the train. The black was alleviated only by flashes of silver—a silver band around his hat and a silver belt buckle. He wore a pistol with an ivory handle and though she had grown somewhat used to seeing armed men over the last couple days, most were wearing their weapons in an understated way. The young man made a show of his pistol.

There was something about him, a cockiness and an arrogance, that she found most unappealing. As he came closer to her seat, she turned to look out the window so as not to make eye contact with him. She inhaled a sharp breath when she sensed he had stopped right beside her seat. She willed herself not to look around, hoping, praying, he would take the hint and pass her by.

"Now, darlin' how do you think that makes me feel, you starin' out the window like that just to keep from lookin' at me?" she heard the man ask. "Why, that's pure insultin'."

"I'm sorry," Janelle said. "I meant no insult."

The arrogant young man laughed. "Oh, I think you did mean to insult me."

The train started with a jerk and the young man had to grab the back of the seat to keep from falling. Janelle tried, unsuccessfully, to smother a laugh.

"Now you're laughin' at me," the young man said.

"Please, won't you leave me alone?"

"You want me to leave you alone, do you?"

"Yes, please."

The young man giggled, not pleasantly, but with an evil cackle. "And what happens if I don't leave you alone?" he asked.

"I'll tell you this, mister. You aren't going to like what happens, if you don't leave her alone," Falcon said, stepping up to the young man.

"Mister, if you don't mind your own business I'm going to—" the young man started, reaching for his pistol even as he was talking. He stopped mid-sentence when he realized his pistol wasn't in his holster.

"Are you looking for this?" Falcon asked, showing the man his pearl handled Colt.

"What? What are you doing with my gun?"

"I'm keeping you alive," Falcon answered.

"What do you mean, you're keeping me alive?"

"If you still had this pistol, you might try and use it on me. And then I would have to kill you."

"Mister, who the hell do you think you are?" the young belligerent asked.

"Mister MacCallister, is there any trouble here?" the conductor asked, coming into the car at that moment.

"No trouble, Andy, as long as you keep this arrogant young fool out of this car," Falcon replied.

"MacCallister?" the young man said, the arrogance and anger on his face replaced by an expression of fear. "Did you call him MacCallister?"

"That's his name," the conductor answered. "Falcon MacCallister."

"Mr. MacCallister, I'm sorry," the young man said. "I didn't mean no harm."

"I'm not the one you need to apologize to," Falcon said. "The person you need to apologize to is the young lady you have been bothering."

The young man turned to Janelle. "I'm sorry, ma'am. I was just, well, I don't exactly know what I was just doin'. But I promise you, I won't be doin' it no more."

"That's quite all right," Janelle said.

Falcon emptied all the cartridges from the young man's pistol, then handed it over to the conductor.

"Hold on to this, will you Andy? Give it back to him when he gets off the train," Falcon said.

"Yes, sir, I'll be glad to do that," the conductor said. "Come along, son. I'll find you a seat in one of the other cars."

Janelle watched as the young man, much less arrogant, meekly followed the conductor out of the car.

"I don't know how to thank you," she said to Falcon.

"My pleasure," Falcon said, again touching the brim of his hat. "I hope the rest of your trip is a pleasant one."

The tall, handsome man, who Janelle could now truly call her hero, returned to his seat in the back of the car, though she wished she had the courage to ask him to join her. Over the next half hour, she went over scenarios in her mind whereby she came up with some clever way of meeting him, but before she could work up the courage to approach him, the train made another stop, and with one final, courteous nod, Mr. Falcon MacCallister, as the conductor had called him, left the train.

Just like that, Janelle thought. Her knight in shining armor was gone, their brief encounter like ships that pass in the night. She would never see him again.

A week later Luke Mueller's horse stepped in a prairie dog hole and Mueller had to shoot him. Throwing his saddle over his shoulder, he began walking. Although his ear was healing, it was still sore, and he knew it must look a sight. With every step he renewed his hatred for Falcon MacCallister. He thought he'd had him back in Idaho Springs, but the man had more lives than a cat. He would get him, though. Or, maybe someone else would kill him. That would be all right too. He didn't care who killed him, he just wanted the son of a bitch dead.

He had walked about two miles when he saw a little trading post that stood all alone, weatherbeaten and drooping. It was the first building of any kind he had seen in the last ten miles. Otherwise indistinguishable from any other desert shack, it was noticeable only because a crudely painted sign had been mounted on the roof, large enough to catch the attention of anyone who might come by.

BLUM'S STORE
BEER – EATS – GOODS

Though it was isolated, the building sat squarely on a much used trail, making it a welcome sight to travelers who might be hungry, or thirsty, or just needing to hear another human voice.

With a sigh of relief, Mueller dropped his saddle on the front porch and went inside. The interior of the store was dark. Light barely filtered through the dirty windows, or the dust-mote laden bars that stabbed in through the cracks between the weathered gray plank walls. The store smelled of the various products offered for sale—salt-cured bacon, flour, dry beans, and stale beer.

A middle-aged, very plump woman was sweeping the floor, and a very thin, bald-headed man was standing behind the counter.

"Your name Blum?" Mueller asked.

"Yes, sir, just like the sign says. My oh my, what happened to your ear?"

"It got bit off by a dog," Muller said.

"All I can say is, that is one mean dog," Blum said.

"Was."

"I beg your pardon?"

"He was one mean dog. I shot him."

"Yes, well, I wouldn't wonder. Now, what can I do for you?"

"I'll have a beer," Mueller said.

"Yes, sir, one beer coming up." Blum picked up a mug, then held it under a spigot that protruded from a barrel. Pulling the handle, the mug was quickly filled with an amber colored liquid, topped with a white, frothy head. He handed the mug to Mueller. "I expect this is goin' to be tastin' awful good to you on this hot day. Most especial, since I seen you walkin' up here, carryin' your saddle on your shoulder. You bein' a little feller an' all, that must have been some load you was a' totin'. I don't mean no disrespect by that, I mean, sayin' you was little and all."

Mueller had a moustache, but no beard. He was in his late thirties, with a face that showed the effects of spending more time outside than in. He had a three corner scar on his forehead and a crescent shaped scar on his right cheek. His right earlobe was mangled and covered with crusty, dark red—almost brown—scar tissue. He had gray eyes, and dirty-blond hair, and as Blum had noted, stood no more than five feet two inches tall.

He blew away some of the foam, then turned the mug up and drained half of it before setting the mug back down. "You seen me walkin', did you?" Mueller asked.

"Yes, sir, I been watchin' you come up for the last ten minutes or so. I pointed you out to my wife over there," Blum said. "Ain't that right, Pearl? Didn't I tell you we got us a customer comin'?" he called over to the woman.

"That's what you done, all right," Pearl answered, though without looking up from her sweeping.

"What happened to your horse, mister?"

"He stepped in a hole and broke his leg, so I had to shoot him.

"Oh, I'm sorry about that. I know folks tend to get real close to their horses. I sure have got close to mine. He's not only fast, he's got a heart so big he can run for hours without ever gettin' tired.

"Yeah, well I ain't goin' to go all weepy eyed, and

start cryin' and blowin' snot over it. It was just a horse," Mueller said.

"Didn't mean to imply that you would," Blum said, somewhat taken aback by the callousness of the man's response. "I was just sayin', losin' a horse is no easy thing, most especial if it leaves you afoot, like this here'n has done you."

"That's true, and it's good you've taken note of that, 'cause, seein' as you know all about it, now, I reckon you also know I'll be needin' a horse."

"I figured you would," Blum said. "Unfortunately, I can't help you with that. Not directly, that is. But I got me a room in the back which I'll let you use for no more'n a dollar, and that'll include your supper and your breakfast. The stage comes through tomorrow mornin' around nine, and it'll take you on in to Piñon."

"Piñon? Colorado?"

Blum laughed. "Piñon, Arizona. You're in Arizona Territory now."

"I'll be damned. I didn't know that."

"No reason you should know it, what with no signs and all. Lots of folks comin' through here don't know if they're in Colorado, Utah, New Mexico, or Arizona. That's 'cause they're all so close together right here. Anyhow, like I was sayin', it'll only cost you a dollar to stay here for the night, an' you can go on into Piñon tomorrow and buy yourself a horse."

"I won't be stayin' here, 'cause I ain't goin' into town," Mueller replied.

"What are you talkin' about, mister? You can't just go a' walkin' through the desert like you was doin' when you come up here. I could tell by lookin' at you that you was nigh on to all done in."

"I want your horse."

Blum laughed. "I reckon you do. Like I said, he's not only the fastest horse around, he's got more endurance than any horse I've ever seen." Blum shook his head. "I'm sorry, mister, but my horse ain't for sale."

Mueller turned the mug up, finished the rest of the beer, then set it down on the counter. With a swipe of the back of his hand, he wiped away the foam that was hanging in his moustache.

"You don't understand. I ain't talkin' about buyin' your horse, Blum. I'm just goin' to take it."

"What?"

"I said I plan to take your horse."

"Are you tellin' me you're figurin' on stealin' my horse?"

"Yeah."

"Like hell you are, you little dried-up son of a bitch!" Blum shouted. Reaching under the counter, he pulled out a double-barreled shotgun, but before he could even swing it around, Mueller drew his pistol and shot him.

"David!" the woman screamed.

Without a word, or a change of facial expression, Mueller turned his pistol on the woman, and shot her, too.

Ten minutes later, with his saddle, thirty-six dollars that he took from Blum's cash box, and a full sack of beans, bacon, and flour thrown across the back of Blum's horse, Mueller rode off. Behind him, Blum and his wife lay dead on the floor of the store.

Chapter Eight

Phoenix, Arizona Territory

It was midafternoon when Janelle stepped down from the train, and so hot she was scarcely able to catch her breath. She had experienced some very warm days in New York, but the wall of heat that washed over her was unlike anything she had ever known before. She moved quickly to get out of the sun and into the shade, but even that offered relatively little relief.

Seeing a bench set up under the roof that extended out over the depot platform, she sat down, then looked around to examine the place.

Why had she chosen Phoenix of all places?

Oh, she knew *why*. Phoenix was a mythical bird that could arise from its own ashes. She considered that allegorical to her own condition. Could she arise from the ashes of her own life?

She thought of her baby, the innocent, and oh so sweet victim of it all. Tears came to her eyes as she realized she had abandoned him, and wondered if she would ever see him again. My God, what a mess she had made of her life!

Struggling to hold on to her composure, Janelle looked around at the place that was to be her new home. She saw an old lady standing near a cart. The woman was dark complexioned, with very black hair and dark eyes. She had a prominent nose and a protruding chin, and she was selling some sort of food, though Janelle had no idea what it was. She watched, with interest, as the woman took out a round, flat piece of bread upon which she put various condiments—Janelle was certain one was some sort of meat, but she didn't have any idea what the others were. The woman put some sort of sauce on all of it, rolled it up, and gave it to her customers.

The other thing she noticed was nearly every man carried a gun, many in a holster that hung from their belt, but nearly as many carried their pistol stuck down into the waistband of their trousers. Surely all these guns weren't necessary, were they? My heavens, was she about to see a gun battle, with half the men choosing one side and the other half choosing the other side?

She had one hundred and forty-one dollars in cash on her person, and she wondered if she should be frightened that one of those armed men would rob her. But, surely, they would not do so in broad daylight, in front of so many people.

She knew the money she had would last her for a while. But what would she do after that money ran out? She had thought only to get away from the shame and disgrace; she hadn't given any thought at all to what she would do to sustain herself.

"No, this isn't right!" a woman cried. She was clearly agitated. "This isn't at all what I ordered!"

"This is the order that arrived on the train for you, Mrs. Buckner."

"Then send it back."

"I'll be glad to send it back if you want me to. But if I send it back, you do understand that you will have to pay the shipping charges, don't you? And from the way I read the bill of lading you have already paid for the product and there is no refund, so all you would be doing is giving the product away."

"But I ordered bonnets." The woman pulled out a hat and held it up. "Does this look like a bonnet to you?"

"No, ma'am," the depot agent said. "Truth is, I don't know what you would call these here things."

"That is called a three-story hat," Janelle said, speaking from her position on the bench.

"I beg your pardon?" the woman asked, looking around toward Janelle.

Janelle put her hand to her lips. "I'm sorry. Please forgive me for butting in where I had no right."

"What did you say this was?" the woman asked. She held the hat out toward Janelle.

"It is called a three-story hat," Janelle repeated. "It is also referred to as a flower pot hat. Bonnets are so passé now. The three-story hat is all the rage."

"Is that a fact? And just where is this place that they are all the rage?"

"I'm sorry, I've said too much already. Please forgive me."

"No, no, my dear, there is nothing to forgive. Believe me, I'm very interested. Please. Have you some involvement with fashion?"

Janelle laughed. "I suppose that depends upon your definition of the term involvement. To hear my father tell it, one would think that my sister and I supported the entire fashion industry of New York. Now, while we were quite active in our shopping, to say that we supported the entire fashion industry would be quite an exaggeration."

The woman laughed with her. "But you do understand fashion, don't you, my dear? I mean, how else would you know about these things? What did you call them, flower pots?"

"Three-story hats, or flower pot hats. Yes, they have become quite popular of late. I'm afraid the ladies in New York consider bonnets to be rather matronly."

"My husband and I own Buckner's Ladies' Emporium here in town. Do you think I will be able to sell these?"

"If you have enough young ladies who want to be fashionable, yes, I'm certain you will be able to sell them."

"You wouldn't like to help me sell them, would you?"

"I beg your pardon?"

"What I mean is, I am offering you a job. What are you doing in Phoenix? Do you have a job? Do you need a job?" The woman put her hand over her own mouth. "Oh, now it is I who should ask for forgiveness. I have no right to impose myself into your private affairs that way."

A broad smile spread across Janelle's face. "No, no, you aren't imposing at all. I don't have a job, and yes, I do need a job."

"My name is Nellie Buckner. My husband, Ken, and I own Buckner's Ladies' Emporium. How would you like to come work for us?"

"I would love to. But first, I have to find a place to live."

"That won't be hard, I can take care of that for you as well, if you would like. I have a friend who owns a boardinghouse. A very nice and genteel boarding house. Come with me, I'll introduce you to her."

"My luggage."

"You'll be taking her to Mrs. Poindexter's?" the depot agent asked.

"Yes, Mr. Donovan. Would you please see to it that Miss"—she paused midsentence and looked at Janelle—"oh my, it would appear that I have just hired you, and I don't even know your name."

"My name is Wellington. Janelle Wellington," Janelle said.

"Please see to it that Miss Wellington's luggage is delivered to the Poindexter House."

"Yes, ma'am."

"Now, Janelle—may I call you Janelle?" Nellie Buckner asked.

"Oh, please do."

"Come with me. We'll get you all moved in, then I'll take you over to the store to introduce you to my husband, and show you where you will be working."

"Oh, before I go, if you don't mind, I would like to send a telegram back to New York to let my family know that I have arrived safely."

"Yes, of course you can. I'll wait right here," Nellie said.

"Western Union is just inside the depot, Miss Wellington," Donovan said.

"Thank you."

Once inside, Janelle wrote her message out on a tablet, then slid it across to the telegrapher. He looked at it, then crossed out the period after the word *spirits,* and added the word *stop.*

"What are you doing?"

"There ain't no code for period, so we use stop," he said. He read it aloud. "I am in Phoenix and in good spirits, stop. All my love, Janelle. Take out the words *I am* and *all my* and *and.* The message would then read, In Phoenix in good spirits stop Love Janelle. Do it that way, and you will save seventy-five cents."

"All right, if you say so."

The telegrapher counted the words. "We don't count the word *love,* we don't count your name. The words that you got left on the paper here will send all the message you are wantin' to send, and this way it will only cost you ninety cents."

"Thank you. That is very kind of you," Janelle said as she handed him a national bank note for one dollar.

"Customer service. That's what Western Union is all about," the telegrapher said as he made change for her.

When Janelle stepped outside, she noticed a

disturbance where she had seen the old woman selling food items from her pushcart.

"Hey, what are you doin' here?" a loud, angry voice shouted at the vendor. The man yelling at the woman who was selling food from her cart was wearing a vest, upon which was pinned a star.

"I'll not have you comin' into my town botherin' the decent citizens," the man said.

"I do nothing wrong, Señor Deputy," the woman said.

"You are breakin' the law," the deputy said.

"Señora Muñoz isn't bothering anyone, Deputy Appleby," Donovan said. "All in the world she is doing is selling tacos, and most of the folks that come here like them. Besides, I gave her permission to be on the railroad property."

"Yeah? Well I ain't give her permission to sell anything in this town," another voice said. A new man arrived on the scene, and like Deputy Appleby, the man, who was bigger and had a bushy moustache, was also wearing a star.

"Marshal Cairns. It's like I told Deputy Appleby, Señora Muñoz has my permission to be on railroad property," Donovan said. "She isn't breaking any law."

"She has no business license. And bein' as I'm the marshal, I'm the one who decides who is and who isn't breakin' the law."

"She isn't breaking any law," Donovan said again. "And she doesn't need a business license as long as she is on railroad property. The railroad has a business license that covers anyone who does business on our property, with our permission," Donovan insisted. "And as I said, I gave her permission to be here."

"Who said she don't need a business license?"

"Why, you can look it up for yourself, Marshal Cairns. It's in the municipal code," the station agent replied.

"If she don't buy herself a license, that means she ain't payin' any taxes. And if she ain't payin' taxes, I'm not gettin' my cut."

"Your cut?"

"Yes, my cut. How do you think me and my deputies get paid? When the city council hired me, they agreed to pay me a base salary, and two percent of all business license fees and taxes."

"That may be, but Señora Muñoz is not in violation."

Cairns nodded at Appleby who, with a loud, cackling laugh, picked one side of the cart and turned it over, spilling the contents onto the ground. The old woman cried out in protest.

"It don't matter now, does it?" Cairns said. "She don't have nothing to sell."

"Marshal Cairns, you shouldn't have done that," Donovan said.

Cairns pointed at the station agent. "Donovan, I'll thank you not to be tellin' me what I should and shouldn't be doin'. I'm the marshal here and I'll do what I damn well please. Let this be a warning to you. Don't be letting indigents come into my town and use your property to get around the law."

"In the first place, she isn't an indigent. She makes enough money selling tacos to support herself and her two children. In the second place, I told you, she is not violating any law. And in the third place, what made this *your* town?"

"I made it my town," Cairns said. "Maybe she ain't breakin' the law now, but I intend to talk to the city council today to get that law changed. If you try and help that Mex woman, or anyone else get around it, I'll throw them *and* you in jail."

After the marshal and his deputy walked away, Janelle went over to help the old woman.

"*Gracias, Senorita, gracias,*" the old woman said as Janelle began helping recover the utensils strewn about. The food she had been selling was scattered on the dirt.

"You are a good woman, Janelle," Nellie said as she and Mr. Donovan joined Janelle in helping the old woman.

"Please don't tell me those awful men were really officers of the law," Janelle said.

"I wish I didn't have to tell you that but, unfortunately, they are," Donovan replied. "Cairns is our city marshal, duly appointed by the city council, and he hired Appleby, who is just as bad."

"I can't help but wonder how in the world the city council could have ever been foolish enough to appoint such an evil man as Mr. Cairns," Nellie said as she continued to help Señora Muñoz recover her utensils. "What they should have done, after Harold Wallace retired, was appoint Deputy Forbis as marshal. He was Marshal Wallace's deputy, and he is a good man."

"John is a good man. But the city council thought he was too young," Donovan said.

"Well if this is what your marshal is like, I certainly hope that I never get on his bad side," Janelle said.

"Oh, honey, you can't help but get on his bad side," Nellie replied.

"What? How?" Janelle asked, concerned about the remark.

"Because he has no good side," Nellie replied and all, including Señora Muñoz laughed.

Finally, with everything recovered, the scattered meats and vegetables cleaned up and put in a trash container, they set the cart back upright. One of the other men who was nearby came over to look at the cart. After feeling the wheels and axles, he stood up and rubbed his hands together. "The cart is undamaged," he said.

"Gracias," Señora Muñoz said.

"Come, dear," Nellie Buckner said to Janelle. "I'll take you over and introduce you to Mrs. Poindexter. She is a wonderful lady and runs a clean and orderly boarding house. I think you will be quite comfortable there."

"I'm sure I will be," Janelle said.

"I cannot get over how cruel that policeman was to that poor Mexican lady," Janelle said as she helped Nellie arrange the three-story hats on a display table."

"We don't have policemen, dear, we call them city marshals," Nellie replied.

"Still, he was incredibly cruel"

"Yes, he was, and he is," Nellie agreed. "I certainly hope you don't think everyone is like the marshal. I would hate for you to get a bad impression about Western men."

"How could I have a bad impression of all Western men?" Janelle asked. "Mr. Donovan is a Westerner, isn't he? And he certainly seems like a very good man."

"Yes, I believe he is, as well."

"And I met a man named Falcon MacCallister on the train," Janelle continued. She hugged herself and smiled.

"You met Falcon MacCallister?"

"Yes. Why, do you know him?"

Nellie shook her head. "I don't know him, but I have heard of him. His name is quite well known throughout the West."

"Really?"

"Yes, really."

"Oh, dear," Janelle said. "Is he an outlaw?"

"An outlaw?" Nellie laughed. "No, my dear, quite the contrary. Although he is not a full-time lawman, he has the reputation of being the nemesis of all outlaws. Some even call him a genuine Western hero."

"I knew it!" Janelle said. "I knew that someone like that couldn't be a bad man."

"Someone like that? My, it sounds as if you did more than just meet him."

"He came to my rescue on the train."

"Oh? Do tell."

Janelle laughed self-consciously. "Well, it was nothing so dramatic; a young man was being a bit more persistent than I wanted. He continued to the point that it was getting quite uncomfortable for me. Mr. MacCallister asked him to leave me alone and the man got quite belligerent. In fact, I honestly believe he intended to draw his gun against Mr. MacCallister but—" she paused mid-sentence and laughed.

"What?" Nellie asked, confused by the laughter. "I hardly think drawing a gun would be cause for laughter."

"It was funny," Janelle said. "You see, he tried to draw his gun—I have no idea how he did it—but somehow when the young man went for his gun his holster was empty, and his gun was in Mr. MacCallister's hand."

Nellie chuckled. "Yes, I can see how that would be funny. I would like to have seen that. Evidently Falcon MacCallister made quite an impression on you."

"He did, I admit. I do believe he is the most handsome man I've ever met. No, I can't say that, exactly. I've seen some very handsome men in New York of course, but most of them are, I'm not sure what expression to use, but, they are what I would call dandies. Mr. MacCallister was handsome, but he was sort of rough looking, too."

Nellie smiled. "Oh my. I think if you stay in our West long enough, you will meet just such a man and stay out here."

"Who knows?" Janelle replied. "I might. When one begins a new adventure, one never can tell what lies ahead."

Every afternoon at two o'clock, Nellie's husband, Ken Buckner, and a few other businessmen met in the Boar's Head Saloon for one beer. Nellie didn't mind Ken's visits. He never abused the situation, he never stayed more than one hour, and she had her own ritual—a morning tea with some of the other ladies in town.

Most of the time Ken's visits were pleasant, with friendly conversation and good-natured bantering. At the moment, Corey Minner, a saloon patron and known bully, was having fun at Ken's expense. He called himself a cowboy, but he had been fired from three outfits already. He was currently unemployed, and nobody knew exactly how he was making a living, though he had coerced some of the cowboys he had worked with in the past to lend him money. He sometimes did odd jobs, and many suspected he was responsible for a string of petty burglaries that had taken place recently.

"Hey, Buckner!" Minner called out, tauntingly. "How come you ain't wearin' a dress?"

Ken didn't answer.

"You heard me," Minner said. "You work in a store for ladies, how come you ain't wearin' a dress?"

Ken started to stand up, but one of the other businessmen put his hand on Ken's arm. "Pay him no never mind, Ken."

"Yes, sir," Minner said. "I think you'd look just real purty in a dress."

Ken stood up then, and turned to face Minner. Minner was a young man, in his early twenties, and Ken was in his late fifties.

"You like thinking about men in dresses, do you, Minner?" Ken said. "I find that interesting. I never knew that about you. Of course, you may find

Phoenix too small a place for someone like you. You might be better off in Denver or San Francisco where there are others of your kind."

The other businessmen laughed and while Minner didn't know exactly what Ken was saying, he realized that somehow, his taunting had been turned back on him, and he was now the butt of the joke.

"You son of a bitch!" Minner said. "You talk to me like that, you better draw your gun!"

"I don't wear a gun, Minner," Ken said calmly.

"Yeah? Well that's your mistake, Buckner, because I do wear a gun!" Minner said.

"So do I," another voice said and looking toward the door, the saloon patrons saw Deputy John Forbis standing there, with his gun in his hand.

"This ain't none of your business, Forbis," Minner said, angrily.

Forbis nodded. "Yeah," he said. "Yeah, it is my business. You see, I'm the deputy marshal. Now, you've got two choices. You can either unbuckle that gun belt and let it fall to the floor, or you can get out of here."

"You can't arrest me, I ain't done nothin'," Minner complained.

"I'm not arresting you," Forbis said. "I'm just telling you to get rid of your gun, before you get yourself into trouble, or get out of here."

Minner glared at Forbis for a long time, then his face broke into a smile. "You don't have to get all mad about it," he said. "I was just funnin' Buckner, that's all." He turned toward Buckner. "No hard feelin's, Buckner. I was just funnin'."

"No hard feelings," Ken replied.

With a shrug of his shoulders, Corey Minner left the saloon.

"Wally, everything goin' all right in here?" Forbis asked the bartender.

"It's goin' fine, Deputy," the bartender replied.

Forbis took a quick glance around, then nodded at everyone before he left the saloon.

"Damn," one of the businessmen said. "Why the hell didn't the city council pick him as the new marshal instead of Cairns?"

Chapter Nine

The Sonoran Desert, Arizona Territory

Luke Mueller had stumbled on a small, intermittent stream of water. It was the Agua Fria River, though he had no idea what the name was. The water was alkaline and relatively bitter, but it was drinkable, so he wasn't in any danger of dying of thirst.

Hunger was another thing. Two days ago he had made four biscuits and cooked four pieces of bacon from the last of the food he had stolen from Blum. He had eaten the bacon and two of his biscuits at the river the day before and one that morning, leaving only one biscuit remaining. He had a decision to make. Should he eat his last biscuit or save it? Even if he saved the biscuit for later, he would still have the next day to contend with. Eating it now might assuage the hunger a bit. If he waited, he would be so hungry the biscuit would do little to take the edge off the hunger.

The question was answered for him when he saw

some sort of structure ahead of him, rising from the ground like another hillock. As he drew closer he saw it was a man-made structure, built of adobe brick and sun bleached wood. The question as to whether it was empty or occupied was answered when he got closer, for a crude, hand-lettered sign nailed to the roof read

Pa Bakers Way Stop
Beer – Eats

Mueller smiled broadly at the sudden, and unexpected improvement of his situation. He had eaten all the food he stole from Blum, but he had not spent one penny of the money he took. He still had all thirty-six dollars in his pocket.

When he reached the other side of the building, he was surprised to see two freight wagons parked out front. Tying his horse off, he pushed through a hanging piece of canvas and stepped inside. For a moment, he thought he had gone blind. Outside the sun was so bright that he had been keeping his eyes at a squint. Inside, he could barely see.

The room was illuminated only by the light that streamed in through two windows and the space between the roof and the top of the walls. He stood for a long moment, trying to adjust his eyes.

"Hee, hee. It do be dark in here when a feller first comes in out of the bright sunlight, don't it?" a man's voice said. Although Mueller's eyes had not yet adjusted enough for him to see who was speaking, the man's high, squeaky voice gave him a very good mental image.

"Don't be worryin' none about it, you ain't gone blind," the voice said. "Just stand there a minute, and you'll see again, soon enough."

True to the scratchy voice's promise, Mueller's eyesight did return, and he saw that, in addition to the bartender, there were two other men in the room.

Mueller walked over to the bar, which consisted of a few boards laid across a couple empty beer barrels.

"What can I do for you, sonny?" the bartender asked.

"Anything wet," Mueller said.

The other two men laughed. "Hell, Pa Baker, don't you have a wet washrag there? Give that to him," one of the men said.

"I wouldn't do that to man or beast," Pa Baker said as he drew a mug of beer from the beer barrel. "If I ever seen me a feller that needed him a beer, it's this here feller. Here you go, mister."

Mueller took the beer without so much as a word of thanks. He had hoped to find the place deserted except for the proprietor. That way he could have done to Pa Baker exactly what he did to David Blum and his wife.

Picking up the mug, Mueller blew off some of the head before he took a swallow.

"I didn't expect there would be anyone here," Mueller said after he pulled the mug away.

"Oh yeah, bein' as I'm on the road between Phoenix and Tempe, I get a lot of business in here," the bartender said. "Mostly from freight wagon men like Frank and Bob over there. That'll be a nickel."

"What?"

"The beer. That'll be a nickel," Pa Baker said. "I didn't say nothin' 'bout it before, seein' as you had quite a thirst on."

Mueller paid for his beer, then turned to the other two men. "Them your wagons parked out front?"

"Yeah," one of the men said.

"Well, they ain't exactly our wagons," the other said. "They belong to the Phoenix Express Company. We just drive 'em."

"Phoenix? What's that?" Mueller took another long, soul satisfying swallow of his beer.

"You ain't never heard of Phoenix?"

"Can't say as I have," Mueller replied.

"Well, it just happens to be the biggest city in all of Arizona, is all."

"Big? How big?"

"I'd say nigh on to three thousand or so live there. Wouldn't you say that, Bob?"

"Three thousand a least," Bob replied. "Or close to, anyways."

"What they got there?" Mueller asked. He took another long swallow, finishing every drop in the mug. He slapped the mug on the bar and another nickel on the bar. "I'll have another," he said.

"Yes, sir," Pa Baker replied. He chuckled. "I knew you was powerful thirsty when you come in here."

"I was. And I'm hungry too. I'd like you to fix me somethin' to eat."

"Yes, sir, you just go over there to one of them tables and I'll bring it out to you directly."

Mueller went over and sat down, then he looked back at the two drivers. "I asked what they got in Phoneix?"

"Why, they got near 'bout anything a man would want," Bob answered. "They got liquor, food, women—"

"And the meanest son of a bitch of a city marshal you ever seen," the other man said.

"City marshal?" Mueller grew instantly alert. "What about the marshal?"

"Are you an outlaw?"

"What?"

"I didn't mean nothin' by askin' was you an outlaw. It's just that, if you was an outlaw, you wouldn't have nothin' to worry about. He don't go after outlaws. 'Bout the only thing our marshal goes after is free drinks at the saloons."

"And findin' ways to get decent folks in trouble so's they have to pay a fine. For things like spittin' in the street," one of the drivers said.

"Frank, you wasn't exactly spittin' in the street," Bob said.

"Well, it was the same as," Frank insisted.

"No, it warn't the same as. What you was doin' was pissin' in the street," Bob said, laughing.

"Well, I was standin' around the corner so's nobody could see me," Frank protested. "He didn't have no call to arrest me. What he was wantin' was the fine. That's what he was wantin'."

"So what you done is, you paid a dollar, just to take a piss," Bob said, and again he laughed.

"It ain't all that funny," Frank said.

"Here's your food, Señor," a Mexican girl said, bringing the plate to Mueller's table.

He paid for the food, then for the next several moments, he was busy eating. The two drivers returned to their private conversation, and Mueller returned to his own private thoughts.

He had never been to Phoenix. He had never even heard of it, so even if there was anybody there who had ever heard of him, there was for sure nobody there who would recognize him on sight. Ever since he had left Colorado, he had been wandering around with no specific purpose or destination. That had all changed. Luke Mueller was going to Phoenix.

MacCallister Valley

In the town named for him, the bronze statue of Jamie Ian MacCallister had arrived by train nearly three weeks ago and was being stored in the Foster-Matthews warehouse. The intent was to keep it out of sight of the public until the actual unveiling on July Fourth, less than a week away.

Falcon and most of his siblings were given a private viewing and, from there, went out to the old homestead. It belonged to all of them but, by consensus of all the others, was occupied by Falcon. He and his brothers, Jamie Ian IV, Morgan, and Matthew, were standing over the graves of their parents. Falcon's sisters, Joleen, Megan, and Kathleen were on their knees tending to the flowers on the graves.

"I wish Andrew and Rosanna were going to be here," Joleen said.

"They can't," Falcon said.

"I know that's what they said. I'm just not sure why they can't, is all."

"Because they're closing one play on the fourth, and they've got a new play opening on the eleventh," Falcon said. "It would be almost impossible for them to be here."

"They could postpone the play, couldn't they?" Morgan asked.

Falcon shook his head. "There is no way they could do that. Those plays cost thousands of dollars to produce. You can't just postpone them."

"Still—" Morgan started but Joleen interrupted him.

"There is no *still* to it," she said. "Falcon has been to New York, he has seen them on stage, we haven't. If Falcon says it's impossible for them to get away, then I'm inclined to believe him. You know full well they would be here if they could."

"I wasn't doubting him. I was just saying that it's too bad Andrew and Rosanna won't be here, that's all."

"Wait, you ought to put those purple ones over there," Morgan said, pointing to a batch of flowers.

"If you think you can do it better, brother, feel free to pitch in," Megan said.

"All right, I will."

Morgan knelt down, repositioned the flowers he was talking about, then grunted, and held his hand up toward Falcon. "*Oomph.* Help an old man up, will you, little brother?" Morgan said.

"Old man? You are only fifty-three," Falcon said.

"Wait until you are fifty-three," Morgan said, grunting again, as Falcon helped him stand.

"Ha," Falcon said. "When Pa was sixty, he single-handedly wiped out Layfield's entire gang."*

"It wasn't quite single-handed," Morgan said. "He had a few men with him."

"A few *good* men," Jamie Ian added. "Preacher and Smoke Jensen among others."

"And a pretty good Shawnee woman as I recall," Megan added. "Hannah was there."

"They've called Bell City, Hell City ever since, because of that fight," Morgan said.

"And Pa's name will forever be linked with it," Matthew added.

"Now, little brother, your name is as well known as Pa's name ever was," Jamie Ian said to Falcon.

"Not quite," Falcon said. "In fact, not even close."

"Never the less, the way you took out the Mueller gang, four to one, is the stuff of legends," Matthew said.

"Here, the rest of us have gone to ground, so to speak," Morgan said. "Ranching, farming, raising kids and grandkids, while you carry on the MacCallister name."

Falcon laughed. "While *I* carry on the family name? It seems to me like you folks have been doing well enough in carrying on the family name with the number of nephews and nieces I have. Good Lord, half of the people in the valley are MacCallisters. Well, not half maybe, but there are what? Fifty, sixty, by now?"

Talons of Eagles

"One hundred and three," Joleen said as she put the last flower in place. As Morgan had before her, she held her hand out and Falcon helped her up, while Jamie Ian helped Kathleen.

"One hundred and three?" Falcon replied. "Can that be right?"

"If Joleen says one hundred and three, you can count on it," Kathleen said. "She is the family historian."

"For a couple of young people barely of age when they came out here, Jamie and Kate made quite a life for themselves," Joleen said, speaking of their parents.

"And for the nine kids they produced," Matthew added.

"Ten, actually," Joleen corrected.

"Yeah, but I'm talking about the nine of us who made it to adulthood."

"When are you going to settle down, Falcon?" Jamie Ian asked.

"I am settled down," Falcon replied.

The others laughed.

"Right," Matthew said. "That little fracas over in Black Hawk was nothing more than a minor disagreement."

"Matthew, the sons of bitches murdered the Reverend and Mrs. Powell. You know that," Falcon said.

Matthew nodded. "Yeah, I know it," he admitted. "And I say good for you for squaring accounts."

"Accounts aren't squared," Falcon said.

"You're talking about Luke Mueller?"

"Yeah," Falcon said. "When I find him, accounts will be squared."

"You could let the law handle that, couldn't you?" Kathleen asked.

"I could. But Luke Mueller has made it personal," Falcon replied.

"Luke Mueller has made it personal?" Jamie Ian asked. "How so?"

Falcon reached into his pocket and produced the reward poster Luke Mueller had put out on him.

"Like I said, Luke Mueller has made it personal."

Jamie Ian read the poster, then passed it around to the others. "Falcon, it's been a while since I wore my guns, but I still know how to use them. If you want me to, I'll come with you."

"Thanks for the offer, Jamie Ian, but there is no sense in getting any more of the family involved in this."

"What are you going to do? Are you going after him?"

Falcon nodded toward the poster that was in Joleen's hands, having been read by all the others. "I don't think that's going to be necessary. Seeing as he has made me a target, all I'm going to have to do is keep my eyes open. I'm pretty sure our paths will cross again some day, and when they do, I'll be ready for the son of a bitch."

"I think you are right," Jamie Ian said. "I think your paths will cross again."

"How do you like your new horse?" Morgan asked, changing the subject now that the topic of Luke Mueller had been fully discussed.

"I like him just fine," Falcon said. "He's a good horse. Of course, the one Luke Mueller killed was a good one, too."

"He's a beautiful horse," Kathleen said as she looked over at the big, bronze stallion. "What have you named him?"

"Lightning."

"Lightning? That was—"

"The name of Pa's horse. Yes, I know," Falcon replied.

Megan looked down at the grave of their father. "I think Pa would like that," she said.

"Yeah," Jamie Ian said. "In fact, I think he would like the fact that Falcon named a horse after his horse a lot more than the idea of having a life-sized statue of him standing in the middle of Kate Boulevard."

"Oh, I don't know," Joleen said. "I sort of think that might please him, too."

"You know Pa wasn't one for personal glory," Jamie Ian said.

"No, but he was real proud of what he and Ma started here in the valley," Joleen said. "I think the statue speaks to that more than anything else."

"I think so, too," Kathleen said. "I just know he will be there with us next Monday."

"What was it he and Ma called heaven?" Falcon asked. "The Starry Trail?"

"Yes, the Starry Trail," Megan said.

"I figure that, come Monday, Pa and Ma will both be lookin' down on us from The Starry Trail."

Chapter Ten

Phoenix

It took Luke Mueller less than two hours to ride from Pa Baker's Way Stop to Phoenix, a bustling community with a surprising amount of traffic in the street, from large heavily laden and lumbering freight wagons to ranch buckboards to surreys. The sidewalks were filled with pedestrians, and in an empty lot he saw several young boys playing baseball. Luke had never played baseball—or any other sport. He had always been too small, and was always the last one chosen. Rather than face the humiliation of such rejection he chose not to play at all.

Just ahead he saw the Boar's Head Saloon and started toward it. Not watching where he was going he rode right out in front of an approaching surrey.

"Hey, watch it, mister!" the surrey driver called, fighting his team, as both horses reared up in fright over the near contact.

Mueller spurred his horse forward and it reacted quickly, carrying him out of danger. Looking back over his shoulder, he saw the frightened look in the face of the lone woman passenger. For some reason that he could not explain, he found her fear of him pleasurable, and he smiled, though not at her.

"Sorry, Mrs. Guthrie," the surrey driver said. "That fool just cut right in front of us."

"That's quite all right, Mr. Conley. You handled the team beautifully," the middle-aged woman replied.

"Thank you, ma'am," the driver said. He stopped the surrey in front of Buckner's Ladies' Emporium. Jumping down, he stepped around to help Mrs. Guthrie exit. "Shall I wait out here for you, ma'am?"

"Yes, please, if you don't mind," she said, taking his hand as she stepped down. "I shan't be too long."

As she opened the door to the Emporium the tinkling bell summoned Nellie from the back of the store and she went up front to greet her customer. "Mrs. Guthrie," she said, recognizing one of her best customers. "How nice to see you."

"Did you see that awful man in the street?" Mrs. Guthrie asked.

Nellie frowned, and shook her head. "No, I'm afraid I didn't," she said.

"He cut right in front of us. Had it not been for Mr. Conley's skillful driving, why, the surrey could have been upset."

"Oh, how glad I am that didn't happen," Nellie replied. "Now, what can I do for you?"

"Mr. Guthrie and I are going to Philadelphia for my niece's wedding, and the gown I wear simply must be of the latest fashion," Mrs. Guthrie explained. "My sister believes that because we are living in the far West we must all dress as savage Indians, and I want to prove her wrong."

"Well, let us see what we can find for you," Nellie said with a professional smile.

Because the saloon was out of the sun, it was a few degrees cooler, but only marginally so. There were several young men in the back corner, along with a young woman whose dress made it evident she was an employee of the saloon. One of the young men said something that Mueller didn't hear, and there was a burst of laughter.

Mueller stepped up to the bar and was greeted by the bartender, who was wearing a smile.

"What can I do you for, mister?" he asked.

"Beer."

More laughter rolled from the table of young men, and the bartender chuckled.

"Ol' Quince is on a roll today," he said as he pulled the handle to draw the beer.

"Quince?"

"You see the young feller there with the fancy gun and holster? That's Quince Anders. He works for Murdock Felton, who owns the Tumbling F ranch. Well, the fact is, all them boys work for Mr. Felton."

"That's quite a holster set he's wearing," Mueller said as he took the beer.

"Yes sir. Well, Quince is really good with the gun, so I reckon the holster ain't out of place."

"What do you mean when you say he is good with a gun? I've been around a lot, but I ain't never heard of someone named Quince Anders.

"Oh, don't get me wrong, he ain't what you would call a gunfighter or nothin' like that. I mean he ain't never kilt nobody. But he's 'bout the fastest I've ever seen, and he always hits what he's shootin' at."

"The hell I can't!" Quince said loudly. "I know damn well I can do it."

"You willin' to put your money where your mouth is?"

"What do you mean?"

"I'll bet you a quarter you can't do it."

Quince shook his head. "Uh-uh. A quarter ain't enough money. You want me to prove it to you, Stanley, it's goin' to cost more than a quarter."

"How much more?"

"Five dollars."

Stanley blanched. "Five dollars? I ain't got five dollars."

"We get paid Saturday," Quince said. "I'll hold your marker 'til then." He smiled. "Of course, you may be right. It could be that I can't do it at all, then you would be five dollars richer."

"Yeah, I would, wouldn't I?" Stanley stroked his chin as he contemplated the offer. "Let's make certain what we're bettin' on," he said. "What you're tellin' me is that you are goin' to hold a glass of whiskey on the back of your hand—out shoulder high—then turn your hand, draw your pistol, and hit the glass before it hits the floor. Is that what you're sayin'?"

"That's what I'm saying," Quince replied.

"And we're talkin' about a whiskey shot glass, not a beer mug, right?"

"Damn, Stanley, you're sure makin' it hard on me," Quince said.

Laughing, Stanley looked at the others. "I didn't think he'd take me up on it."

"Oh, I didn't say I wasn't goin' to take you up on it. I just said you were making it hard on me. Is it a bet?"

Stanley nodded. "Yeah," he said. "It's a bet."

Quince picked up a whiskey glass and put it on the back of his hand, then held his hand out.

"Wait a minute, hold it!" the bartender shouted. "Quince, you ain't plannin' on doin' that in here, are you?"

"Why not?" Quince replied.

"Why not? 'Cause it's dangerous shootin' inside, that's why not. You're likely to hit someone. At the very least, you'll be puttin' a bullet hole in my floor."

"Come on, Wally, it ain't like you don't have about a dozen holes in your floor already," Quince said. "'Sides, look at it this way. "Once I do this, folks will be wantin' to come here to have a drink in the saloon where the great Quince Anders done the best shootin' that's ever been done."

Mueller turned his back to the bar so he could have an unrestricted view of what was going on.

Wally laughed out loud. "I'll say this for you,

Quince, you sure have a high opinion of yourself. All right, go ahead, try it. If you can do it, you're right, it might be a good advertisement for my place. And if you can't do it, well, it'll be good to see you gettin' your comeuppance."

"There ain't goin' to be no comeuppance, old man. You can count on that," Quince replied.

Mueller watched as Quince Anders put the glass on the back of his hand, his arm stretched out full at shoulder height.

"Somebody need to count or somethin'?" Stanley asked.

"No need to count," Quince replied. "Just hush and let me do this."

The saloon grew very quiet then as the other patrons in the saloon realized what was about to take place. All eyes were on Quince.

Quince turned his hand and the whiskey glass started toward the floor. Suddenly there was a shot and the whiskey glass shattered, but it wasn't Quince who fired. It was Luke Mueller.

Gasps of shock and surprise escaped from all those who had been watching. Since it was obvious Quince had not been the one who broke the glass, they were puzzled.

"I'll be damned," Wally Cook said. "I ain't never seen nothin' like that."

Looking over at Wally, the mystery was solved when the others saw Luke Mueller standing with his back to the bar, holding a pistol, with a small stream of smoke drifting from the barrel.

"Mister, what the hell did you do that for?" Quince demanded. "You messed up my trick."

"Wasn't much of a trick," Mueller said. "You seen how easy I shot the glass."

"Yeah? Well let me tell you what I'm goin' to do now. I'm goin' to come over there and whip your scrawny ass, you little shit."

Mueller put his pistol back in his holster, then smiled a cold, humorless smile at Quince.

"I don't think you want to do that," Mueller said.

"Why don't I want to do that? You just cost me five dollars, is what you done."

"I'll give you a chance to get your five dollars back," Mueller said.

"How?"

"Shoot against me," he said.

"For five dollars?"

"Or more."

"What will we shoot at?"

"Oh," Mueller said easily. "I thought you knew. We would shoot against each other."

"What? Are you crazy?"

"I might be," Mueller said. "After all, you've been telling everyone how good you were. I'd have to be crazy to want to go against you, wouldn't I?"

Quince suddenly realized that he had stepped into a lot more than he had bargained for. "One of us could get killed if we did that," he said, his words squeaking out of a throat constricted by fear.

"Yes," Mueller replied. "That's generally the way it happens. One of us always gets killed. So far it hasn't been me."

What had started as lighthearted entertainment had suddenly turned deadly serious and all eyes were on the two principals.

"What will it be, cowboy? Shall we settle this little dispute between us?"

Quince stared at Mueller for a long moment, as if unable to believe he had gotten caught up in such a deadly game.

"No!" Quince said, holding both hands out in front of him, palms facing outward. "No, I ain't goin' to do this!" Quickly, he turned and ran from the saloon.

"You didn't leave him much there, partner," Wally said quietly. "He wasn't harmin' nobody."

Mueller picked up his beer, drained it, then put it down. "Give me another beer," he said.

Wally refilled the mug, then put it on the bar in front of Mueller. "What's your name, mister?"

"My name ain't none of your business," Mueller replied.

"No sir, you're right. It ain't none of my business," Wally said, quickly. "I didn't mean nothin' by askin'. I was just bein' a mite friendly, is all."

"I don't need no friends," Mueller said.

"No sir, I don't reckon you do," Wally said, walking to the far end of the bar.

Mueller took his beer mug over to the most distant table, then sat there alone. He did not want anyone to know who he was, nor did he want to be bothered by anyone. It was for that reason he had shot the glass Quince dropped. That little exhibition had the desired effect; it had generated fear and respect in everyone who saw it.

* * *

Over in Buckner's Ladies' Emporium, Mrs. Guthrie was standing in front of a mirror, looking at herself. She was wearing a gown that Nellie Buckner had recommended to her.

"What do you think?" she asked Nellie.

"Let me have you consult with Miss Wellington," Nellie said. "She has recently come into my employ and has a wonderful eye for fashion."

"It can't just be pretty, you understand," Mrs. Guthrie said. "It must be up to date with the latest fashions from the East."

"Miss Wellington has recently arrived from New York. I think you will find her suggestions most helpful. Janelle, won't you come speak with Mrs. Guthrie?" she called.

"Yes, of course," Janelle answered from the back of the store. "Oh, that's a lovely gown," Janelle said as she approached.

"Yes, but is it fashionable?" Mrs. Guthrie asked.

"She is going to a wedding in Philadelphia," Nellie said. "She must be very up to date."

"I see. In that case . . . Mrs. Guthrie, is it?"

"Yes."

"Perhaps you wouldn't mind a couple suggestions?" Janelle asked.

"I wouldn't mind at all."

"Then I would say extend the bustle even farther in the back."

"Really? It seems quite large enough to me," Mrs. Guthrie said.

"Oh, but they are even larger now," Janelle said. "Then, we'll add several layers of brightly colored material in beautiful colors: magenta, gold, brilliant green, and red, all in a waterfall effect." As she spoke, Janelle grabbed up bolts of cloth and skillfully draped them to give the illusion she was describing.

"Oh, yes!" Mrs. Guthrie said, looking at the effect in the mirror. "Yes, that would be beautiful, wouldn't it? And this is what they are wearing in New York?"

"Not everyone in New York," Janelle replied. "Only the most fashionable ladies are wearing it."

"Only the most fashionable, you say?"

"Yes, during the season there are a bevy of balls, dinners, parties, receptions, and other activities, many of them hosted by Mrs. Astor, or Mrs. Gould. Only the most elite members of the Four Hundred attend such events, and they are always wearing the latest and most fashionable designs. With a few slight alterations to this gown, why, you would fit right in with the Four Hundred."

"What is the Four Hundred?"

"The Four Hundred are the most elite of New York society," Janelle explained. She chuckled. "I have heard that the number was selected because that was how many people could fit in to Mrs. Astor's ballroom."

"Oh, my. Someone has a ballroom large enough to hold four hundred people?"

"Mrs. Astor does."

"Have you ever seen anyone who belongs to this Four Hundred you are talking about?"

Janelle and her family were members of the Four Hundred, but she did not think it was proper to make that claim, so she demurred somewhat. "I have seen them," she said, without further explanation.

"Then surely I must wear this gown to my niece's wedding. Nellie, how soon could you have the gown ready?"

"When are you leaving for Philadelphia?"

"Monday morning."

"Heavens, this is Friday. That doesn't give us much time. And Monday is the Fourth of July. Do you mean to tell me you are going to miss all the festivities?"

"I'm afraid so," Mrs. Guthrie replied. "But, I will gladly pay extra to have the gown done in time."

Nellie looked over at Janelle. "Do you think we could have it finished tomorrow, Janelle?"

Janelle nodded and smiled. "Yes, we can have it ready for you by tomorrow."

"Nellie, wherever did you find this lady? What a wonderful addition she is to your emporium. You must never let her go," Mrs. Guthrie said.

"I found her as soon as she came to Phoenix," Nellie replied. "She will be a valued employee of the emporium for as long as she wishes."

"I cannot wait until I wear it. Oh, the people in Philadelphia will be absolutely pea green with envy," she said as she left.

Chapter Eleven

Shortly after Mrs. Guthrie left, Ken Buckner came in, wearing a broad smile. "I just entered Vexation in the horse race for the Fourth of July," he said.

"Oh, Ken, after that spill last year, I thought you weren't going to do that anymore," Nellie said.

"Don't worry, I learned my lesson. I won't be riding Vexation, I will have someone else ride for me."

"Who?"

"I don't know yet, but I'm sure I can find someone before Monday."

"I will ride for you," Janelle said. She was busy gathering up the material she was going to add to Mrs. Guthrie's dress.

"I beg your pardon?" Ken said. "Did you say you would ride Vexation?"

"Yes. I'm quite a good rider, if I say so myself."

Ken laughed out loud. "Forgive me for laughing, my dear. But I'm talking about a horse race, not a ride through the park. I don't think you could race, sitting sidesaddle."

"Oh, I wouldn't be riding sidesaddle. I will ride astride," Janelle said. "Where is Vexation? Shall I give you a demonstration?"

"Women can't ride astride," Ken said.

"Oh, if you are worried about the propriety of such a thing, don't. I have a special riding skirt that will allow me to do so, while still preserving modesty," Janelle said.

"It isn't a matter of modesty. Woman can't ride astride because their thighs are too rounded," Ken insisted.

Janelle laughed, then, when she saw the expression on Ken's face, she apologized. "Excuse me for laughing," she said. "But I have never heard such a thing."

"Everyone knows that," Ken said.

"Then everyone knows something that just isn't true," Janelle replied. "And I can prove it to you if you let me."

Something that Janelle had shared with nobody since her arrival in Phoenix, was the fact that she was an expert horsewoman. Her father kept a stable of horses that were specifically bred for fox hunting, and very quickly, Janelle became the most adept rider, male or female, in the Long Island Hunt Club.

"Are you serious about this?"

"Oh, I'm very serious. Where is Vexation now?"

"I board him down at Housewright's Livery," Ken said.

"I brought my riding habit with me," Janelle said. "If you want a riding demonstration, I'll just hurry back to my room and change."

"All right. If you are dead set on demonstrating this to me, I'll go down to the livery and get Vexation saddled."

"I'll meet you there," Janelle said.

"Ken, Janelle, listen to the two of you," Nellie scolded. "Have you both gone daft? There is no way a lady, especially a well-bred lady from the East, can ride in a horse race. Ken, you know how dangerous it is. You were nearly killed last year."

"I wasn't nearly killed, I broke my arm."

"In two places," Nellie reminded him. "And it could have just as easily been your neck."

"I need a rider for the race on Monday, and she wants to ride. If she can do it, I say good for her."

When Marshal Cairns stepped into the Boar's Head Saloon, he signaled Wally Cook, the bartender.

"Yes sir, Marshal Cairns, what can I do for you?" Wally asked.

"I heard tell there was a man in here who did some fancy shootin' a half hour or so ago."

"Yes, sir. Damnedest thing I ever seen. He was standin' right where you are now, and Quince was way over there in the middle of the floor. Quince got to braggin' as to how he was goin' to drop a whiskey glass, then shoot it before it hit the floor. Well sir, he talked it up 'til he got some folks ready to bet on it, then dropped the glass just like he said. Only the thing is, this here feller that was standin' right where you are now, shot it right out of the air his ownself."

"Where's this fancy shooter now?"

Wally nodded toward the shooter who was still sitting alone at the table he had chosen on the far side of the room.

Cairns looked in the direction Wally pointed, then he chuckled quietly. "Well I'll be damned," he said. "What the hell is he doing here?"

"Do you know him, Marshal?" Wally asked, surprised by Cairn's reaction.

"Yeah, I know him," Cairns said. "Give me a bottle of whiskey and two glasses."

"Mostly you just get a beer," Wally said.

"What?"

"I mean, well, I don't never charge you anything for the beer, bein' as you are the city marshal and all. But a bottle of whiskey, that's a little more expensive."

"If you have a complaint, take it to the city council," Cairns said, gruffly.

"No, no, I don't have no complaints," Wally said, pulling a bottle of whiskey from beneath the bar. He took two glasses down from the shelf and handed them to him as well. "I was just commentin' is all."

"Well, keep your commentin' to yourself," Cairns said.

"Yes, sir," Wally replied meekly.

Taking the bottle of whiskey and glasses from the bar, Cairns walked over to join Mueller. Mueller watched, a surprised look of recognition on his face. Then, seeing the lawman's star on Cairns's vest, the look of surprise changed to one of absolute shock.

"Hello, Luke," Cairns said quietly. He filled the two glasses, then slid one over in front of Mueller. "Long time no see."

Without a word of thanks, Mueller picked up the glass and drank it quickly. Putting the empty glass back on the table, he wiped his mouth with the back of his hand. "Who the hell ever made you a deputy?" Mueller asked.

Cairns smiled, and shook his head. "I ain't a deputy. I'm the city marshal." Cairns noticed the missing earlobe and the jagged, still purple mass of flesh. "What the hell happened to your ear?"

"A dog bit it off."

Cairns laughed. "What? A dog bit it off? How did you let a dog bite your ear off?"

"What happened to my ear don't make no never mind," Mueller answered gruffly. "Are you serious? Are you really the marshal?"

"Yeah, I'm really the marshal."

"Well I'll be damned. Is this the same Egan Drumm I know? Is this the same Egan Drumm that held up a train in Missouri, killed a shotgun guard and a passenger during a stagecoach robbery in Kansas, and rustled cattle down in Texas? Is this the same Egan Drumm that was ridin' with me an' my brother when we stoled that hog money from Dumey, then wound up killin' him and his whole family? Yeah, seein' as I was there, I would say this is the same Egan Drumm I know. So my question to you is, how the hell did Egan Drumm become a city marshal?"

Cairns chuckled. "Well, that's just it, Luke," he

said. "My name ain't Egan Drumm. Leastwise, not no more it ain't. It's Jimmy Cairns."

"Jimmy Cairns? Wait a minute, wasn't that Wyatt Earp's deputy back in Wichita?"

"Yeah, it was. When I got here it come in just real handy to borrow his name," Drumm said. "There was one or two here that had heard of him, but nobody that had ever actually seen him, so it was real easy to make the city council think I'd been a lawman in the past. They needed a city marshal and that got me this job."

"Ha!" Mueller said. "Wouldn't they be surprised if they know'd who you really was, and that you was wanted for robbery and murder in three states?"

"They think that I—that is, Jimmy Cairns—killed Drumm. And in a way, you might say that I did, seein' as how I don't use that name no more. I've got a sweet deal here, Mueller. I wouldn't want anything to happen that would mess it up." Drumm poured Mueller another whiskey.

Mueller took a swallow of it, then held his glass out. "So you expect to buy me off with a couple glasses of whiskey, is that it?"

"Not exactly," Drumm said. "Truth is, I reckon we can sort of scratch each other's back, so to speak."

"How?"

"Well, to begin with, I have paper in my office that says you are a wanted man. It seems you and your brother held up a bank in MacCallister, Colorado, and you kilt a couple of people doin' it. Sorry to hear about what happened to your brother, by the way."

"You've got paper on me, you say?" Mueller said, taking another swallow of his whiskey.

"Oh yes. Fresh paper with a new reward. You're worth fifteen hundred dollars, Luke. Did you know that?"

"I reckon I did know that. So, what are you gettin' at?"

"Just this. You are goin' to need a safe place to hang your hat, a place where you don't have to keep lookin' behind you," Drumm said. "You can stay here, there ain't nobody goin' to bother you."

"You said you have paper in your office. What if someone recognizes me?"

"I've got two deputies, one will recognize you and one won't."

"Which one will recognize me?"

"Bert Appleby."

"Appleby? He's here? He's a deputy?"

Drumm chuckled. "Yep. I had to take him on as a deputy. I didn't have no choice. He seen who I was, right off the bat."

"Maybe he won't recognize me. I ain't seen him since we pulled that job together back in Missouri. That's been five years ago, at least. And as I recall, we wasn't exactly good friends then."

"There ain't no way he won't recognize you. You ain't exactly an easy man to forget."

"Like I told you, we didn't get along all that good. What if he decides to tell folks who I am?"

"Ha!" Drumm said. "Appleby is wanted for murder back in Missouri his ownself. He ain't likely to want to open that can of worms."

"I reckon not. But what if someone else recognizes me?"

"As far as I know, there ain't nobody else in town that would actually know you, other than Appleby. But if anybody thinks they recognize you from your description or something, I'll just tell them that they are wrong. I'll tell them that I've met the real Luke Mueller, and while you might look somethin' like him, you ain't him. I'll tell folks you are my first cousin."

"What do you want for that?"

"Like I said, we'll be scratchin' each other's back. I won't tell anyone who you are, and I don't want you to tell anyone who I am," Drumm said. "In addition, from time to time, I might also require some, uh, let us say special services done, the kind of services that a man in my position, bein' as I'm the marshal an' all, can't do. Something that someone like you can perform for me."

"There any money to be made from these services?"

"What do you need money for? From what I heard, you got a pretty good haul from that bank holdup. Am I hearin' wrong?"

"Yeah, but you may have heard that an hombre by the name of MacCallister got on our trail. He's the one that kilt Clete, and the others. That caused me to have to leave town pretty fast, and I left the money behind."

"I read that MacCallister recovered most of the money, I figured that meant you managed to keep some of it."

Mueller shook his head. "Nary a cent. The only

money that wasn't recovered was what we had already spent." Mueller chuckled. "I'll tell you this though, we was havin' us a fine time with the money we was a' spendin'."

"Until MacCallister butted in, right?"

"Yeah, until MacCallister butted in." He finished the second glass of whiskey then as he had before, wiped the back of his hand across his mouth. "That's why I put out a thousand dollar reward to anyone who would kill the son of a bitch."

"You've got a thousand dollar reward out for MacCallister?"

Mueller chuckled, a low, growling kind of laugh. "Yeah, ain't that rich, puttin' out paper on him?"

"I thought you didn't have any money."

"I don't have the money. That reward ain't nothin' but a bluff."

"What would you do if someone did kill him and tried to collect?"

"I just want the son of a bitch dead," Mueller said. "So I reckon if it happens, I'll have to cross that bridge when I come to it."

"Then you damn sure do need to stay here for a while, don't you?"

"I reckon I do," Mueller admitted.

"Do we have a deal, Luke?"

"Yeah, Drumm, we have a deal."

"It ain't Drumm."

"I mean Cairns."

"Come on down to the jail with me now."

Mueller got a strange look on his face. "What do you mean, come down to the jail with you? What have you got in mind?"

"I ain't got nothin' in mind," Drumm insisted. "I'm just going to introduce you to my deputies now, that's all."

Mueller started to get up, then he stopped and stared hard at Drumm. "You better not be pulling a fast one on me," he said.

Drumm held up his hand and shook his head. "You don't have to worry about that. I told you, I've got as much to lose as you do."

Mueller was silent for a long moment, then he nodded his head. "Yeah," he said. "Yeah, I reckon you do at that, don't you?"

Janelle walked from Mrs. Poindexter's Boarding House to the livery stable. She had changed clothes, and was wearing a riding skirt which was split into panels that would allow her to button off the panels to either side, thus creating riding breeches. She drew several looks of surprise along the way.

Ken had saddled Vexation by the time Janelle arrived. "You sure you want to do this?" he asked.

"I'm sure," Janelle said.

"What's going on here?" Housewright, owner of the stable, asked, walking over to join them.

"Murray, I'm going to let Miss Wellington ride Vexation around in your corral if you don't mind."

"She's going to ride Vexation in them clothes?"

"I imagine she is, since she's about to ride him, and that's what she's wearing."

"I ain't never seen nothin' like that."

"It's called a riding habit," Janelle explained. "It allows me to ride astride."

"Women can't ride astride. Their thighs is too rounded. They can't stay in the saddle," Housewright said.

Janelle laughed, and looked at Buckner. "So I've heard. But I'd sure like to give it a try, to prove you are wrong."

"All right, go ahead," Housewright said, waving his arm as he surrendered the argument. "When you get right down to it, I think this is somethin' I'd like to see, anyway."

Smiling, Janelle took the reins from Ken and mounted the horse. She slapped her heels against its side and Vexation bolted forward as if shot from a cannon. Seeing a watering trough that protruded out from a windmill she headed directly for it, intuitively feeling the horse under her gathering itself for the jump.

"Look out, miss, you're about to—" Housewright cut his yell midsentence when he saw the horse spring from the ground with its legs extended fore and hind. It sailed over the watering trough as if it had wings, then landed gracefully on the other side, continuing at full gallop.

There were three others present at the livery and, upon seeing the graceful jump, they all applauded.

Janelle gave the horse its head, allowing it to race all the way around the paddock, staying close to the fence. Finally she guided Vexation back to where Ken Buckner, Murray Housewright and the others were standing, eyes wide open in shock over what they had just seen.

Janelle brought the horse to an abrupt halt, then

leaped adroitly from the saddle. "He's a good horse," she said, handing the reins back to Ken.

"Do you really want to ride in the race, Monday?" Ken asked.

"Yes, sir," Janelle replied, a broad smile spreading across her face.

"Well, I have to say, that's some of the best riding I've ever seen. So if you want the job, it's yours."

"Thanks," Janelle said, smiling broadly.

Janelle changed clothes again and returned to the emporium, where Ken and Nellie were engaged in conversation. Nellie smiled at her.

"Well, I must say, my dear, you made quite an impression on Ken. He is now saying he actually thinks you might win the Fourth of July race on Monday."

"I certainly hope so," Janelle replied. "I will be riding to win, I know that."

"Oh, by the way, Janelle, I stopped by the post office before coming back to the shop. You have a letter," Ken said.

"Thank you, I'll read it later," Janelle said, taking the letter, then slipping it under the counter. "Mrs. Buckner, if you will give me Mrs. Guthrie's dress, I will go into the back and work on it now," she added.

The Buckners watched her gather up the brightly colored material and the dress, and head into the back of the store where sat the most valuable commodity of the store, the sewing machine.

"She won't, you know," Nellie Buckner said quietly, after Janelle left.

"She won't what?" Ken replied.

"She won't read the letter."

"How do you know?"

"Because she has already received four letters since she started working here, and all four are right there, under the counter, unopened and unread.

Chapter Twelve

The Eagle Theater was decorated in patriotic flags and bunting appropriate for the occasion. The set on the stage resembled the parlor of an elegant house. Rosanna McCallister, costumed as a very wealthy lady, stood in the middle. With one leg slightly in front of the other so as to best accent her feminine form, with her left arm down by her side and her right arm extended, the fingers curled just so, Rosanna, as Mrs. Abernathy, delivered the last line of the play. "Alas—now we know—he truly was an English gentleman."

She held that position for a long moment until the curtain came down. The applause from an appreciative audience was thunderous as they paid homage to the final performance of a long and successful run of the play, *The English Gentleman.*

After a moment, the curtain drew open again. The actors rushed onto the stage to take their curtain calls, the minor players first, coming out together. As it moved up the cast in order of importance, the players began to come out one at a time to louder applause. The loudest applause of all was reserved for the two principal actors; Andrew MacCallister bowed deeply to applause and cheers, then stepped aside and with a sweeping motion of his arm saluted Rosanna as she moved quickly and gracefully to the front of the stage. As Andrew had before her, she received thunderous applause from the crowd. Joining hands, brother and sister bowed once more as the curtain closed for the final call.

"Thus endeth the triumphant run of *The English Gentleman*," Andrew said.

"And a wonderful play it was," Rossana said.

"With a wonderful cast," Andrew said, turning toward the others to applaud them. Rosanna joined him.

"Oh, Mr. MacCallister, Miss MacCallister, I can't tell you what a thrill it was to appear in a play with you. I shall always remember this night," a very pretty young woman said.

"My dear," Andrew replied with a gracious smile. "I have no doubt in my mind but that, one day, and soon, I shall be bragging to my friends that I appeared in the same play as Katrina Kirby." He reached for the young actress's hand, then raised it to his lips to kiss it.

"Oh," the young actress said, obviously flustered by the unexpected attention. "You are—too kind, sir."

"Not at all, not at all."

"He isn't kind, my dear, he's just an outrageous flirt," Rosanna said, teasingly.

"Why shouldn't I be flirtatious? After all the young lady is both beautiful and talented."

"Andrew, will you be available after a while?" Rosanna asked.

At that moment a young man from back stage moved quickly toward Katrina and the two shared an intimate embrace.

"Evidently I will be available," Andrew said with a thwarted sigh.

"Really, brother, she is much too young for you. Now I want to ask you to get out of costume quickly. I will call on you directly."

"You know what, Rosanna, I think you should change your name," Andrew said. "How can I get any young woman interested in me, when they all think you are my wife, rather than my sister?"

"Thank you, no, I like the name I have. You change yours," Rosanna said with a laugh, throwing the remark over her shoulder as she hurried off-stage to her dressing room.

Fifteen minutes later, Andrew MacCallister was sitting in front of the mirror in his dressing room. Picking up a jar of cold cream, he began applying it over the stage makeup he was wearing, when there was a light knock on his door.

"Andrew, are you decent?" Rosanna called, her voice somewhat muffled.

"Yes, Rosanna, come on in."

Rosanna was still in costume and makeup when she came in.

"What? Here, you asked me to hurry, but you haven't changed yet. Are we not going out? Have you forgotten we are to meet Edwin Booth for dinner at Delmonico's?"

"We will, we will. I just haven't had time to change yet, because Emma Wellington was in my dressing room when I got there. We've been talking," Rosanna said. "Andrew, I feel so sorry for her. She is very upset."

Emma Wellington was the wife of Joel Wellington, who had not only financed *The English Gentleman*, but was also the financier for *The Ideal Suitor*—the next play in which Andrew and Rosanna were to perform. It was definitely to their advantage to keep the Wellingtons happy. If Mrs. Wellington was upset, they needed to do whatever they could do to make her feel better.

Having applied the cold cream to his face, Andrew used a towel to take it off. "What is troubling her?" he asked, his voice smothered by the towel.

"It's her daughter, Janelle," Rosanna said. "You may remember there was some family—difficulty a couple months ago."

"Yes, I do remember her. Quite an attractive young lady, as I recall," Andrew said, his face devoid of all stage makeup. "I never knew exactly what the family crisis was, but I figured it was not our business to get involved."

"You were right, it wasn't our business to get involved"—she paused for a moment—"then."

"Then? What do you mean, it wasn't our business to get involved *then*?" Andrew asked.

"I mean that at the time it came up, it was none of our business."

Andrew chuckled. "Something tells me, little sister, that you have now come to believe perhaps this *is* our business."

Andrew and Rosanna were actually twins, but she qualified as his "little" sister, by virtue of the fact that he was the first to be delivered. Rosanna followed him into this world by less than five minutes.

"I have indeed. I absolutely, positively, think it is time for us to get involved," Rosanna said.

"Absolutely, positively, huh? That's pretty definite."

"Definitely," Rosanna replied.

Andrew laughed. "All right, Rosanna, what would you have us do? Give Janelle a good talking to?"

"That wouldn't be a bad idea," Rosanna replied. "But first we have to find her."

"Find her? What do you mean, find her? Where is she?"

"According to a telegram the Wellingtons received, she is in Phoenix," Rosanna said. "That's where they have been sending all their mail."

"Phoenix? As in Arizona?"

"Yes. Phoenix, as in the middle of the desert, Arizona."

"Well if they know where she is, and if they are exchanging letters, why don't they just ask her to come home?"

"They aren't exactly exchanging letters. They've sent her several letters, but they have gotten only one letter back from her—written on the train while she was on her way out there, and one telegram saying she had arrived safely in Phoenix. There has been nothing from her since, despite the many letters they have sent her. The Wellingtons feel the only way she is going to respond is if someone else speaks to Janelle personally, on their behalf. That's where we come in—the someone else."

"Rosanna, we can't just hop on a train and go to Phoenix. Remember, we have a new show opening in only four weeks, and rehearsal begins tomorrow."

"Who said anything about us going to Phoenix?" Rosanna asked, a small smile beginning to spread across her lips.

"You just said that's where we come in."

"Yes, but I meant this is where we get involved. I didn't mean that we had to go to Phoenix ourselves."

"Well, how else are we going to find her if we don't—" Andrew stopped mid-question as the smile on his face, mirrored that of his sister's. "You're talking about Falcon, aren't you?" he asked.

Rosanna nodded. "You know how much he likes to come to New York to see our plays. He's the only one in the family who ever does."

"Oh, what a devious mind you have, little sister. We're going to invite him to the grand opening, and then spring this on him, aren't we?" Andrew asked.

"Yes."

"You're going to do this, even though we turned down the invitation to go to MacCallister for the unveiling of Pa's statue? Which is today, by the way, in case you have forgotten."

"I have not forgotten and it isn't unfair, Andrew. You know why we can't go. We closed this play today, and we have a brand new play opening next Monday on July eleventh. It was impossible for us to be there, unless we could somehow telegraph ourselves there."

"Telegraph ourselves there," Andrew said with a little chuckle. "Whoa, now wouldn't something like that be great? One could go into a telegraph office, somehow be wired up, and then sent, with the speed of light to one's destination."

"Be serious."

"Me be serious? You're the one who said we should telegraph ourselves there. Anyway, I understand why we can't go and you understand why we can't go, but I'm not sure all of our siblings understand."

"Falcon understands," Rosanna said. "And that is enough. He will make the others understand as well."

Andrew nodded. "I believe he does understand. But, don't you think what you have planned is a little unfair to Falcon?"

"You do want to keep Joel Wellington happy, don't you?" Rosanna asked.

"Yes, but not at Falcon's expense. He is our brother, Rosanna."

"I know he is our brother. That is why he will do this for us," Rosanna said confidently. "If we ask him, he will find her, and he will bring her back."

"Shall we write him a letter, then?"

"I think the situation requires more urgency than a letter."

"A telegram?"

Rosanna nodded. "A telegram."

"All right, all right, if you say so. Go now, and change. We'll send the telegram on our way to the restaurant."

Superstition Mountain

It had been almost three weeks since Rhoda turned up the little pile of gold nuggets, and in that time Ben Hanlon had dug under every mesquite tree, every saguaro and cholla cactus, and every rock. He had dug into indentations at the base of the mountain and scrambled halfway up the side of the mountain, looking for a washout area that could have dumped the nuggets down to the ground below—all without success.

It was midafternoon. He sat with his back against a large rock and examined what he had found on that first day—forty-six pecan-sized nuggets, each nugget being half to three quarters gold. Hefting them in his hand he figured they weighed about four pounds total. If half of the weight was gold, he had thirty-two ounces of gold. Gold was heavier than the rocks themselves, so if he had four pounds, more than half of it was gold, but he wanted to be cautious, so he figured it at half. At twenty dollars an ounce, that was six hundred forty dollars.

"Whooeee!" he said aloud, throwing his head back. "Rhoda, that's more money 'n we brung in, in the last five years! That's fantas—" he stopped midsentence. The shadow of Weaver's Needle just passed by the face of Superstition Mountain exposing an opening about five hundred feet up the side of the mountain. The opening was shaped like a grinning mouth, not very wide from side to side, and not very high. In fact, he was sure that one could only enter that opening by crawling through.

Why had he not seen that before? He had been on and around Superstition Mountain for more years than he could remember and he had camped right in this very spot more times than he could count, but he had never seen—

It was gone! Even as he stared, it disappeared. How could that be? Unless it wasn't really there at all. Had he really seen it? Or was it just his imagination?

Hanlon had heard of men going crazy out on Superstition. Maybe they went crazy seeing things that weren't there. Maybe there was no opening, maybe it was just a mirage.

Hanlon climbed up the side of the mountain the next day, taking the better part of two hours. As he was climbing, he didn't see the opening until he was right on it. He wriggled inside and, back a little way from the opening saw the gold, flashing in the sunlight.

When Hanlon climbed back down more than an hour later, his stomach was rolling, and his head was spinning with excitement, but he was very careful. What a foolish thing it would be to fall, after having made his discovery.

When he got back down to the foot of the mountain, he looked up and saw nothing, even though he knew exactly where to look. Then, suddenly, the opening appeared to him, as clear as day, though it was visible for less than a minute before it disappeared.

"I'll be damned, Rhoda. I've got it all figured out now," he said. He knew that talking to Rhoda made no sense. Rhoda was a mule, after all. But he wanted to say the words aloud, he wanted to hear them spoken. Somehow, talking to Rhoda didn't seem quite as crazy as talking to himself.

Hanlon pointed. "You see, Rhoda, it's like this. Because of the angle of the opening, and because of the shadow cast upon the opening by Weaver's Needle, the mouth of that there cave is only visible for a few minutes each day."

He had no calendar, but, by looking at the position of the sun, he knew it was probably late June or early July.

"In fact," Hanlon said, continuing with his explanation to the mule, "I'll just bet that as the sun changes position during the seasons, the actual opening would only be visible for a few minutes each day, and only for few days in early summer. Within another couple weeks you won't be able to see it again, until next year. No wonder it has been lost for so many years."

Hanlon drew out a quick claim on a piece of paper, put it in an empty peach can, then buried the peach can under a pyramid of rocks. On the claim he was purposely vague about the location of the mine. In that way he was able to establish his claim, without giving away so much specific information that anyone who might see the quick claim would actually be able to find the gold.

On a second piece of paper, Ben Hanlon drew out an extremely accurate map. He wanted to make certain he could find the cave later, especially since he now knew how hard it was to find.

Then, with a leather pouch filled with enough nuggets to tide him over until he returned, he stashed all of his mining equipment and started the long trek into Phoenix.

Chapter Thirteen

MacCallister

The sun had scarcely risen on the morning of the Fourth of July when the residents of MacCallister Valley started coming into town. By horseback, in surreys, buckboards, and wagons they came, from individuals to whole families, from babes in arms to the very old. Most brought picnic lunches, for this was to be a daylong celebration.

The front of all the buildings, as well as the lantern poles, were decked out in red, white, and blue bunting. Kate MacCallister Boulevard, MacCallister's main street, ran east and west. Two huge banners were spread across the boulevard, one at each end of the street. The one that greeted visitors who were arriving from the west read

OUR NATION CELEBRATES ITS BIRTHDAY.

At the east end of Kate MacCallister Boulevard, or The Katie as the locals called it, was another banner.

We Honor Our Founder
Jamie Ian MacCallister

The Katie had been closed off to horse and vehicle traffic so those who were coming into town from out in the valley were directed to park their conveyances in a huge open area behind Shultz Mercantile Store. Leaving their wagons, buckboards, and surreys behind them, they poured into town, joining with the growing throngs.

Already, people were setting off firecrackers and the pops could be heard from all over town, generally followed by squeals of laughter. The town's children who were running through the street, in and around people, vending booths, and kiosks, were joined by children just arriving from the valley. The Katie was awash with the aromas of grilled sausages, freshly made fudge, baking pastries, and popped corn. Lemonade, sarsaparilla, and beer were being sold at the street booths, though a city ordinance had declared that whiskey could only be sold in the saloons.

Like every other town in the West, MacCallister made a special holiday out of the Fourth of July. But this year the excitement was even greater, because they would also be dedicating a statue to the memory of their founder and namesake, Jamie Ian MacCallister, the patriarch of the MacCallister clan. The bronze statue, commissioned of Frederic Remington, was mounted on its pedestal in a specially constructed median in the middle of Kate MacCallister Boulevard. A stage had been erected just to one side of the statue, which was under a shroud, pending its official unveiling.

The guest of honor for the day was the honorable Frederick Pitkin, Governor of the state of Colorado. As it was Independence Day, several cities and towns in the state had requested the Governor's presence, nearly all of them larger than MacCallister. It spoke volumes of the Governor's respect for Jamie Ian MacCallister and the MacCallister clan that he chose to go there. Governor Pitkin had arrived by train from Denver the day before, and spent the night in the Morning Star Hotel, which was the finest hotel between Denver and San Francisco.

The Governor's special train, consisting only of an engine, a tender, and a private car, sat on a side track at the depot. The engine was dark green, with brass fittings and gold-painted striping. The spokes of the wheels were red, and it became an object of attention as many of the valley people walked down just to have a special look at the beautiful train. The name painted in gold script on the side of the engine was *The Columbine*. The columbine was a flower that many wanted to become the official state flower of Colorado.

Across town in the Morning Star Hotel, a special reception was being held in the hotel ballroom. The reception room was absolutely packed with men, women, and children. Except for the Governor, his personal staff, and the employees of the hotel itself, every person present was a member of the MacCallister family—the children of Jamie and Kate, all the way down to their great-grandchildren.

"It is a wonderful day," the governor said as he stood near the buffet table, holding a cup of coffee.

"Yes, it is," Falcon said. "I just wish Reverend Powell could be here. I know that he was really looking forward to giving the invocation."

"Do you think your father is here?" Governor Pitkin asked.

Falcon thought for a moment, then he realized what the governor was asking. He nodded. "Yes, there is no doubt in my mind but that Pa is here."

"Then so is Reverend Powell. No doubt, they are sitting together over in some corner, catching up on stories of old times."

Falcon smiled. "Yeah," he said. "I think you might be right."

"Ladies and gentlemen!" someone shouted. "Would you all please come outside? The festivities are about to begin!"

Falcon, the governor, and the others were led outside, then up onto the stage. Looking out over the street, Falcon was amazed at how many people were there. Though the population of MacCallister was only a little over three thousand, he estimated there were at least five thousand or more people in the crowd.

The city band, outfitted in their red and black uniforms, had been playing marching music all morning long, but it quieted when Joe Cravens, MacCallister's newly elected mayor, stepped to the front of the stage. Holding up his hands for quiet, he waited until the buzz of conversation stilled, then he introduced Reverend Pyron to give the invocation.

Pyron was not yet out of his twenties, but all those who attended his church admitted that the young parson was a "go-getter." He had a strong voice which could be quite easily heard by most of those present. "Before I begin the invocation, I would like to take a moment to remember the man who was supposed to do this. He was my friend and mentor, and a personal friend of the man we are all here to honor today. If you would, please, keep the Reverend Charles Powell and his wife, Claudia, in your thoughts as we bow our heads, please."

Quietly, respectfully, the audience bowed their heads as the Reverend Pyron began the invocation. He offered thanks for the life of Jamie Ian Mac-Callister, and prayed for God's blessings on his family, and on the valley and town which bore his name. He asked, also, that all who might view this statue in the years to come would be inspired by the life of the man the statue represented. "Amen," he concluded.

"Amen," the crowd responded.

At the conclusion of the invocation, Mayor Cravens once more stepped to the front of the stage. "Ladies and gentlemen, I now have the distinct honor and personal privilege of introducing to you our governor, the honorable, the esteemed, Frederick Pitkin."

To the applause of the crowd, Governor Pitkin stepped up to the podium. He stroked his full beard as he waited for the applause to subside, then he began to speak.

"Jamie Ian MacCallister was but a boy, living in Ohio, when a Shawnee war party killed his parents. The same Shawnee who killed his parents adopted him into their tribe where he learned the warrior's way. Although he learned much from the Shawnee, he escaped from them and, at the tender age of twelve, began his life on his own. Soon after, he met Kate Olmstead. He and Kate married in the small river town of New Madrid, Missouri, then came West. Jamie fought with the defenders of the Alamo, leaving with a packet of letters the night before the Alamo fell.

When the great Civil War struck our country, the MacCallister family became a microcosm of this nation for, just as our country was divided, so was the MacCallister family. Following their hearts, some fought for the North and some for the South but, at the end of the war they were fully reunited, just as was our great nation.

We are here today for a special dedication. It is our intention for this beautiful work of art to project into the ages yet to come, the dream, the aura, and the spirit of Jamie Ian MacCallister!"

At that, the cover was drawn away, revealing a bronze statue of a man who had broad shoulders, narrow hips, and massive arms. The statue of Colonel Jamie Ian MacCallister depicted him holding a pistol in each of his large hands.

The crowd applauded loudly. Then the band began playing "Dixie," as tribute to Jamie MacCallister's service as a colonel in the Confederate army.

Afterward, the guests on the stage mingled

with the crowd. Many wanted to interact with the children of the great Jamie MacCallister and, for nearly an hour The Katie was teeming with people.

Finally Falcon managed to extricate himself from the well-wishers and, mounting Lightning, started home.

"Falcon, wait a moment, would you?" Gary Baxter called out from the Western Union office. He waved a piece of paper. "I have a telegram for you."

Weary of the morning's seemingly endless activities, Falcon wanted nothing more than to just keep riding, but he angled his horse toward the telegrapher.

"It came about an hour ago," Baxter said, "but there were too many in the crowd for me to find you."

"Thanks," Falcon said, dismounting and walking over to take the message from the telegrapher.

"I heard you lost your horse. I was sorry to hear that. How's the new one working out?"

Falcon patted Lightning on his neck, and the horse dipped its head a couple times. "He's a good horse," Falcon said. "But so was the other one. I hated losing him like that."

Baxter nodded toward the still unread telegram. "As you'll see when you read it, that's from your brother and sister in New York. That sister of yours is sure one pretty woman."

"Thank you, I'm sure she would be flattered," Falcon answered as he unfolded the paper. "I imagine this is some comment about the unveiling of Pa's statue."

"No, it isn't that," Baxter said. "Yes, sir, Rosanna is a pretty woman with a pretty name. She's never gotten married has she?"

"She was married to a Frenchman for a while, but he was sort of a puny fellow and he got sick and died," Falcon said.

"Oh, I'm sorry to hear that."

"He wasn't all that popular with the rest of the family," Falcon said.

"And she has never remarried?"

"Nope. There's still hope for you, Gary," Falcon teased.

"Oh, shucks," Baxter said, embarrassed. "I didn't mean me. Not with someone like your sister, that is. Though I must say, it does make one wonder what's wrong with the men in New York, letting such a pretty woman stay single this long."

"Who knows? Could be my sister would prefer a good Western man to those effete fellows she sees in New York." Falcon chuckled as he began reading the telegram.

AS YOU KNOW ROSANNA AND I OPEN
NEW PLAY ON JULY 11 STOP PLAY SAID
TO BE MOST IMPORTANT IN NEW YORK
THIS SEASON STOP WOULD GREATLY
APPRECIATE SOME FAMILY SUPPORT FROM
OUR FAVORITE BROTHER STOP ANDREW

"Are you going?" Baxter asked.

"What?" Falcon asked, glancing up from the telegram.

Baxter pointed to the telegram. "To New York to see the new play, I mean. Are you going?"

"I didn't think you were supposed to read other people's telegrams," Falcon said.

"I'm not supposed to," Baxter admitted. "But you tell me this. If I'm the one that gets the message and writes it down, how can I not read it?"

Falcon chuckled. "I'm just teasing you, Gary, you're right. There's no way you can write out the telegram without reading it."

"So, you aren't sore with me?"

"Of course not."

"Then I'll ask you again. Are you goin' to New York?"

"I don't know," Falcon replied. "I guess I'll have to think about it for a bit."

"Better not think too long. It'll take you five days to get there. And I expect you'll want to be a day or so early, which means you are just about going to have to leave today," Baxter said.

Of all the MacCallister siblings, Falcon was the only one to have actually gone to New York to visit Andrew and Rosanna, and he had done that on several occasions. In addition, he had hosted them in their rare visits back home, once to perform at a theater in Colorado Springs, and once to entertain Custer's Seventh Cavalry at Ft. Lincoln, Dakota Territory. His brother and sister seemed to enjoy their visits back West, though in truth, neither regarded Colorado as home anymore.

Falcon considered the invitation. Should he accept it?

Why not? Now that the dedication of his father's statue had taken place, there was no reason not to go. He loved his brother and sister, and admired and respected their talent. But for the life of him, he could not understand how they could choose New York as a place to live. And they chose it, not only as a matter of the necessity of their chosen profession, but, he realized, because they had developed a degree of attachment that was as strong for the city as was his to the wide open spaces of the West.

"If it were me, I would be going," Baxter continued. "I mean if for no other reason than to tell them about the dedication of the statue to Colonel MacCalliser. I saw that Mr. Dysart was taking photographs of it. Andrew and Rosanna might like to see what it looks like."

"Thanks, Gary, that's a good idea—getting a picture from Dysart," Falcon said. "Maybe I will go. I always enjoy my visits to New York, and I would like to see Andrew and Rosanna again."

"Listen, Falcon, tell your sister that if she ever gets back to MacCallister and wants someone to take her around to show her all the sights, and have a good time, why, I'd be more than glad to do it."

"I'll tell her," Falcon promised.

"Really, you'll tell her?"

"Sure."

"I, uh, no, wait, don't tell her. She'd just wonder what sort of damn fool would say such a thing."

"I think she would find the offer flattering, Gary," Falcon said. "And I would be glad to tell her."

"Thanks," Baxter said. "You're good people, Falcon."

Having made up his mind to go, Falcon rode to the depot to make arrangements for his trip. The morning train had already passed through and there wasn't another train due until the afternoon, so for the moment, the train station was empty.

The depot building consisted of a small waiting room with two wooden benches, a wood-burning stove which, though cold, still had the lingering smell of last winter's wood smoke hanging about it. A counter separated the waiting room from the depot office, and a short, bald man, wearing sleeve garters and a green visor, was working behind the counter. He looked up and smiled as he recognized the town's leading citizen.

"Mr. MacCallister," the ticket agent said, "How good to see you. Are we about to take a trip?"

Falcon laughed. "I don't know, Sid, are you going to join me?"

"What? No, I—" Sid started, then he laughed as well. "You got me on that one, Mr. MacCallister," he said. "Yes, sir, you got me good. Now, where are we"—he stopped—"I mean where are *you* going?"

"New York, New York," Falcon said.

"New York, New York. My, my, how I would like to see New York some day. I work here, making out tickets for people to go to wonderful places like New York, St. Louis, Washington, Chicago, Boston—but I'm afraid that writing out these tickets is about as close as I will ever get to actually seeing one of those places. Will you be coming back to MacCallister?"

"Why do you ask?" Falcon teased. "Is there some reason why I shouldn't come back?"

"What? No, I didn't mean anything like that. I just meant will it be round-trip?"

"Yes."

The ticket agent got out a book of pre-printed ticket forms, then began writing in the destinations; from MacCallister to Denver, from Denver to St. Louis, from St. Louis to Columbus, Ohio, then to Philadelphia, and finally to New York, each destination requiring a separate ticket. When he finished filling out all the ticket forms, he picked up a leaden stamp, pressed it into an ink pad, then slammed it down on each of the tickets, applying the official seal of the Colorado Central. In that way, each subsequent railroad, from the Denver and Rio Grande, to the Union Pacific, to the Missouri Pacific, Illinois Central, Chesapeake and Ohio, Pennsylvania Central, and New York Central, would be able to submit the stamped tickets back to the originating railroad, in order to collect their own fees. When all the stamped tickets were assembled, Sid slipped them into an envelope and passed them across the counter to Falcon.

"Here you go, Mr. MacCallister. You are all set," he said. "The fare comes to a grand total of forty-two dollars and seventy-five cents."

Falcon paid the fare with a fifty dollar bill.

"The eastbound will be leaving the station at two-thirty this afternoon," Sid said as he gave back the change to Falcon. "From all the reports by telegram we have been receiving, it is running on time, so I wouldn't be late if I were you."

"Thanks," Falcon said. "I'll be back in time."

Leaving the depot, Falcon rode out to the ranch to pack a grip. He was about to leave when Jamie Ian and his wife, Carolyn, came driving up in a surrey. Seeing Falcon with a suitcase, Jamie Ian stopped just in front of the porch.

"Where are you going?" he called.

"I'm going to New York to see Andrew and Rosanna in their new play."

"Oh, that will be nice," Carolyn said with a broad smile. "Do you really think you will need your gun?"

"Oh," Falcon replied with a sheepish grin. "I didn't even realize I was wearing it."

"Tell them we said hello," Jamie Ian said.

"I'll take them greetings from everyone," Falcon promised.

As soon as he returned to town Falcon stopped at the Dysart photography studio. Stepping inside, he saw a little sign that read, I AM IN THE DARKROOM, PLEASE WAIT OUT FRONT.

While he waited, Falcon examined some of Dysart's display photographs which were in a book that sat on the counter. He recognized citizens of the town and valley, many of them members of his own family, seated in a wide variety of poses. Some were sideways to the camera, others were angled or facing directly into the camera. Some showed only the upper body, others were full length. He was looking at a particularly good picture of Joleen and her family when the curtain separating the front from the back parted and Don Dysart came through. He was wiping his hands dry, though Falcon could smell the developing solution.

Dysart smiled when he saw Falcon. "Falcon, my friend," he said. He started to extend his hand, then pulled it back. "I've still got solution on my hands," he explained. "What brings you here?"

"I understand you took some pictures of the statue of Pa."

"That I did, and I just developed them. They came out beautifully. Would you like to see them?"

"Yes."

"I'll bring them out."

Dysart disappeared for a moment, returning with a handful of photographs. He spread them out on the counter for Falcon's perusal. One picture in particular caught his eye. It captured, in great detail, the entire statue which depicted the no-nonsense demeanor of Jamie MacCalliser.

"Could you make me an extra copy of this one?" Falcon asked, holding up the photograph.

"No need to make an extra copy," he said. "I've already made plenty of them. That one is yours."

Falcon started to reach for money to pay for it, but Dysart held up his hand to stop him.

"No charge," he said. "It's the least I can do. Your father was a great man and, though most don't know this, he helped me get my business started when I first came here. Here, let me put that in an envelope for you so it doesn't get damaged."

"I thank you, Mr. Dysart," Falcon said.

Ten minutes later Falcon dismounted in front of the livery, then gave the liveryman a dollar. "Have someone take Lightning back to the ranch, would you? My hands will look after him, and I think he'll be more comfortable there."

"Sure thing, Mr. MacCallister," the liveryman replied.

He had an hour before train time, so he crossed the street to have lunch at the City Pig Café, crowded with people still celebrating the Fourth. So many came to shake his hand and congratulate him on his father's statue, he barely managed to eat before having to catch the train.

Chapter Fourteen

Phoenix

"What do you mean a woman is going to ride in the race?" one of the riders asked. "There ain't no way that's goin' to happen."

"Why not?" Mayor John Alsop asked. He was in charge of all the festivities of the town for the Fourth of July celebration.

"What do you mean, why not? 'Cause it just ain't right, that's all," the young cowboy said.

"There is no rule or law against it," Mayor Alsop said. "As the mayor of this town, and the chairman of the Fourth of July celebration, I am saying that Miss Wellington can ride in this race."

"What's the matter, Ellis? You afraid you'll be beaten by a woman?" one of the other riders asked.

"It ain't that," Ellis said. "It's just that—well, ridin' in a race can be dangerous. You seen what happened last year when Collins and Mr. Buckner run into each other. Mr. Buckner broke his arm and Collins had to destroy his horse."

"That don't mean it's goin' to happen this year."

"It might, if you get someone that don't know how to ride."

"Believe me, Ellis, the young lady can ride," Housewright said.

"How do you know?"

"Because I have seen her ride, that's how I know," Housewright replied. "Look, you can complain all you want about whether or not a woman should ride, but don't be sayin' it's 'cause she don't know how."

"What's it goin' to be, Ellis?" Mayor Alsop asked. "Are you going to ride or not?"

"Am *I* goin' to ride? That ain't the question."

"Yes, it is the question," the mayor said. "Because I tell you now, Miss Wellington is going to participate in this race. So if you don't like it you have two choices: either accept it and ride, or don't accept it, and don't ride. So which will it be? Are you going to ride, or not?"

"Yes, I'm goin' to ride. There ain't no way I'm not goin' to ride, but I tell you plain and I tell you true, it ain't right for a woman to be in the race."

"Then I suggest you get ready, because I'm goin' to start the race in about three minutes."

Although Janelle had said nothing during the long discourse as to whether or not she could ride, she had heard every word while standing alongside Vexation. When she heard the mayor's final decision in her favor, she smiled with pleasure, mounted her horse, and rode over to the starting line.

The race would be down Central, starting at McDowell Road. The riders would go to Indian School Road, then turn around and come back. The first rider to cross McDowell on the way back, would win.

As the horses were lined up for the start, Janelle looked down the road and saw hundreds, maybe as many as a thousand or more people crowded on both sides of the street. Most, she knew, would be against her because she was a woman, and like Ellis the protesting cowboy, they did not believe that a woman should ride.

But she had a small galley of supporters: Mr. and Mrs. Buckner, Mrs. Poindexter, and the other residents of the boarding house. She heard them shouting their encouragement, saw them waving at her. She gave them a small wave in return.

Mayor Alsop climbed up onto a small stand at the edge of the street, even with the starting line.

"Gentlemen!" he called. Then with an embarrassed smile and a nod toward Janelle, he amended it. "And lady. Get ready!"

Janelle heard a scattering of sniggers from those of the crowd who were nearest the starting line.

Alsop pulled the trigger, the gun banged, and the horses leaped forward. Although most of the horses were cowboy favorites—the fastest from the various ranches—only Vexation had actually been trained as a racehorse. Shooting away like a cannon ball, he got the best start.

Janelle had pulled the stirrups up very high to keep her feet up, her knees bent and close in. She leaned forward from her waist with her head and shoulders only inches above Vexation's neck.

He was all strength and sinew, and as he galloped down the road she felt almost as if she were one with his musculature. The crowd on either side of the road flashed by with such speed they were a blur. She would not have been able to identify anyone's face, even if she had known them, for she was going too fast to see.

When she reached Indian School Road she turned and started back. She was pleasantly surprised to see that she was at least one hundred yards ahead of her nearest competitor, Ellis. Because he was so vocal in his protest over her riding, Janelle figured he probably had the most to lose.

As he drew closer she moved over slightly, to give the cowboy room to pass, but he followed her. At first she thought it was because he was trying to avoid her. But when she turned again, she saw that it wasn't an accident, he was purposely trying to run her down!

Janelle was left with three choices—give way by riding off the road, in which case she would be disqualified, run into a vending stand which was protruding into the road, or cross the road into the path of the other horses.

To everyone's surprise, she headed right for the vending stand, urging the horse up. Vexation cleared it by inches, coming down in full stride on the other side. Even those who had been against her, began cheering her, and booing Ellis, who they saw trying to run her down.

Janelle crossed the finish line first. When she

looked back she was surprised to see that Ellis was nowhere close. He had broken off the race after Janelle jumped the vendor's booth. As the other riders crossed the finish line, they rushed over to Janelle and congratulated her, not only for winning the race, but also for avoiding the trap Ellis had set for her.

The Buckners ran up to her and both of them embraced her. "You were magnificent!" Ken Buckner said, enthusiastically. "I've never seen anything like that."

"Vexation is a very good horse," Janelle said, wrapping her arms around the horse's neck. "I've never ridden a better horse."

"He is good, isn't he?" Ken Buckner said. "I'm so proud of him. But I must say, I'm just as proud of you. In fact, I'm so proud of you, that I'm giving you the one hundred dollar prize money."

"Oh!" Janelle said. "You don't have to do that, Mr. Buckner. It was your horse that won."

"I know, and I'm going to keep the trophy," Ken said. "I think I shall keep it in the window of the Emporium so that everyone who sees it will be reminded that it was a woman who rode the winning horse in the Fourth of July race."

MacCallister

The station that had been empty earlier was full of passengers holding tickets, friends, and family saying good-bye. There were also people waiting to greet passengers arriving on the incoming train. And a rather large contingent of townspeople tended to gather at the arrival and departure of *any* train, drawn by the excitement of it.

"You got here just in time, Mr. MacCallister," the ticket agent said. "Your train is pulling into the station now."

As if to underscore the ticket agent's observation, Falcon heard the whistle of the approaching train. The 4-4-2 engine rushed into the station, its four huge driver wheels pounding, the steam gushing from the cylinders, and burning embers dripping from the firebox. Finally, with a squeal of steel on steel, the train came to a halt. It sat there, not as some inert iron contraption, but alive with sight and sound. Black smoke roiled up from the stack and wisps of steam glistened in the afternoon sunlight as it escaped with loud, rhythmic hisses from the actuating cylinders. While journals and bearings popped and snapped as they cooled, men shouted at each other as they off-loaded and then loaded luggage at the baggage car. The engineer leaned out the window of the cab, a long-stemmed pipe clutched between his teeth as he surveyed from his lordly position those who had gathered on the depot platform.

Falcon watched as the arriving passengers detrained and were greeted by those who had come to meet them.

When the last passenger had stepped down, the conductor raised his hand to his mouth. "All aboard!"

Falcon waited until the others were boarded, then he climbed the steps and started down the center aisle of the car. It was a day car only, though once he reached Denver he would be able to take advantage of a Pullman car.

Finding a seat by the window, he sat for a few minutes until, with two long whistles, the train started forward with a jerking, halting motion until all the slack was taken out of the couplings. The motion smoothed out and he looked through the window, watching the depot slide by. It was the beginning of what would be a four night, five day journey.

Phoenix

The day after Independence Day Janelle was busy spreading a display of colorful material in the window. True to his promise, Ken Buckner had put the silver cup winner's trophy in the window, and it was Nellie's idea to combine that with business.

"If people are going to come look at the trophy, we may as well let them see what kind of material we have for sale," she said.

Ken agreed, and the two of them left it up to Janelle to construct an artistic display, rather than just lay out bolts of cloth. Janelle had risen to the task and the window had become a veritable meadow of color, with cascading browns, carpeting greens, billowing yellows, and floating blues all designed to draw attention to the display.

As she was working on the display she saw a grizzled old man riding a mule down the street, and she laughed out loud.

"What is it?" Nellie asked.

"That man," Janelle said, pointing. "I've never seen anyone who looked like that before."

"Oh, that's just a prospector," Nellie said.

"A prospector?"

"Someone who is looking for gold," Nellie explained. "Or silver, or turquoise, or whatever they can find. They spend months, sometimes years out in the desert."

"Why on earth would anyone ever do such a thing? Do they actually think they will find something?"

"Sometimes they do," Nellie said. "Not very often, but evidently often enough to keep the hope alive in poor souls like that one."

"Poor soul?"

"Yes, look at him, Janelle. You can tell by looking that he is barely able to keep body and soul together. Why, I'll bet he doesn't have five cents to his name."

"Oh, how terrible. How does such a person live?"

"Oh, honey, you don't really want to know that." She laughed.

"I'm ashamed, now, that I laughed at him. I wish I could give him some money."

"No, dear, you don't want to do that," Nellie said.

"Why not."

"Those type of men are fiercely independent and very proud. If you offered him money—especially coming from someone like you—he would be mortified."

"Oh, well, I wouldn't want to do anything like that," Janelle said.

"I know you meant well. I'm just telling you how things are, is all."

"Thanks," Janelle said.

At that moment the bell on the door tinkled, and a tall gray haired, distinguished looking man came in.

"Good morning, Mr. Montgomery. May I help you?" Nellie asked.

"I'm shopping for my wife's birthday," Montgomery said. "Let me look around a bit."

"Go right ahead." She turned her attention back to the window. "Oh, Janelle, that is beautiful," she said, complimenting Janelle's artistic display.

After wandering around a bit, Montgomery picked up one of the hats Nellie had recently received. He spent a long moment examining it, as he held it in his hand.

"Tell me, Mrs. Buckner, do you think my wife would like this?" he asked. "The reason I ask is, I thought I might get her a bonnet, but I've never seen anything like this."

"That is called a flower pot," Mrs. Buckner said.

"A flower pot? You plant flowers in it?"

Mrs. Buckner laughed. "Janelle, please come over here and tell Mr. Montgomery about this hat, will you?"

"Of course," Janelle said, coming away from the window.

"You," Montgomery said, pointing at Janelle and smiling broadly. "You are the young lady who rode in the race yesterday, aren't you?"

"Yes, I am."

"Well, I must tell you the entire town is proud of you."

"Thank you."

"Do you work here?"

"She does," Nellie said. "She has the most marvelous eye for fashion. And, she also keeps our books."

"This young lady keeps your books?"

"She does indeed," Nellie said. "Now, you wanted to ask her opinion about that hat?"

Montgomery turned his attention back to the hat. "Yes, I do."

"What would you like to know?" Janelle asked.

"Is it stylish?" Montgomery asked. "I mean, if we went to some big city like Denver, St. Louis, or New Orleans, would she be—I'm not sure what the word is I am looking for, but—would she be out of place?"

"She would not be out of place at all," Janelle said. "That hat is very stylish." Janelle put the hat on her own head and tilted it just so. She smiled as she was modeling the hat, and the smile lit up her face.

"Oh, my that—that is beautiful," Montgomery said, almost reverently.

"I assure you, Mr. Montgomery, if your wife wore this hat, she would be fashionable not only in Denver, St. Louis, or New Orleans, but I have seen this same hat perched on the head of the most fashionable ladies of New York, and Paris as well."

"New York and Paris, you say? You have been to those places?"

"I have."

"And at the price of two dollars, you won't get a better bargain," Nellie added, trying to close the sale.

"Two dollars? Isn't that a bit high for such a small bit of straw?"

"A small bit of straw? Mr. Montgomery, calling this a small bit of straw is like calling Michelangelo's statue of David a small piece of marble," Janelle said.

Montgomery laughed out loud. "You make a good point, Miss—? I didn't get your last name, and it would hardly do for me to call you by your Christian name."

"It is Wellington. Janelle Wellington."

"I see what you mean, Mrs. Buckner, when you tell me she has an eye for fashion. And you say she also does your books?"

"Yes, she does."

"Tell me, Miss Wellington, are you an educated woman? And by that, I mean have you attended a school beyond the normal public school?"

"Yes, my father believed in education, even for women. I matriculated from Cornell, one of the few private colleges that will admit women."

Montgomery smiled and nodded. "Cornell, yes, I have heard of it. It is a very good school. And, good for your father. He is, truly, a man ahead of his time. I think the time will come when men and women are given equal opportunities for education."

Mrs. Buckner laughed. "What a foolish idea. Beyond the ability to read, I see absolutely no reason for a woman to have an education."

"Unfortunately there are a great number of people who feel just as you do. Therefore it might be quite some time before my prediction comes true," Montgomery replied.

"Do you wish to buy the hat, Mr. Montgomery?" Janelle asked.

Again, Montgomery laughed. "You are a woman with a mind for business, Miss Wellington, and I appreciate that. Yes, I will buy the hat."

Chapter Fifteen

C. D. Montgomery was President of the Sun Valley Bank and Trust, and after having his purchase gift wrapped, he took it back to the bank with him. He pictured the look on his wife's face when he gave it to her after the birthday dinner he had planned. He let himself into his office through a side door, and so didn't see the long-haired, scraggily bearded, disheveled man in the raggedy clothes sitting out front, waiting for him. Immediately after stepping into his office, there was a light knock on his door, and his secretary, Jarvis Depro, stuck his head in.

"Mr. Montgomery, there is someone waiting to see you. I told him I'm sure you wouldn't be interested in meeting with him, but he wouldn't go away. I'm afraid he is rather insistent."

"Why do you think I wouldn't be interested in seeing him?"

"Because he is most—unkempt—sir," Depro said. "He may be the filthiest man I've ever seen. And he smells."

Montgomery chuckled. "Jarvis, have you been around some of our leading citizens? The fact that the person waiting to see me smells is not particularly significant. Please, show him in."

"Very good sir," Depro said.

Leaving Montgomery's office, Depro walked back to the front of the bank. For a moment he just stood there looking at the strange scruffy little man, then he walked over toward him.

"Mr . . . ?"

"Hanlon. Ben Hanlon."

"Mr. Hanlon, Mr. Montgomery will see you now."

"Thank you, sonny. I'll remember you in my will," Hanlon said with a high, cackling laugh.

A few minutes later Ben Hanlon was scratching his scraggly beard, feeling one of the lice move quickly to escape his clawing fingers as he sat in the office of the president of the bank. Leaning back in the chair he examined the room. The calendar on the wall said it was Tuesday, July 5, 1885.

1885?

That surprised him. He thought it was sometime in the 1870s, maybe '78 or '79. Damn, that meant he had been prowling around on Superstition for what? Ten years, maybe? He wondered how long it had been since he had slept in a real bed, or spent the night under a roof. It didn't really matter how long it had been since he had done it, the important thing was how long would it be before he did it again. He had a feeling that it would be no longer than that night.

Ben's chair was on one side of the desk, and the bank president was on the other side. For the last few minutes, Montgomery had been studying a paper Ben had given him.

"I don't know, Mr. Hanlon," Montgomery finally said, speaking for the first time in several minutes. "What you are asking is highly unusual."

"How come that?" Ben asked. "This here is a bank, ain't it? An' don't banks lend money to folks."

"Yes, we are here to lend money to people. But only to people with a good prospect of being able to pay it back. Oh, and of course, people with collateral," Montgomery replied.

"What's that mean? Collateral?"

"It means that in order to get a loan, you have to put up something of value, generally of the same, or more value than the amount of money you are asking for."

"Well, hell, ain't that what I just done?" Ben asked, pointing to the piece of paper on Montgomery's desk. "Didn't I just give you that?"

"I can't make heads or tails of this," Montgomery said holding out the piece of paper. "What is it?"

"It's what you was askin' for," Ben said. "It's collateral."

"It's a piece of paper."

"It's a map," Ben said. "It's a map to the richest gold mine what has ever been found. I aim to put that map up so as to borrow enough money to start workin' the mine. I'll be needin' me some food, and by that I mean some real store-bought food, not the desert rats and cactus fruit I been eatin'. An' maybe a couple more mules, seein' as I'll be haulin' out more ore than Rhoda can carry by herself. Oh, an' I'll be a' wantin' me some new duds, too. These here clothes is plumb wore out. And I'll be a' needin' some—"

Montgomery held up his hand. "Hold it, hold it, slow down here," he said.

"What?"

"Mr. Hanlon, I'm surprised at you, paying good money for a map like this. Do you have any idea how many maps there are to the Peralta mine? Where did you buy this?"

"I didn't buy it nowhere," Ben answered indignantly. "I drawed that there map my ownself. It tells you exactly where at the gold is."

"Are you telling me you know where the gold is?" Montgomery asked.

"Yes, sir, that's exactly what I'm a' tellin' you. An' I need me some money to buy some new supplies. An' like I said, maybe some more clothes and a couple of mules."

Ben began scratching under his shirt. "An' I might even get me a bath," he added. "Lord, I reckon it's been some twenty years or so since I've had me a proper bath, I mean in a bathtub with soap and all."

"Do you have any proof that you found the mine? I mean, other than this map?"

"Yes, sir, I got me some proof," Ben said. He unbuttoned a couple shirt buttons, then reached his hand inside. Pulling out a small rawhide sack, he dumped the contents on Montgomery's desk. "These here is nuggets I took from the mine," he said. "An' they's a lot more where these come from."

Montgomery picked up one of the rocks, cleaned it off, then began turning it in his hand. He stopped turning when he saw a streak of yellow metal.

"This—" he started, then stopped. Opening a drawer to his desk, he pulled out a knife and began digging at the yellow metal. After a couple probes, he gasped. "This is gold!" he said. "This is real gold!"

"Yes, sir, that's what I been a' tryin' to tell you all along," Ben said. "To tell you the truth, Mr. Montgomery, I reckon you might say that I'm a rich man. Only I ain't quite figured out how a rich man's s'posed to act, I mean, all high falutin' and sech."

"How much gold do you have, Mr. Hanlon?"

"Right now, all I got is what's in this here bag, but like I said, there's a heap more where this come from. I figure the rest of it would be safer where it is, rather than me bringin' a lot of it into town. That is, seein' there don't nobody but me know where at the gold is. 'Ceptin' now, maybe you, you havin' the map an' all."

"Yes, I think you may be right," Montgomery said. "All right, Mr. Hanlon, I'll take the map as collateral, and I'll make you that loan."

St. Louis, Missouri

Falcon stared through the window as the train crossed the bridge over the Mississippi River. At that moment the conductor was passing through the car, and seeing Falcon staring so intently, he stopped beside his seat.

"I'll bet you never thought the Mississippi River could be bridged, did you?" the conductor asked.

"It is quite a feat," Falcon replied, although it was not his first time to cross the river at St. Louis.

"Yes, sir, this is some bridge," the conductor said, enjoying his role as the purveyor of technical information. "What you are looking at is a true marvel of modern engineering and science. It's called Eads Bridge, and it's the longest arch bridge in the world. Over sixty-four hundred feet it is. Why, that's almost a mile and a quarter. Think of it. Here we are, riding comfortably in a train that is propelled by its own means of locomotion, crossing such a bridge. Yes, sir, we live in a marvelous age."

"We do indeed," Falcon replied, responding in a way that was courteous, but offering the conductor little opportunity to expand the conversation.

"Yes, sir, a marvelous age," the conductor repeated, then satisfied that Falcon was suitably impressed, he moved on through the train to find another audience for his accolades of Eads Bridge. Falcon settled back in his seat to read the newspaper he had picked up at Union Station in St. Louis. He was slightly less than halfway through his journey and began reading, his attention drawn to one of the articles.

Luke Mueller and Egan Drumm
Still Missing

Word has reached the *Dispatch* of the involvement of Luke Mueller and his brother Clete, in a bank robbery in MacCallister,

Colorado. Subsequent to the robbery, the thieves were hunted down by Mr. Falcon MacCallister who, while not normally a lawman, was apparently acting as some sort of deputy at the time. In a confrontation between Deputy MacCallister and the four brigands, MacCallister discharged his pistol but four times, each shot however finding its mark with devastating effect, killing all four outlaws. Among those killed was Clete Mueller. However, Luke Mueller, who is known to have been part of the bank robbery and double murder, was not present at the time of the confrontation. Because of that, the brigand escaped his due, and remains at large, a scab on humanity.

Informed readers of the *Dispatch* will remember that the Mueller brothers, as well as Egan Drumm, are wanted for a murder and robbery most foul in Jackson County, Missouri where they did shoot down Mr. Chris Dumey, his wife and two children, all for the purpose of stealing the money Mr. Dumey had just received from the sale of his hogs. Dumey lived long enough to write on the floor, using his own blood, the names of those who killed him.

Egan Drumm is not believed to have been a part of the MacCallister bank robbery, and indeed has not been seen since leaving Missouri. There is an unsubstantiated claim that he may have been killed somewhere in Kansas, but most believe that the brigand is still at large, and some believe he may still be keeping company with Mueller.

It is hoped that justice will soon be brought to these evil men, perhaps the same kind of justice which Deputy MacCallister delivered to Clete Mueller.

Falcon spent four nights en route. On the morning of the fifth day his train reached the Hudson River, swept down its eastern bank for 140 miles, flashed quickly by a squalid row of tenement houses, then dived with a roar into the tunnel which passed under the glitter and swank of Park Avenue before emerging at Grand Central Station. Once the train reached the track complex in the depot rail yard, it stopped, then began backing up. Falcon watched through the window as they slipped in between two other trains on adjacent tracks. The bright sunlight disappeared when the car in which Falcon was riding passed under a long roof into the car shed. Finally the train came to a halt with a rattling jerk of fittings and connectors.

"New York, folks," the conductor said, passing through the car. "This is Grand Central Station in New York. Everyone out here."

When Falcon stood, he reached toward his side in an automatic gesture to check for his pistol. For just a second he was disturbed that the familiar weight of the revolver wasn't there. Quickly, he realized guns weren't worn in New York as if they were a part of his anatomy.

Seeing an attractive young mother struggling to control her rambunctious child while also trying to retrieve something from the overhead storage rack, Falcon moved quickly to her assistance.

"Thank you, sir" she said, flashing him a smile as he handed the bag to her.

With a polite nod of his head and an inviting sweep of his arm, Falcon indicated that she could go before him.

"Hurry up, lady," an irritated male voice said from behind. "I don't intend to spend the entire day standing here, waiting for you to get off the train."

Falcon turned and looked at the man. Though he made no overt threat, not even in the form of his facial expression, the fact that someone as powerfully built as Falcon was looking at him, caused the man to look aside, sheepishly.

It was a warm, muggy, summer day and the smoke and the steam from the dozens of engines working the tracks in the huge, cavernous car shed rose to the roof, only to be forced down again in swirls of smoke and steam that burned the eyes and irritated the throat. Sounds were amplified and magnified—the ring of steel wheels rolling on steel track, the clanging of bells, the hollow puffing of vented steam, and the yells of railroad men, shouting instructions for the various switch tracks.

Once inside the terminal he saw the young mother he had helped and her child being greeted by a tall, well-dressed man. The little boy opened his arms wide, and the man, who Falcon presumed was the boy's father, picked him up.

There was much to be said for Falcon's lifestyle, his freedom of movement without the constraint of a family. Since his Indian wife, Marie, and their two children had died, he had never seriously contemplated remarriage. But there were times, like that moment as he watched the obviously happy reunion, when he thought it might be good to have a family.

Ahh, what am I thinking? I do have a family. Andrew and Rosanna are my family. That's why I am here in New York.

Stepping onto the street, Falcon saw a glut of hansom cabs and horse-drawn jitneys lined up outside the four-story redbrick building that was the Grand Central Depot. He stretched to work out the kinks in his body wrought by spending the better part of a week on the train. The bright sunshine caused him to blink a few times as he looked around to take in the scene. Across the street from the depot was the Park Avenue Oyster House, and the aroma of fried oysters hung in the air. Omnibuses, trolleys, and pedestrians made a kaleidoscope of movement and color on East Forty-second Street.

"Falcon! Over here!"

Looking toward the sound of the woman's voice, Falcon saw his sister and brother, standing beside a carriage. Smiling, he picked up his luggage and walked toward them.

"Oh, it is good to see you," Rosanna said, giving him a big, welcoming hug. Andrew shook his hand.

"We appreciate you coming to see us," Andrew said.

"Heck, I didn't come to see you, I came to see the new play you are in," Falcon teased.

Brother and sister laughed.

"Whatever it takes to get you here, brother," Rosanna said.

The driver of the carriage put Falcon's suitcase into the boot as the three MacCallisters climbed in.

"I have something to show you," Falcon said, and from his bag he removed an envelope.

"What is it?" Andrew asked.

"Look inside."

Andrew opened the envelope, then pulled out the photograph. "Oh, my," he said. "Look at this, Rosanna."

For a long moment, Andrew and Rosanna stared at the photograph of the bronze statue of their father.

"I wish we had been able to be there," Rosanna said, as she wiped a tear from the corner of her eye. What a wonderful tribute to Father."

Falcon smiled. Everyone in the family referred to him as Pa. Only Andrew and Rosanna had ever called him Father.

"I do hope everyone understood why we couldn't come," Andrew said.

"Don't worry about it, Andrew, everyone understands perfectly," Falcon said. "There were no hard feelings."

That wasn't quite true, but Falcon saw no need to tell them otherwise. It was obvious they very much wanted to come, and would have come had they been able to.

It took only ten minutes to go from Grand Central Station to Shoemaker's Dining Salon on Sixth Avenue, located next door to the Eagle Theater, where Andrew and Rosanna would star in the premiere performance of *The Ideal Suitor.*

"Mademoiselle and Monsieur MacCallister, what a delightful treat it is for us to serve you on the day before your opening," a rather effeminate maitre d' said by way of greeting when they stepped into the dining room. *"C'est un honneur pour accueillir tel thespians du distinguised à notre resturant."*

"Merci Jacques. C'est notre frère, Falcon, venez nous visiter de l'Ouest." Andrew said. Then, continuing in English, "And I would advise you not to anger him. He is a man of no small repute in the Wild West."

"Yes, I can see that," Jacques said, continuing in English. "He is as powerful looking as he is handsome."

Sensing that the maitre d's effusive compliments of Falcon were making his brother uneasy, Andrew spoke up quickly.

"Have Mr. and Mrs. Wellington arrived yet?"

"Ah! Indeed they have," Jacques replied. "They are waiting for you in the private dining room." Jacques snapped his fingers and a young man approached. "Jefferson, please show the MacCallisters to the Golden Room, would you?"

"Yes, sir," Jefferson replied.

The Golden Room was a private dining room located on the top floor of the three-story building. There was no mystery as to how it got its name, for the textured ceiling was overlaid with a thin layer of real gold. The walls were wainscoted; cherrywood below and textured wallpaper above with a pattern of fleur-de-lis in green and gold. A rich green carpet covered the floor, while the table was covered in a gold-colored cloth. Expensive gold-rimmed china, silverware, and crystal sparkled in the light from the gas lantern chandelier.

A man and woman rose to greet them as they

entered. Both were late middle age, though they looked much younger.

"Falcon, this is Joel and Emma Wellington," Andrew said. "And this is my brother, Falcon," he concluded, directing the latter remark toward the middle-aged couple.

"It is so good to see you, Andrew and Rosanna, and a great privilege to meet your esteemed brother," Joel said. He smiled at Falcon. "I have heard so much about you. Your brother and sister are convinced you hung the moon."

"My brother and sister tend to exaggerate," Falcon said.

"Oh, I wouldn't know about that," Joel said. "They make their case brilliantly."

"Falcon, Mr. Wellington is the angel for our new play," Andrew said. "In fact, if truth be told, he is responsible for our very careers."

"I'd hardly say I was responsible for your careers," Joel said, dismissing Andrew's comment. "You two are the most talented couple in New York. All that was needed was the opportunity for you to show others what you could do. After that, you were both on your own."

"But who provided us with that opportunity? It was you, and the many plays and performances you backed."

"I consider it an investment," Joel said. "With the way you two bring theatergoers to the plays, the investment has more than paid off."

The mutual compliments shifted to other subjects, then Joel cleared his throat and looked at Andrew. "Have you mentioned it to him?"

"No," Andrew replied. "Not yet."

Falcon noticed that all four were looking directly at him and he put down the glass of wine he had just picked up. "What is it?" he asked.

"I told Joel you would help him," Andrew said. "I mean, considering how much he has done for Rosanna and me, I figure we owe him."

"*We* owe him?" Falcon asked.

"Well, by we, I meant that Rosanna and I owe him," Andrew said, clarifying his comment. "But we have always stuck together as a family, have we not? And you, especially, have always gone out of your way to help others."

"Mr. MacCallister, you may be our only hope," Emma Wellington said, and her eyes misted over with the sincerity of her plea.

Falcon smiled pleasantly at the attractive woman. "Well then, if I am your only hope, I had better do all that I can, hadn't I?"

"I will pay you any amount—" Joel started, but Falcon held up his hand to interrupt him.

"If I understand my brother and sister, you have already contributed more than enough in helping their careers. If it is something I am capable of doing, I'm more than willing to give it a try, and no pay is necessary."

"Bless you, Mr. MacCallister," Emma said.

"And thank you," Joel added.

Again, Falcon smiled. "It's about time I found out what I'm supposed to do, isn't it?"

"It's our daughter," Joel said.

"We want you to find her," Emma added.

"She's somewhere out West," Andrew said.

"That's why I suggested you would be the right person to look for her."

"Somewhere out West? That covers a lot of territory." Falcon said.

"We received a telegram from her, informing us that she was in Phoenix, in the Arizona Territory. Do you know that area?"

"Yes, I've been there a few times," Falcon said.

"Do you think you can find her?" Joel asked.

"Do you think she is still in Phoenix?" Falcon asked him.

"I have no reason to think otherwise."

Falcon nodded confidently. "Phoenix is not that large a place. If she is still there, she shouldn't be very hard to find."

"Yes, well, finding her is not the only problem," Joel said.

"There's another problem?"

Joel nodded. "You may have a problem in getting her to come home."

"Mr. Wellington, I'll do what I can to talk her in to coming home," Falcon said. "But I hope you don't expect me to force her to come back, because I won't do that."

"No, nor would I expect you to," Joel replied.

"Perhaps if you tell her she has nothing to be ashamed of, that her mother and father love her, and that we want her, she'll come back," Emma suggested.

"You say she has nothing to be ashamed of?"

"Not a thing," Joel said, and Emma shook her head in general compliance.

"Why would she think she should be ashamed?"

"I-I hesitate to say," Joel said.

"Nonsense, Joel," Emma scolded. "On the one hand you say she has no need to be ashamed, then on the other, you are too ashamed to speak of it."

"I suppose you are right," Joel said. He took a deep breath. "The thing is, Mr. MacCallister, Janelle had a child out of wedlock. She thought she loved the father, and she thought he loved her. The scoundrel's name is Boyd Zucker. He was a business partner of mine, younger than I, but substantially older than our daughter and I don't think he ever had the slightest idea of marrying her. When the rogue learned of Janelle's, uh, confinement, he claimed to have no part in it. He refused to marry her."

"If it's any consolation to you, I'm sure that isn't the first time an evil man took advantage of an innocent young woman, then abandoned her," Falcon suggested.

"I tried to tell her that, but her shame knew no bounds," Joel said.

"Shortly after her baby was born, she gave him to her sister, then she went West, claiming she could not face the shame," Emma said.

"We could have done more to stop her," Joel said. "It is true she left without our knowledge, but I think if he had been more—understanding—we could have prevented her from leaving. But the truth is, I think we were feeling a little shame as well."

"Please, Mr. MacCallister, say that you will find her," Emma said, her anguish showing in her eyes. "I can't imagine how she must feel, abandoned first by the evil Mr. Zucker, and then by her own parents."

"We didn't abandon her," Joel said resolutely.

Emma reached across the table to put her hand on Joel's. "Yes, my dear, we did abandon her," she said.

"I-I suppose we did," Joel agreed reluctantly. "Mr. MacCallister, please say that you will help us."

"I'll—" Falcon started, then stopped. He almost said he would *do what he could,* to find her, but he knew that would be scarce comfort. "I will find her," he promised.

"I hope you can," Emma said.

"Mrs. Wellington, if my brother says he will find Janelle, you can count on it," Rosanna said. "Falcon never goes back on his word."

"Oh, thank you, Mr. MacCallister," Emma said, relief evident in her eyes and her voice. "I don't know how to thank you enough."

Falcon knew he had just declared an absolute—something he rarely did. But he knew, also, that he could not let these people down, and he derived a great satisfaction from seeing their reaction to his promise. It was one of contentment—and he made a promise to himself to see to it their confidence in him was not misplaced.

"You will be going to the grand opening of the play tomorrow night, won't you?" Joel asked, changing the subject.

"Of course I will, that's why I came to New York," Falcon said. He chuckled. "I mean, that's why I thought I came to New York."

"It is why you came," Joel said. "I want you to have a wonderful time while you are here. Please allow me to pay for your hotel and dining expenses.

It's the least I can do to repay you for what you are doing for Emma and me."

"Oh, well, if I had known you were going to pay for the hotel, I would have gotten the finest suite available," Falcon teased, and the others laughed, the more so because Andrew and Rosanna knew he had taken a suite at the Grand Central Hotel, perhaps New York's finest.

Chapter Sixteen

Phoenix

The very first thing Ben Hanlon did when he left the bank with money in his pocket, was buy himself a new change of clothes. After that he went to the bathhouse and bought himself a bath. When he was clean, really clean for the first time in a very long time he went to the Boar's Head Saloon.

As he stepped inside he stood there for a moment, looking around, savoring actually, the fact that he was in a saloon, and he actually had money in his pocket. A piano stood at the back of the room, but there was no one playing it. Because it was early afternoon, the saloon wasn't very crowded.

There were three bar girls, but they were together in a cluster at the far end of the bar, talking among themselves. There were only four others in the saloon, the bartender, and three men who were sitting at a table.

Hanlon stepped up to the bar, then pulled out a ten dollar banknote and slapped it down.

"Barkeep, I would like to buy a drink for everyone in the house," he said.

"The girls too?" the bartender asked.

Hanlon looked down at the three girls, and smiled. "Especially the girls," he said.

"Thank you, mister," one of the girls said.

"Ben," Hanlon said. "The name is Ben."

"Maxine," the bartender said, handing one of the girls a bottle. Go refill the drinks of the gentlemen at the table."

"All right, Wally," the girl said. She flashed a wide smile at Hanlon. "But don't you go away, Ben. I'll be right back."

"I'm not going anywhere, darlin'," Ben replied.

The bartender looked at Hanlon. "And what would you like?"

"You got any Champagne?" Hanlon asked.

Wally laughed. "Champagne? This is Phoenix, not San Francisco. We've got beer and whiskey."

"Then that is what I will have."

"Which? Beer or whiskey?"

"I'll have beer and whiskey," he said.

The barkeep put both drinks in front of him, and Hanlon tossed the whiskey down, then chased it with the beer.

Within a very short time, Ben Hanlon was drunk. It wasn't just that he couldn't handle his liquor, which was true, or that it had been over a year since he had last had a drink, which was also true. It was because he was trying to make up in one night for the dry spell that had lasted for so long. He was in the Boar's Head Saloon, spending the money so freely the soiled doves gathered around him were being rewarded by having bills stuffed in the tops of their low-cut dresses.

"Old-timer," Wally said after pouring another drink for Hanlon. "I'm happy to take your money as long as you want to spend it, but don't you think you ought to slow down a bit?"

"Don't you be a' worryin' none 'bout me, sonny," Hanlon replied. "I got money all right. I got me more money than you ever seen before."

Hanlon took out his little leather pouch and poured out a few gold nuggets. "You see this here? Just one of these nuggets would pay for ever'thing I done spent in this here saloon so far tonight."

The bartender examined the nugget for a moment, at first with skepticism, then with surprise. "This is real."

"It sure as hell is real."

"Where did you get this?"

"Ha! Wouldn't you like to know?"

"You think you can find it again?"

"Damn right I can find it again," Hanlon said. "I got me a map that will take me, or anybody that looks at it, right to where I found this gold."

"A map, huh?" Wally said with a chuckle. "Now Ben, you ought to have been around long enough by now to know better than to buy a map."

"I didn't buy it, sonny, I drawed it up my ownself."

"Yeah? Where is this map now?"

"It's in a safe place."

"You got it hid out, have you?"

"No, it ain't hid. It's down to the bank. That's where you're s'posed to keep valuables, ain't it?"

"I reckon that's so," the bartender said.

Luke Mueller came into the saloon then, and though he came in too late to hear any of the conversation about the map, he did see the gold nuggets Hanlon had scattered out on the bar.

"Yes, sir," Hanlon said, as he scooped the nuggets up and put them back into a small, rawhide bag which he stuck under his shirt. "Bet you ain't never seen nothin' like this, have you?"

"I can't say as I have," Wally replied, then moved down the bar to Mueller. "Yes, sir, Mr. Jones, what'll it be?"

"I'll have a beer," Mueller said. He nodded toward Hanlon, who had gone back to talking with the three soiled doves. "What's that ol' fool got that has them women buzzin' around him like flies on a turd?"

"Gold," the bartender said. He turned around and drew a mug of beer, then set it in front of Mueller.

"Gold?" Mueller asked.

"Yes, sir, gold. He's got himself a whole sack of gold nuggets."

"Well, I reckon somethin' like that would get the ladies' attention."

Wally chuckled. "Yes, sir, I reckon it would."

Talk of the gold had gotten Mueller's attention, too, and he nursed his beer as he watched Hanlon out of the corner of his eye. Hanlon was drinking heavily and soon, Mueller knew he would get his chance.

It took no more than fifteen minutes before the opportunity presented itself.

"I gotta go outside and take myself a pee," Hanlon announced. "You ladies wait right here 'til I come back. That is, lessen one of you would like to come along with me, maybe help me hold on to it," he added with a ribald chuckle.

"Really now, what kind of girls do you think we are?" one of them asked, giggling at Hanlon's comment.

"Oh, darlin', I know what kind of women you be," Hanlon replied as he started toward the back door. "You be the kind I can buy if I got enough money, and that, I got. I'm just decidin' which one of you I want."

"Hurry back now, Ben, honey," Maxine called out to him. "If you are nice enough, and spend enough money, you can have all of us."

"All of you?" Hanlon laughed. "Well now, I ain't never thought of nothin' like that. Could be, maybe I might just want to try that."

No one noticed that as Hanlon left by the back door, Marshal Cairns' cousin, Jesse Jones, was moving quickly toward the front door.

Hanlon walked back to the outhouse, stepping inside even as Luke Mueller hurried around back. Looking around to make certain there was nobody watching, Mueller waited by the door of the outhouse until Hanlon came out again, buttoning his pants as he did so.

"Was you waitin' to get in?" Hanlon asked. "Sorry. But I'm all done now."

"Thanks," Mueller said in a gruff voice and he put a foot on the step as Hanlon walked away. Then, from behind, Mueller brought the butt of his pistol down hard on Hanlon's head, and the old prospector collapsed to the ground in front of him. Working quickly, Mueller took what was left of

Hanlon's cash money, as well as the little bag of gold nuggets.

He hefted the bag in his hand and from the weight of them, he figured he had to have at least two or three hundred dollars worth of gold. The problem would be in getting rid of it. The old fool had been too eager to show it off, and everyone in the saloon had seen it. But he also had almost fifty dollars in cash, and Mueller could spend that money anywhere. He went back into the saloon and retook his seat. It had all happened so quickly, he didn't think anyone even noticed he had left.

"Bartender," he called.

"Yes, sir, Mr. Jones," Wally replied.

"Another beer. He nodded toward the bar girls. "And something for the ladies," he added.

"Wally, what do you think is takin' Ben so long?" Maxine asked.

"He's an old man," one of the other women said. "You know how old men are. Sometimes it takes them a real long time to pee."

"Doris, you are awful!" Maxine said, but she and the other girl were both laughing at Doris's comment.

When more than ten minutes went by and Ben hadn't returned, Maxine asked Wally about him again. "Now I'm beginning to get worried," she said. "Do you think the old man is all right?"

"Yeah, I'm sure he is," Wally said. "He was drinking a lot. I wouldn't be surprised if he didn't get outside then realize just how drunk he is, and how much money he was spending. He probably just went somewhere to sleep it off."

"I hope he is all right. I thought he was cute," Maxine said.

"Ha. You just liked the money he was spending," Wally said.

"Yes, I did. But I also thought he was cute. And I do hope he is all right."

Deputies Forbis and Appleby were making their rounds with Appleby on one side of the street and Forbis on the other. When he looked into the alley behind the Boar's Head, Forbis thought he saw something lying on the ground so he went back to check.

It was a man, lying facedown on the ground.

Forbis thought he was dead, and he dropped down to one knee to check him out. The man let out a little groan.

"Appleby!" Forbis shouted. "Appleby, over here!"

Responding to Forbis's call, Appleby trotted across the street, with his pistol drawn.

"You won't be needing that," Forbis said.

"What is it?"

"This man has been hurt."

"Hurt? More'n likely he's just passed out drunk."

"Help me get him up," Forbis said.

"What for? Just leave him here."

"We can't do that, Bert. Come on, help me get him up. We'll take him down to the jail, just so he'll have a place to sleep it off tonight."

With Forbis on one side, and Appleby on the other, the two deputies managed to get the old man on his feet.

"Rhoda," he said.

"Rhoda? Who's Rhoda?" Forbis asked.

Appleby snorted what might have been a laugh. "Prob'ly the whore that got him drunk."

"Rhoda is my mule. I want Rhoda."

As they half carried, and half facilitated his walk, they came back out to the street. Glancing toward the front of the saloon, Forbis saw, tied at the hitching rail with four horses, one mule. "Is that Rhoda?" he asked.

"Yes. She will be worried if I don't come back."

"Don't worry, old man," Forbis said. "I'll take care of Rhoda for you."

"My head hurts. Someone hit me."

"Nobody hit you old man. You're just drunk," Appleby said.

"Someone hit me."

When Ben Hanlon woke up, he wondered for a moment where he was. He was lying in a bed, or at least a bunk, but he didn't remember checking in to a hotel. In fact, he couldn't remember anything since standing at the bar in the saloon, talking to the bar girls. He sat up, and as he did, his head began to spin. He fought a bout of nausea and felt a rather severe pain in the back of his head. Looking around he saw that he was in a little room, and, upon further examination, realized he was in a jail cell.

"What the hell? Hey!" he called out. "Hey! Anybody here?"

"Keep it quiet back there."

"Hey, what is this, a jail? What for am I in jail?"

A broad-shouldered man with a bushy moustache came back to the cell. He was wearing a badge over his left pocket.

"Who are you?" Hanlon asked.

"My name is Cairns. Jimmy Cairns," Drumm said. "Maybe you've heard of me."

"No, I ain't never heard of you."

"I'm the mashal here. Who are you?"

"Ben Hanlon is who I am. What I want to know is, what am I a' doin' in this here jail?"

"You don't remember?"

"I don't remember nothin' since I was down at the Boar's Head, talkin' with all the girls," Hanlon said. "What did I do? Did I do somethin' wrong? I don't remember doin' anything wrong. Why am I in jail?"

"You're in jail because you are an indigent. We found you passed out in the alley behind the Boar's Head Saloon."

"What's an indigent?"

"That means somebody that don't have no money, and no way of takin' care of themselves. I don't like folks like that in my town. They're the kind that winds up stealin' from the decent folks."

"Yeah? Well, I'll have you know I got me some money," Hanlon said. "Fac' is, I got me lots of money."

"Do you now?" Drumm asked with a sarcastic chuckle.

"I sure as hell do."

"Let me see it."

"It's right here," Hanlon said, reaching inside his shirt. He stopped when his hand didn't encounter the little leather bag. "What the hell?"

"What is it? What's wrong?" Drumm asked.

"The money," Hanlon said. "It ain't here."

"Of course it ain't there, 'cause it never was there," Drumm said. "Like I said, you are an indigent."

"I ain't no such a' thing!" Hanlon said. "I got me lots of money. Why, I got me more money'n you done ever seen."

"If that's so, just where is it?" Drumm asked.

"I had me some money that I got from the bank, and I had me a sack of gold nuggets."

"Gold nuggets, huh? You expect me to believe that?"

"Yeah, I expect you to believe that. I had lots of 'em. Why, you could ask Mr. Montgomery over to the bank. How else do you think I got the money I was spendin', iffen I didn't get it from the bank?"

"Are you tellin' me you sold some of the gold to the bank?"

"No, I didn't sell none of my gold. What I done was, I borrowed money agin' the map I showed him for"—Hanlon stopped midsentence while he searched for the word—"collateral."

"What is this map?" Drumm asked.

"It is a map to the richest gold mine there ever was," Hanlon said.

"Where is it now? The map, I mean."

"Montgomery's got it," Hanlon replied. "Like I said, I give it to him for collateral."

"Hello, Marshal Cairns," Wally Cook said, as the lawman entered the Boar's Head.

"Was there sort of a wrinkled up old man in here last night with some gold nuggets?" Drumm asked.

"Yeah, Ben was his name. He may have give his last name, but I don't recall it."

"He had a sack full of gold nuggets?"

"He had some gold nuggets all right."

The Boar's Head was quiet at that time of morning, and the bartender was washing glasses. Only one of the bar girls was downstairs. She was sitting alone at a table, drinking a cup of coffee. An old Mexican man was mopping the floor.

"Fac' is, he had a lot of 'em. You can ask Maxine over there, she seen 'em, same as I did. Hell, we all did."

"That true?" Drumm called over to the woman at the table.

"That's true, Sheriff," Maxine said. "He had a whole sack full of 'em."

"What happened to them?"

Wally shook his head. "I don't know. He said he had to go take a leak and he went out back, but he never come back in. Why do you ask?"

"My deputies found him passed out drunk last night," Drumm said.

Wally chuckled. "Passed out, huh? Well, I ain't surprised. He put away enough whiskey last night to make three men drunk."

"He said he hadn't had a drink in over a year, and he had some catchin' up to do," Maxine said.

"Your deputies that found him, did they say anything about the gold?" Wally asked.

Drumm shook his head. "There wasn't nothin' on him when they found him."

"You say both your deputies found him?"

"Yes."

"If it had just been Appleby who found him, I'd be suspicious. But if Forbis was with him, then he probably didn't have any gold on him when they found him."

"What do you mean by that?"

"Come on, Marshal, you know what I mean," Wally said. "Forbis is an honest man. I wouldn't trust Appleby as far as I could throw him. For the life of me, I don't know why you put him on as one of your deputies."

"You've got Appleby all wrong," Drumm said. "He's a good man."

"I guess you are entitled to your opinion, bein' as you are the marshal and all. But like I said, if Forbis said there wasn't no gold when they found him, then more than likely what happened is that Ben went outside and passed out, drunk as he was. Somebody passin' by must've seen 'im and when he went over there he discovered the gold and all the money the feller had on him."

"Yeah," Drumm replied. "You may be right about that."

"'Course, you could ask your cousin about it," Wally said.

"My cousin?"

"Ain't this little feller that's come new to town, Jesse Jones, ain't he your cousin?"

"Oh, yeah, he's my cousin."

"Well, he was in here last night, he seen ever' thing that was goin' on. Maybe he's got an idée as to what happened."

"At least Ben didn't have the map on him, so they didn't get that," Maxine said.

"The map? What map?"

"He's got him a map, that he drew himself, locating the mine where he got all that gold," Maxine said.

"Do you believe there really is such a map?"

"I don't know," Wally replied. "All I know is, he got that gold from somewhere. If he claims he has a map showin' where it is, then I'd be inclined to believe him."

"Well, thanks for the information," Drumm said, finishing the free beer he had taken as the *right* granted him by being sheriff.

From the saloon, Drumm walked over to the livery barn. Mueller had taken a part-time job mucking out stalls in exchange for a room that was just off the back of the barn.

He saw one of Housewright's hands working on some harness.

"You," Drumm said. "Cooper, isn't it?"

"Yeah, Cooper. What do you need, Marshal?"

"I'm lookin' for Luke."

Cooper looked up. "Who?"

"I mean Jesse," Drumm corrected. "Jesse Jones."

"He don't have to come to work 'til noon. He's in his room back there," Cooper said, nodding toward the back of the barn.

"Thanks."

Going to the little room at the back of the barn, Drumm pushed the door open without knocking and saw Mueller sleeping on the canvas cot.

"Wake up," Drumm said.

Mueller snorted once, and turned over.

"I said wake up!" Drumm said, louder that time.

Mueller opened his eyes and seeing Drumm standing there looking down at him, sat up quickly.

"What is it?" he asked. "What do you want?"

"How much money did you get off him?"

"What are you talking about?"

"You know what I'm talking about. I'm talking about the prospector that was in the saloon last night. They say he was spending money like it was water."

"What's that got to do with me?"

"They also say you was there in the saloon at the same time."

"I reckon I was."

"He was robbed. How much did you get?"

"What makes you think I done it?"

"How much did you get?" Drumm asked again.

"All right, all right. I got maybe thirty dollars offen him."

"How much gold?"

"What gold?"

"How much gold?" Drumm repeated.

"I don't know how much gold. Whatever is in this sack." Mueller reached over to pick up his hat, revealing a small pouch underneath. He poured the contents of the little sack out onto his cot. "It ain't worth nothin', though."

"Why not?"

"Ever'one in the saloon seen the gold. I can't spend none of it without it bein' known that I stole it."

"Give it to me."

"Why should I give it to you?"

"You just said you can't spend it, didn't you?"

"Well, yeah, for now. But I figure the time will come when I can spend it."

"I tell you what. I'll give you fifty dollars for the gold right now. You can also keep whatever money you got off him. You'll need it in order to get out of town."

"Why do I need to get out of town? I thought you said I would be safe here."

"That was before you killed that prospector."

"What do you mean I killed him? I just knocked him out, is all."

"Yeah, well, one of my deputies picked him up last night and brought him to jail. He died this morning, which means you killed him."

"Now hold on, Drumm, I did no such thing," Mueller said.

"I told you, my name isn't Drumm. Now, get out of town like I told you, or I'll be forced to arrest my own cousin."

"Ha! You won't do that. Not unless you want me to tell ever'thing I know."

"That's why I'm tellin' you that you need to get out of town."

"Yeah, all right, I was gettin' a little tired of hangin' around here anyway."

His deputy wasn't on duty when Drumm returned to the sheriff's office. Ben Hanlon was still sitting on the bunk in the jail cell, and he looked up when Drumm stepped inside.

"Did you talk to Montgomery?" he asked. "Did he tell you about the map?"

"You know bankers don't get up this early," Cairns replied. "I did talk to the bartender down at the saloon though. He says you had a bag of gold nuggets on you."

"Yeah, I did. But I don't have 'em now. Someone must've stole 'em from me, but if they did, I don't 'member nothin' about it." Hanlon chuckled. "'Course, what they don't know is, they didn't get hardly nothin' a'tall just by takin' them nuggets. The real treasure is the gold mine I found, and it's all marked out on that map."

"This map you are talking about. Are you tryin' to tell me that it's real?"

"Sheriff, I ain' a' *tryin'* to tell you no damn thing a' tall. I *am* tellin' you that it is real Just as real as me sittin' here."

"You say you gave that map to Montgomery?" Drumm started.

"I didn't exactly give it to him. Well, I did give it to him, but what I done was I just give it to him to hold for a while so's I could borrow some money from the bank," Hanlon said. "That's called collateral."

"Did he lend you money?"

"Hell yes, he loaned me some money. How else do you think I got these here new duds?" Hanlon asked, proudly showing off his shirt and trousers.

"If Montgomery loaned you money against the map, he must've thought it was real," Drumm said.

"Well, I reckon he does think it is real, seein' as how it is real."

"All right, the map you did give to him. Where did you get it?"

"I didn't get it nowhere," Hanlon said. "I drawed it up my own self."

"Just where is this gold mine you say you found?"

"I ain't just a'sayin' I found it. I did find it. You ever hear tell of the Lost Dutchman mine?" Hanlon asked.

"Are you talking about Jacob Waltz? That old fool?" Cairns asked.

"That's the one. I don't hold nothin' agin' you for callin' him an old fool. Not after as much time as I've spent cussin' him out over the last few years because I figured he was a fool and a liar as well. But then I found that same gold mine my ownself."

"Where did you find it?"

"It's at Weaver's Needle, just like folks has been sayin' all along."

Drumm shook his head. "No it ain't. Hell, I've been out there a dozen or so times my ownself. There ain't nothin' there."

Hanlon smiled. "Oh yes there is," he said. "You just got to know where to look for it, is all."

"This map you are talking about. Does it tell exactly where to look?"

"Sure it does. Wouldn't be much of a map if it didn't tell you how to find the gold now, would it?"

"How do I know you are tellin' the truth?"

"Where do you think I got the gold nuggets from?" Hanlon asked. "Anyhow, what do I care whether you think I'm tellin' the truth or not? You ain't the one that loaned me the money, so it don't really matter none whether you believe it or not.

Mr. Montgomery is. He knows I'm tellin' the truth, and soon as he finds out you got me locked up in here, he'll tell you I ain't no . . . what was that word you used? Indigent?"

"Yes, indigent."

"Well, sir, you go see Mr. Montgomery soon as he gets into the bank. He'll tell you that I ain't no indigent. What you ought to be doin' is, you ought to be lookin' for the feller what did this to me. I was hit over the head and stoled from, but I'm the one you got in jail. That ain't no way right, and you know it."

Drumm stroked his chin for a moment. "Yeah," he said. "Yeah, I guess you are right."

"So, when are you goin' to let me out of jail?"

"Right now, I reckon," Drumm said.

"Thanks."

"Don't forget your hat."

Hanlon turned back toward the bunk to get his hat, and didn't see Drumm draw his pistol. He brought the gun down hard on Hanlon's head. Hanlon went down and Drumm dropped on his knees beside him. It took only a moment to determine that he was dead.

Drumm picked Hanlon up and put him back in the bunk, then he put Hanlon's hat over his face. After that, he returned to his desk. He was sitting at his desk, calmly drinking coffee and looking at some posters, when Deputy Forbis came in a few minutes later.

"'Mornin', Marshal Cairns," the deputy said.

"Good morning, Forbis," Drumm replied. He nodded toward the cell. "I haven't heard anything from our drunk this morning. Why don't you go back there and wake him up. We may as well let him go."

"All right," the deputy answered. The deputy got the key ring down from a wall hook, then walked back to the cell.

"Want a cup of coffee, Deputy?" Drumm called out, cheerfully.

"Yes, sir, that would be nice," the deputy replied.

Drumm was pouring a cup of coffee for his deputy when Forbis called out to him. "Sheriff?"

"Yeah, Forbis, what is it?"

"This here feller is dead."

"What's that? He's dead, you say?"

"Yes, sir."

"How the hell did that happen?"

"I don't know," the deputy replied. "But I'll say this. He was complainin' of a headache last night when Deputy Appleby and I brought him in. I'll just bet you he was hit over the head. He must have died durin' the night."

"Yeah, I reckon so," Drumm said.

"What do we do now?" the deputy asked.

"What else can we do? He's an indigent, so I don't reckon anyone will be comin' for the body. I guess that means the town will have to pay for the buryin'. You'd better get the undertaker down here."

"Yes, sir," the deputy said, grabbing his hat as he started out the door.

"Oh, and Forbis?"

"Yes, sir?"

"See if you can find my cousin."

"Jesse?"

"Yes, Jesse Jones. If you can find him, bring him down to the jail. And if he don't want to come, arrest him."

"Arrest him? What for?"

"I went down to the saloon this morning to see if any of them knew anything about our drunk," Drumm said. "It seems Jesse was in there all night and he saw all the money our drunk was passin' around."

"Money? Are you kidding? Are you talkin' about our drunk?"

"Yes. It seems the old coot found gold."

The deputy looked back toward the body lying in the cell. "It's a damn shame," he said. "He found gold, and he doesn't get to spend it."

"What would an ol' coot like that do with it anyway?" Drumm asked, exhibiting no compassion at all.

Dalton O'Dell was the undertaker and he arrived no more than five minutes after the deputy left. "Deputy Forbis said you had a task for me," O'Dell said.

"He's back here in the cell."

O'Dell walked back to the cell with Marshal Cairns. "Who is it?" he asked.

"I don't know his name. The deputy brought him in last night. I think someone hit him over the head before the deputies found him. He must have died durin' the night."

O'Dell reached down to touch the body, then he

shook his head. "More'n likely he died this morning," he said. "Probably not more'n an hour ago."

"How can you tell?"

"His skin is still supple, no rigor mortis, no post-mortem pooling of the blood. He was alive all this time and you didn't know it."

"I didn't know he was dead until Forbis discovered it this morning. I guess I should have checked on him, and maybe got the doc over to take a look at him."

O'Dell looked at the head wound. "It wouldn't have mattered. With this wound he would have died anyway. I've got my wagon out front, I'll get him down to the mortuary. Who is paying for it?"

"The city will pay for it. So keep it cheap."

"I'll keep it inexpensive," O'Dell said. "Cheap is not a word I like to use with my subjects. It lacks a certain dignity."

"As long as it don't cost much," Cairns said.

"Sheriff?" Deputy Forbis said, coming back into the office then. "He's gone."

"Who's gone?"

"The feller you sent me after. Your cousin. Housewright said he rode off this mornin' without so much as a fare-thee-well."

"I'm not surprised," Drumm said. "Help O'Dell get the stiff into his wagon."

Chapter Seventeen

The men and women who took rooms at Mrs. Poindexter's Boarding House were provided bountiful meals, served communally in the oversized dining room. Most of the residents had had their breakfast and departed the premises for their various occupations, leaving Janelle Wellington alone with her light breakfast of coffee and a biscuit. She was thinking about the possibility of working at Mr. Montgomery's bank.

When C. D. Montgomery bought the new hat at Buckner's for his wife's birthday, he had been so impressed by Janelle's social graces and her intelligence he asked her to come interview with him for a position in his bank. It was rare that a woman would hold such a position, but he was certain she could do it.

Janelle very much wanted to take the position, but she felt a sense of obligation to Mrs. Buckner who had given her a job shortly after she arrived in Phoenix. She thought back to her conversation with Mrs. Buckner.

"*Don't be silly, my dear, take the job,*" Mrs. Buckner had told her. "*It is a wonderful opportunity for you. And don't worry about me. I got along without you before, I can do so again if need be. Though, from time to time I may ask you to help me with my bookwork.*"

"*I'll be glad to, Mrs. Buckner,*" Janelle said. "*That is, assuming I get the job.*"

"*You'll get the job. Mr. Montgomery was quite impressed with you. He would be a fool not to hire you and I know him well enough to know that he is no fool.*"

A grandfather clock in the hall of the boardinghouse marked the time as eight o'clock, its loud chimes reverberating throughout the house.

"What time is your appointment, dear?" Mrs. Poindexter asked.

"It's at eight-thirty," Janelle said. She drained the last of her coffee. "But I think I'll leave now so I can get there a little early."

"That's probably a good idea," Mrs. Poindexter replied. "I know Mr. Montgomery, and I know he places great value upon punctuality." She picked up a couple plates and carried them into the kitchen as Janelle left the dining room table.

Central Street was filled with the traffic of commerce as Janelle walked from the boardinghouse to the bank. She saw the undertaker's wagon backed up to the mortuary, and she said a quick prayer as the undertaker and his assistant removed a body from the wagon and carried it inside. A stagecoach starting its run to Mesa rolled by, the driver whistling at the team. The shotgun guard was eating an apple, and a young boy inside the coach was looking out the window.

"Hey!" he called to her. "You're the lady that won the horse race, ain't you?" He waved enthusiastically at Janelle, and with a broad smile, Janelle returned his wave.

The coach met a convoy of three arriving freight wagons, one week out of Tucson, the harness jangling and the wheels groaning in protest as they turned under the heavy load. Farther down the street a group of carpenters were building a new feed and seed store, the sound of their hammers and saws invading the morning. Mr. White, the druggist, was sweeping his front porch, the scratching sound of his broom adding to the overall cacophony. There was a dog lying on the porch of the apothecary, so secure in his position that he made no effort to move, forcing Mr. White to sweep around him.

A buckboard stopped in front of Shainberg's General Store, and a husband, wife, and three anxious children climbed down to start their day of adventure in town.

"I'm goin' to get me some horehound candy drops!" one little boy shouted excitedly.

"Don't forget, Timmy, you've got to share," the mother said.

Janelle took it all in with a smile that was almost patronizing. Used to the frenetic pace of life in New York, the bucolic tempo in Phoenix was quite a contrast. If you had asked her about Phoenix one year ago, she would have thought only that it was a mythical bird, rising from the ashes. Never, in her wildest imagination, would she have thought she would find herself in a sleepy western town by that name, not just as a visitor, but as a resident.

But that was before she became pregnant. As she walked she thought of her last year in New York.

"Pregnant? Are you sure?"

"Oh yes, Boyd, I am quite sure," Janelle said. "Isn't it wonderful?"

"Wonderful? How can it be wonderful? You aren't married. You will be a disgrace to your family."

"Not if I am married. Boyd, we could get married now—right away. By the time the baby is born, we will have been married long enough that only the most hateful will have their tongues wagging."

"Married?" Zucker replied. "Married? No, I don't think so. Right now, marriage isn't an option. My career—I don't have time to get married. I have too many things scheduled."

Janelle chuckled. "Perhaps you had better prepare yourself for it," she said. "The baby has its own schedule."

Zucker shook his head and held up his hand, as if pushing her away from him. "You shouldn't have gotten yourself pregnant."

"I shouldn't have gotten myself pregnant? Well, that's just it, Boyd. I didn't do this all by myself, you know. You had a hand in it as well."

"Really?"

"Yes, really," Janelle replied, growing anxious over

the direction of the conversation. "Boyd, what are you saying?"

"I'm saying, how do I know the baby is mine?"

"What? How dare you? Of course the baby is yours!"

"Yes. Well, we can't be sure of that now, can we?" Boyd said. He shook his head. "You had better make some other arrangement, Miss Wellington, because I have no intention of marrying you."

Janelle did not tell anyone of her pregnancy until it was no longer possible to keep it a secret. After much persuasion she finally told her family who the baby's father was.

"What?" Joel asked angrily. "Why didn't you say something before? I would have kept that scoundrel here, and I would have forced him to marry you."

"I know, Father," Janelle said. "That's exactly why I didn't tell you. I could not marry someone who does not want to marry me."

Janelle went into confinement shortly after that, staying in her room and seeing no one. When it came time for her delivery, her father found a doctor who didn't know them, nor moved in their social circles, extracting a promise from him to say nothing of the bastard boy child.

Two months after the baby was born, without consulting with her parents, Janelle made the decision to leave New York. She took her baby to her sister, then left town that same day.

* * *

Pulling herself out of her reverie, she realized she'd been in Phoenix for two months trying to make a new life. She thought of her baby—the baby she had abandoned, not by choice, but by necessity. She told herself that once she was established in a good paying job, making enough money to not only buy a house, but to hire a full-time nurse for the baby, she would ask her sister to bring the baby to her. She was determined that one day she would reunite with her baby. She could see them living in one of the houses on the outskirts of town.

She smiled broadly, and wrapped her arms around herself. With the prospect of a job at the bank, a job she was sure would pay well, she might very well be able to fulfill that dream. Oh, what a joyous thing that would be. For the first time since leaving New York, for the first time since giving birth, she felt a sense of intense joy and anticipation. She had to get the job. She simply had to.

When she reached the bank she saw a sign on the front door of the building, informing the public that the establishment would not be open for business until nine o'clock. It was exactly as she had expected. Mr. Montgomery had said he would leave the side door open for her.

Janelle started up through the little pathway that separated the bank from the Phoenix Tonsorial Salon, stepping around the red and white striped pole that advertised the profession. Three quarters of the way to the rear of the bank building she saw a door that opened onto the little pathway and when she reached it, she tapped lightly, and called out, "Mr. Montgomery?" Getting no answer she tapped again, then she turned the doorknob and pushed. The door opened easily, and Janelle stepped inside. "Mr. Montgomery?" she called again, though not loudly.

"You have no right to it," a man's voice said. Even though the voice was angry, Janelle recognized it as belonging to C. D. Montgomery.

"The man died in my jail. The city is out the expense of his burial. Now, if he has anything of value, I am claiming it in the name of the city," another voice said. There was no anger in the voice. It was cold and calculated. Janelle recognized it as belonging to City Marshal Cairns.

She walked up to the office door. It was open just a crack and she peeked through. Mr. Montgomery and Marshal Cairns stood in the middle of the room, confronting each other.

"Before he died, he told me he had left a map with you."

"What if he did? A map in itself has no direct value," Montgomery replied.

"It must have some value, or you would not have loaned him any money against it. You did loan him money, didn't you?"

"Suppose I did?"

"Then that means the map has some value, and as I said, I am now, officially, confiscating it."

"Not without a court order you aren't going to confiscate it. Do you think having that city marshal's badge gives you the authority to confiscate private property?"

Drumm pulled his gun and pointed it at Montgomery. "Oh, but you forget, Mr. Montgomery, I am not only a city marshal, I am a city marshal with a gun," he said with a laugh so evil it made Janelle shiver.

"Put that gun down, Cairns. Do you think you can frighten me with that? There is no way you are going to shoot me. How would you explain it?"

"That won't be hard. I will just tell them I came in here and caught you robbing your own bank."

"You are out of your mind."

"Give me the map," Drumm demanded again.

Suddenly, and unexpectedly, Montgomery leaped toward him.

"You crazy fool!" Drumm shouted. He jumped back even as he was pulling the trigger. Janelle saw flame and smoke leap from the end of the barrel. The roar of the gunshot was deafening. It covered Janelle's loud gasp as she saw a red hole suddenly appear in Montgomery's chest as he fell down.

"Why didn't you just listen to me? If you had given me the map, this would not have had to happen," Drumm said in a growling voice. He leaned over and took something from Montgomery's jacket pocket, then raised up and looked around.

Realizing that he was about to come toward her, Janelle moved quickly away from the door and hid behind a settee as the marshal came through the outer office to exit through the same door she had just entered. As soon as the marshal left, Janelle went into Montgomery's office, then knelt beside him. He was still alive.

"Miss Wellington, I've been shot," Montgomery said, his voice strained as he looked up toward her.

"I'll get the doctor."

"No, there's no time for that. Get the map."

"I beg your pardon?"

"It's behind the picture on the wall. Get it. It must not fall into Cairns' hands."

"What map?"

"Please, get the map," Montgomery gasped out.

Curious as to what he was talking about, but anxious to fulfill his wish, Janelle looked behind the picture, and seeing an envelope glued to the back of the picture, she removed it and took it back to show him.

"Is this what you are talking about?" Janelle asked.

"Yes," he said, the word coming out as a sigh at the exhalation of his last breath.

"Mr. Montgomery?

There was no answer.

"Mr. Montgomery?"

The banker was no longer breathing.

"Mr. Montgomery?"

"Montgomery, you son of a bitch. What are you trying to pull? This isn't the map!" the marshal's voice came from the outer office.

Janelle quickly stuffed the envelope into the bodice of her dress, managing to do so just before Cairns came back into the room.

Startled at seeing Janelle, he stopped. "What are you doing here?" he asked.

"I had an appointment with Mr. Montgomery," Janelle replied. "You killed him. I saw you shoot him."

For a second the marshal's face reflected shock, then, inexplicably, a smile spread across his face and Janelle shuddered. Had the devil incarnate appeared before her, his smile could not have been more satanic.

"No, my dear," Drumm said. He pulled his pistol and pointed it at her. "I saw *you* shoot him. It will be my word against yours, and I am the law.

There was a loud knock on the front door of the bank.

"Mr. Montgomery, are you all right? We heard shooting! What's going on in there?"

Drumm turned his head toward the front and when he did, Janelle dashed out the side door. Drumm pointed his pistol at her and pulled the trigger. Janelle felt her stomach leap to her throat in fear—then she heard the click of the hammer falling, but no shot being fired. It was either a misfire, or he was out of bullets.

Once outside the bank, Janelle ran down the pathway toward the alley behind the bank. Turning south, she ran down the alley until she reached Adams Street. There, she saw two freight wagons rolling slowly out of town and—unseen—she slipped into the back of the second wagon, then slid under the tarpaulin.

Miraculously, she had gotten away.

Chapter Eighteen

Drumm considered going after Janelle, but he was reasonably certain she would not get away. Hurrying to the front of the bank, he opened the door. There were four or five people standing there, customers who had heard the gunshot while waiting for the bank to open.

"Did you see her?" Drumm shouted, holding his pistol in his bent arm as he pushed through the crowd.

"Did we see who?" Sullivan asked. Like some of the others, he was there to draw enough money from his account to operate his store.

"The woman who works at the Buckner Emporium. Wellington, I think her name is."

"Are you talkin' about the lady who won the horse race last week?"

"Yes, that's the one I'm talkin' about. Did you see her?"

"No, I didn't her. She didn't come this way," Sullivan said.

"She had to come this way!" Drumm argued in

an agitated voice. "I seen her shoot Montgomery, then run this way. I tried to take a shot at her, but my gun misfired."

"Wait a minute? Are you sayin' Miss Wellington shot Mr. Montgomery?" Sullivan asked incredulously.

"That's what I'm sayin'."

"I don't believe it. Why would she do that?"

"Are you callin' me a liar, Sullivan? How do I know why she did it? She just did it, that's all. And I seen her do it!"

"Mr. Sullivan, it isn't that far-fetched when you stop to think about it," the apothecary White said. "I mean, we all saw her ride in the race and you have to admit, that is certainly nothing any normal lady would do."

"Yeah, well, if she did do it—and I still don't believe she did—she didn't come this way," Sullivan said.

"Maybe she left by the side door," White suggested.

"Yeah, that could be," another added.

"Come on, let's go. We've got to catch her before she gets away. She kilt Montgomery," Drumm shouted.

"Mr. Montgomery's dead?" someone who was just arriving asked with a gasp.

"Yeah, he is," Drumm answered, his voice void of all expression.

"Come on, fellers, we can't let her get away!" called out one of the many who had gathered around the front door of the bank. At the call, the others spread out, running through the town, calling out to still more to join in the hunt for the woman who murdered Mr. Montgomery.

Smiling with a degree of self-satisfaction over the way things were panning out for him, Egan Drumm watched the frantic motions of the impromptu, but growing posse. He removed the misfired cartridge from his pistol and stared at it. The firing pin had clearly struck the detonator, but the bullet had not fired. If it had, it could have all been put away neatly.

It still might work out all right for him. He was sure the woman would be found within an hour or so, and with any luck, she would be killed in the process, saving the trouble of a trial.

His two deputies, John Forbis and Bert Appleby came running up with their guns drawn. "What happened?" Appleby asked.

"C. D. Montgomery has been killed."

"Who done it, do you know?"

"Yes, I know. It was the Wellington woman, the one who works over at Buckner's Ladies' Emporium."

"Damn, are you talkin' about that good lookin' woman that won the horse race last week?" Forbis asked.

"Yes, that's who I'm talkin' about."

"I don't believe it."

"You don't believe what?"

"I don't believe Miss Wellington killed Mr. Montgomery."

"I seen her do it with my own eyes, Deputy," Drumm said. "Are you calling me a liar?"

"No, sir, I'm not calling you a liar, it's just—"

"Just what?"

"It's just that it doesn't seem possible she did it, is all," Forbis said.

"Possible or not, she did it. And it just happened, so she couldn't have got far," Drumm said. "I've got the whole town out lookin' for her. You two go out as well. If you find her, bring her to me."

Drumm watched his deputies run down the street to join the others, then turned and went back into the bank. He had to find that map. He started searching Montgomery's office, jerking open the drawers of his desk and a cabinet. He brushed the shelves clean, dumping papers, pictures, and bric-a-brac on the floor, but the map was nowhere to be found.

On the wall he noticed the picture hanging askew and hurrying to it, he took it down. A small piece of paper adhered to the back of the picture, as if a larger paper had been glued there, and left a bit of residue when it was pulled off.

"Damn!" Drumm said aloud. "She has the map!"

"Marshal, are you back here?" someone called.

"Yeah, I'm back in the office."

O'Dell came in then. "This has been a busy day," he said. "First your prisoner, and now Mr. Montgomery."

"Yeah, you ought to do real well today," Drumm said.

"Marshal Cairns, I resent that, sir!" O'Dell said indignantly. "It isn't a matter of money, it is a matter of respect."

"Respect, huh? But you don't do it for free, do you?"

"All professions deserve some compensation," O'Dell said. It wasn't until then he noticed the condition of the office. "My oh my, what happened here?"

"I think Miss Wellington was looking for something, and when Mr. Montgomery came in and saw her, she panicked and shot him."

"What a shame, what a shame. Poor Mrs. Montgomery. I saw the two of them at the restaurant last night, celebrating Mrs. Montgomery's birthday. She was wearing a new hat he bought her. She will be devastated."

"Everyone who dies has someone who is devastated over them," Drumm said flatly. "Get the body out of here."

"Yes, sir."

Nellie and Ken Buckner were arranging bolts of cloth on a display table.

"Do you think the red looks better here, or over there?" Nellie asked.

"Here, there, it doesn't matter," Ken replied.

"What do you mean it doesn't matter? Of course it matters. Oh, never mind. I'll ask Janelle. She has a good eye for such things."

"She doesn't work for us anymore, remember? She works for C. D. Montgomery."

"Well, he hasn't hired her yet, though I'm sure he will. Anyway, Janelle said she would drop by from time to time, and I wouldn't be at all surprised if she didn't come by today, after work. She'll be so excited that she will have to come by and tell us all about it."

Ken chuckled. "She'll do that, all right." He got pensive for a moment. "Nellie, have you ever thought that if little Melinda hadn't caught the fever when she was six months old, she would be about Janelle's age?"

Nellie smiled and nodded. "I have thought about it, Ken. I think that's one of the reasons I've enjoyed having her around so much."

The little warning bell on the front door rang as it was opened and Ken and Nellie looked toward the front.

"We're back here," Nellie called.

Deputy Bert Appleby came to the back of the store. He had never been in the store before and Nellie was surprised to see him, but that surprise changed to concern when she saw that he was holding his pistol in his hand.

"Where is she?" the deputy asked, his voice stern and demanding.

"Where is who?"

"The woman that works for you. Janelle Wellington. Where is she?"

"She doesn't work for us anymore," Nellie said. "At least, not after today. She will be working over at the bank for Mr. Montgomery. Why do you have your gun out?"

"You don't mind if I look around your store, do you? Just to make certain?" Appleby said. He made no effort to holster his pistol.

"Look for what?" Ken asked.

"Look for that woman."

"We told you, she isn't here. What is this all about?" Ken asked, the curiosity in his voice changing to one of irritation.

"I told you what it's about. I'm tryin' to find Janelle Wellington."

"And we told you that she isn't here. If you want to find her, try the bank. Ask Mr. Montgomery where she is."

Appleby shook his head. "Can't do that."

"What do you mean you can't do that?"

"C. D. Montgomery is dead."

"What? Mr. Montgomery is dead?" Ken gasped. "When? How?"

"This mornin'," Appleby replied. "He was kilt by Janelle Montgomery."

"No! That's impossible! She would never do anything like that," Nellie cried.

"What makes you so sure?"

"Because I know her. Why, a sweeter girl never lived."

"Uh-huh, so you say. But the truth is, C. D. Montgomery caught her red-handed tryin' to steal somethin' from his office, so she shot him."

"With what?"

"What do you mean, with what? With a pistol of course."

"What I mean is, where did she get it? Janelle didn't have a gun. Why, I doubt she's ever even held one in her hand."

"Well, she held one in her hand when she kilt the banker. The marshal seen it with his own eyes."

"Are you saying the marshal is claiming he actually saw Janelle kill Mr. Montgomery?"

"I don't know if he actually seen it, or just seen her standin' there afterward with the gun in her hand."

"So there's no proof that Janelle did it," Ken said.

"Well, she run from the marshal. Seems to me like that's about proof enough," Appleby said.

Forbis came in then. "She's not over at the Poindexter place," he said.

"They say she ain't here neither," Appleby said. "But I ain't searched the place yet.

"No need to search," Forbis said.

"What do you mean there ain't no need to search? The Marshal told us to search for her."

"If Mr. and Mrs. Buckner say she isn't here, then she isn't here."

"Thank you, Deputy Forbis," Ken said.

Forbis touched the brim of his hat. "Sorry to bother you folks," he said. "Let's go, Appleby."

With one last glare at the Buckners, Appleby holstered his pistol, then left the store with Forbis.

"I don't care what the marshal says, I don't believe it," Nellie said after the deputy left. "Why, a sweeter girl never lived than Janelle Wellington."

"Yes, but still . . ." Ken said, letting the sentence hang.

"Still what?"

"You have to wonder why she came here from New York."

"She said she wanted to see the West. Do you doubt that?" Nellie asked.

"No, it's just that . . ." Again, he let the sentence hang.

"Just that what?"

"There are those letters. The ones she gets from home, but never opens. There is something in her past that she's running away from."

"Yes, I forgot about those," Nellie said. "Still, I don't believe for one moment that she killed Mr. Montgomery. Oh, poor Mrs. Montgomery. Here we have been concerned about Janelle and haven't even thought about Mrs. Montgomery."

The bell on the door tinkled again and looking toward it, they saw Mrs. Poindexter coming in. "Did you hear?" she asked, an expression of horror on her face. "Deputy Forbis was just over at my place asking about Janelle. He said she is wanted for murder. It can't be true, can it?"

"No, it isn't true. I don't believe it for a minute," Nellie said.

"But practically the whole town is out looking for her."

"If you ask me, the marshal is behind this," Ken said.

"But why would Marshal Cairns do such a thing?" Mrs. Poindexter asked.

Ken shook his head. "I don't know why," he said. "But there's not the slightest doubt in my mind but that he is behind it."

It had been at least two hours since Janelle climbed into the back of the freight wagon. She figured they were far enough away from town that she was probably safe from the sheriff. She had no idea where she was, or what was outside but she was getting hungry and thirsty. However she dare not show herself as long as the wagon was in motion. Finally, the wagon stopped.

With the creaking of the wagon wheels silenced, she could hear the two men talking.

"What you stoppin' for, Bob?" the driver of her wagon called out to the driver in the lead.

"I'm goin' to walk over there and water the lilies," Bob called back.

"Yeah, I'll go with you. I've had to pee for the last half hour or so."

"Well hell, Frank, why didn't you say somethin'? I would have stopped."

"I don't know. I reckon I was just goin' to see how long it would take you to stop, is all."

Bob laughed. "If I had know'd it was a contest, I never would have stopped."

"You'd do that too, wouldn't you, Bob? You'd sit right up there in your wagon and piss in your pants a' fore givin' in."

The conversation drew more indistinct as the two men walked away from the wagon.

One of the horses whickered, and stamped its foot, and Janelle heard the harness rattle.

Satisfied that she was alone, she stuck her head out from under the canvas, and looked around. Both men were standing about ten yards away from the road, their backs to the wagons as they urinated. Janelle had to urinate as well, and for a moment she envied the fact that men could accomplish that operation so quickly and easily.

Moving as quietly as possible, Janelle slipped out from under the white canvas covering. She started to move away from the two wagons when she saw a sack marked DRIED APPLES.

She didn't relish a diet exclusive to dried apples, but that was better than starving, so she took the sack, then stepped down into the ditch that ran parallel to the road. Seeing that the men were starting back, she lay down in the bottom of the ditch and stayed there quietly, until she heard the wagons drive away.

Not until the wagons were nearly out of sight did Janelle stand up and look around. She saw nothing but rolling desert land, dotted with saguaro and prickly pear. A hot, dry wind whistled though the mesquite and it suddenly dawned on her that, while she had some dry apples, she had no water. She could die of thirst before she died of hunger.

She should not have left the wagon. She had no idea where they were going, but wherever they were headed, she was sure there would be water there. And there would be food too, other than the sack of dried apples she was carrying.

She was not dressed for an extended excursion in the desert. She had put on her best dress and her best shoes in order to meet with Mr. Montgomery, and while they would have been perfectly appropriate for working in the bank, they were extremely uncomfortable, to say nothing of impracticable, under her present circumstances.

By her estimate, plodding along at a steady rate of about five miles per hour, she had come about ten miles from Phoenix while still in the wagon. She debated with herself as to whether or not she should go back to Phoenix. It was a finite distance, it was civilization where there would be food and water, and it was a town she knew.

She thought about Mrs. Poindexter's Boarding House. They were probably sitting down to a lunch of fried ham and potatoes. There would be tea, too. Cooled in a ceramic crock, the tea would be served sweetened. Janelle's mouth would have watered at the thought of the tea, if she had not been too dry to form saliva.

She decided that it would be too dangerous to return to Phoenix. She couldn't face Mrs. Poindexter, nor anyone else in town. She was sure Marshal Cairns had spread the word that she was the one who killed poor Mr. Montgomery, and that the accusation had taken on a life of its own.

Janelle didn't know where the wagons were headed, but she was certain they were going toward civilization of some sort, so she resumed the journey, walking, rather than riding, in the same direction the wagons had been heading.

Early in the afternoon she ate a few of the apples, and though they assuaged her hunger, they did nothing for her thirst. In fact, eating them made her even thirstier, and she considered throwing the sack away, just so she wouldn't have to deal with the bother of carrying it. But if she did, she would have no food at all, and while she might be lucky enough to find water somewhere, she was sure she wouldn't be able to find food.

She walked for the rest of the day, having no idea where she was, or how far she had gone. Her feet were sore from dozens of needle pricks, her dress was soiled and torn by interaction with cactus, and her lips were swollen from lack of water. Finally, thankfully, the sun got lower, providing her some relief from the heat, and giving her an absolute bearing. The sun was setting in the west—behind her. She was walking almost due east.

"Ha! I'm going east!" she said, speaking the words aloud just to hear a human voice, even if it was her own. She was surprised at how hoarse her voice sounded. "If I keep going this way long enough, I'll just walk back to New York." She laughed at the absurdity of her statement, and though it wasn't really that funny, it did provide her with a bit of comic relief.

Comic relief.

She thought of her father, and of the many stage productions he had sponsored. She enjoyed them, especially the plays and musicals in which Andrew and Rosanna MacCallister performed. Oh, why couldn't she have fallen in love with someone like Andrew MacCallister, instead of Boyd Zucker?

MacCallister. Could Andrew MacCallister be related to the Falcon MacCallister she had met, oh so briefly, on the train?

Why was she thinking that? Were the sun and the thirst causing her to lose her senses?

Chapter Nineteen

Janelle felt water running into her mouth and she coughed and choked, then began swallowing deeply.

"Easy, now, miss, easy," a man's voice said. "You don't want to be drinkin' too fast now."

It was not until that moment she realized a man was holding a canteen to her lips. He pulled the canteen away but she reached for it and pulled it back.

"Here now, miss, go easy like I said, otherwise you're a' goin' to be pukin' your guts out."

Janelle took a few more swallows, and when he pulled the canteen away again she didn't fight him.

"Thank you," she said.

"How did a fine dressed lady like you get here?" the man asked.

"I don't know," Janelle said.

"Yes, well, it ain't all that unusual you bein' kinda dizzy and out of sorts like that. Happens to lots of people when they start wanderin' around in the desert like you done. One minute you're bright eyed and bushy tailed, and the next moment you're lyin' on the ground, just a'wonderin' where you are."

"That's what I'm doing now," Janelle said, "wondering where I am."

"You're in the Sonoran Desert, is where you are. The question I'm askin' is, how did you get here?"

"I'm not sure," Janelle answered, though as she spoke the words, she had a vision of herself being in the back of the wagon.

What was she doing in the wagon?

"Sounds to me like you got what they call the amneasy," the man said. "Do you think you can walk?"

"I-I don't know. I suppose I can, now that I have had some water."

"Let me help you up."

It wasn't until she stood up that she got a close look at the man who had come to her rescue. He had long stringy white hair and a long, scraggy white beard. She couldn't begin to guess his age, though she suspected he might look older than he actually was. Even in the dark, she could see a warm and inviting sparkle in his eyes, so she wasn't frightened.

It was dark!

When had it gotten dark? The last thing Janelle could remember was wandering around in the bright sun.

"Where did you come from?" Janelle asked.

"I have a place not too far from here," the man said. "I was out takin' an evenin' stroll when I seen you. At first, I wasn't sure what it was I was lookin' at, then when I seen you was a young woman, I wasn't sure you was alive. But you are alive."

"Yes, I'm alive."

"Let's see if you can walk."

Janelle took a couple steps then stumbled, and would have fallen had the man not kept her up.

"Sorry," she said.

"Well, there's your problem," the man said, pointing to her feet. "I don't know how you got this far wearin' them shoes like that."

"I can't very well go barefoot," Janelle said.

"You would probably be better off iffen you was barefooted. Sit down and take them shoes off."

"You aren't going to make me go barefoot, are you?"

"No. What I'm goin' to do is make you shoes you can actually wear. They won't be nothin' pretty that you can wear someplace fancy, but they'll help you walk through the desert."

Janelle chuckled.

"What is it? What's so funny?"

"I'm not likely to be going anyplace fancy right away, am I? But I am in the desert."

The old man chuckled as well. "You're all right, missy, if you can laugh at yourself. Let's get them shoes off and I'll see what I can do."

Janelle sat down and watched as the man removed both her shoes. He began cutting on them and within moments, the stylish shoes were redone as comfortable, if unattractive moccasins.

Janelle laughed again.

"You found somethin' else funny, have you, girl?"

"I was just wondering what my sister would think

right now if she saw what was happening to these shoes. She bought them on Fifth Avenue at Madam Demorist's Fine Fashion Mart for my birthday."

"I've never been to the place," the old man said. After another moment he tied the little strips of leather onto her feet. "Here, try to walk now."

Once again Janelle stood up and when she began walking she noticed the difference immediately. "Oh, this is wonderful," she said. "Thank you. It is so much easier to walk now."

"What's your name, girl?" the man asked.

"Ja—" Janelle started, then stopped mid-sentence. The man had been very nice to her—more than nice, he had saved her life. But if the sheriff back in Phoenix really did make the claim that she had murdered Mr. Montgomery, there was likely to be a reward out for her. It could be the old man would keep her alive just long enough to take her back to Phoenix and claim the reward.

"Ja? Your name is Ja?"

"It's Jo."

"Joe? That seems like a funny name for a woman."

"It's spelled without the e," Janelle said.

"What e?"

"Never mind. I suppose it is a strange name," she said. "What is your name?"

"Cornbread."

Janelle laughed out loud. "Cornbread? You tease me about my name, and your name is Cornbread?"

"Well, it ain't the name I was borned with," Cornbread said. "The name I was borned with is

Cornelius. But I reckon Cornbread is what I been called purt' nigh all my life. It seems I liked it a lot when I was a wee one, and Cornelius and Cornbread kinda goes together. Besides which, I make the best cornbread you ever et. Fac' is, I got a pone back at the house now, and unless I miss my guess, you're probably right hungry."

"I am hungry," Janelle admitted.

"Got some bacon and beans, too. It'll be good to have someone to eat with."

They walked through the desert, much more comfortable with the blazing sun and the heat of the day gone. Without the maddening thirst that had plagued her, she almost found the situation pleasant. Looking up into the sky she saw a display of stars unlike anything she had ever seen before. They were so bright and so close she felt as if she could reach up and grab one. The magnitude of the stars gradually decreased from the brightest to those so distant they could only be viewed in total. They seemed to spread a luminous powder that made the night sky glow.

"Purty, ain't they?" Cornbread said.

"What?" Janelle replied, surprised by his comment.

"I seen that you was lookin' up at the stars. That's one of the reasons I sometimes take me these walks at night. In the daytime the desert can be awful bothersome hot, but at nighttime, it can be powerful purty."

Though Cornbread's description fell short in its grammatical construction, Janelle was moved by the passion of his words.

* * *

Janelle awakened the next morning to the smell of frying bacon. For just a moment she thought she was back at Mrs. Poindexter's Boarding House. Then she remembered the ordeal of the day before—recalling in great detail everything that had happened—from seeing Mr. Montgomery killed, to being accused of the killing by City Marshal Cairns, the very man who had actually committed the murder. She remembered her escape from the marshal. She remembered vividly the sound of the hammer falling when he pulled the trigger as he tried to shoot her. She remembered crawling into the back of a wagon to flee Phoenix, and finally, she recalled nearly dying of hunger and thirst, only to be rescued by a strange man.

It had been the middle of the night when she was taken to the cabin. It was too dark and she was too exhausted to see much then. In the light of day, she was able to peruse her surroundings. She was lying in bed and, for a moment, wondered if she had anything to be concerned about. Almost as quickly as she had that thought, she put it away as being ungrateful. If she had not been found, she might very well be dead. As to whether or not she had been compromised in any way, she knew that wasn't a worry. She was still wearing her dress, and as she looked over in the far corner of the room, saw a mussed blanket which suggested her rescuer had slept there during the night.

Though the cabin was quite rustic, it was exceptionally neat and well cared for. The floor was swept clean, there was no clutter anywhere, and the walls were covered with newspapers. With a start, she saw her father's name on one of the papers, then saw that it had to do with his shipping line.

Her eyes landed on her rescuer. What was the name he had told her? Cornbread? Yes, Cornbread, she was sure that was it. Examining him more closely, she saw that he was about five feet eight inches tall, and was wearing a red and black plaid shirt and denim trousers. Unlike many of the men she had seen in the West, Cornbread was not wearing a pistol strapped to his belt.

He had his back to her, unaware she was awake. He opened the door to the oven on the small stove to check on its contents and Janelle saw a pan filled with rising and browning biscuits.

"I thought your specialty was cornbread," she said.

He jumped, startled by her words. "Lord 'a mercy, girl, don't go a' scarin' me like that," he said. "I plumb forgot there was anyone else in here."

Janelle laughed out loud. "Surely you didn't forget I was here? Or do you always cook that much breakfast?"

Cornbread shook his head. "No, you just scairt me for the moment is all. I didn't actually forget you was here, that's why I'm cookin' a big breakfast. As far as my bakin' biscuits is concerned, well truth is folks could have just as easy commenced to callin' me Biscuit, 'cause my biscuits is ever' bit as good as my cornbread. As you are about to see."

"It smells heavenly," Janelle said.

From a cupboard, Cornbread took down plates and cups, as well as knives, forks, and spoons.

"Oh, my, these plates are beautiful," Janelle said.

Cornbread ran his finger around the silver and blue trim of one of the plates. "My wife picked 'em out," he said, pensively. "When Sherman's troops come through they burned our house and most of our things, but Marthy Lou saved these plates by buryin' 'em in the barnyard. I wasn't there, seein' as I was off fightin' in the war my ownself, but folks told me she stood on the porch holdin' a shotgun, just darin' Sherman's men to dig up them dishes. She put a big store in 'em, and it was purt' nigh the only thing we brought with us when we come out here from Georgia."

"Your wife is—" Janelle didn't want to say the word *dead*.

Cornbread understood the implied question and nodded, then pointed outside. "Marthy Lou is lyin' buried on that little hill out back. The fever took her some four, maybe five years back."

"I'm sorry. From the way you talk about her, you must have loved her very much."

"I still do," Cornbread said. "Just 'cause some has died, that ain't no reason you got to stop lovin' 'em. She was a wonderful woman, Marthy Lou was. Maybe you'll think I'm a bit crazy in the head, but I sometimes still talk to her, even though she's been gone for all this time."

"Why are you out here all alone? Are you a farmer or rancher?"

Cornbread chuckled. "I wouldn't be much of a farmer out here, now would I?" he asked. "Can't nothin' grow out here but cactus and mesquite. Land ain't much good for ranchin' either. No ma'am, what I do is, I work for the railroad. I'm a track rider."

"What's a track rider?"

"That's someone that rides alongside the track to make certain there ain't no bad rails. If I find something I put up a signal for the engineer. One day I'll ride ten miles north, then come back. The next day I go ten miles south, then come back. I only cover twenty miles of track, but I have to ride forty miles doin' it."

"You don't say. You know, when you are on a train, you never think about such things, but it's people like you who keep the travelers safe. You ought to get more credit."

Cornbread shook his head and smiled. "No, I like it that people just take it for granted that the track is safe. That means that me'n the other track riders are doing our job."

After breakfast, Janelle walked outside with him. She watched while he saddled his horse in preparation of his ride for the day. He carried a couple biscuit and bacon sandwiches with him for his lunch.

"You can fix anything you want to eat while I'm gone," he said. "I'll be back before nightfall."

"Thanks," Janelle said.

She watched Cornbread ride away, then returned to the cabin, Though it was very warm, she was at least out of the sun. With the window and the door open, she was able to enjoy a cross breeze.

She thought of Mrs. Montgomery. Though Janelle had never met her she'd heard from Nellie that the woman had been thrilled with her new hat. Leaving Phoenix Janelle had been concerned only for herself, but now that she was in no immediate danger, she thought how difficult things must be for Mrs. Montgomery.

She wished she could go to her and say a few words of comfort, but she knew she couldn't. She figured the marshal had told Mrs. Montgomery that Janelle was responsible for Mr. Montgomery's death. With no one to contradict the marshal, Mrs. Montgomery would have no choice but to believe it.

Janelle hated that—the fact that Mrs. Montgomery would believe such evil of her—almost as much as she feared the consequences of being found and arrested for the murder. She had seen Marshal Cairns murder Mr. Montgomery, but the marshal was right, nobody would believe her over the city marshal.

Why did the marshal do that?

The map!

Reaching down inside her bodice, she found the envelope she had taken from the back of the picture. Stuffed between her dress and the camisole underneath, it had been protected and was not soiled with sweat.

Janelle took the map from the envelope and spread it open.

At first she could make nothing of it but as she looked more closely she saw that the lines and squiggles were identified, though in a few cases she had to work to decipher the spelling. On the side of the mountain near Weaver's

Needle was an X beside which was annotated
HOL IS HEER.

Map to gold Mine

Follow the salt river til you reech
superstishen montan. Find Weevers Nedel,
then look at the montan bhind the nedel.

You haf to clum up the side of the montan to
find it cuz the hol that gos into the mine can
only be seed for a cupel minits in the aftrnun,
and only for a cupel days in the erly sumer but
evn if you caint see it, dont meen it aint ther
caus tis. This heer X is the hol that gos into the
mine. You haf to git down on yur belly and skiny
thru to git inside wherats the gold.

This heer map was drawd by Ben Hanlon

Once Janelle managed to interpret the terrible
spelling, she was able to decipher the map quite
easily.

"Oh, my," she said aloud. "No wonder the marshal killed Mr. Montgomery to get this map. This is
a real map to a real gold mine."

Folding the map up and putting it away, Janelle
looked around the cabin to find something to
occupy her time. Cornbread had said she could fix
anything she wanted to eat and looking through all
his possibilities, she saw that by using the dried
apples she had brought, she would be able to make
an apple pie.

By late afternoon, the cabin was filled with the
scent of cinnamon and baked apple. A pie, overlaid

with strips of brown crust, sat on top of the stove—brown, aromatic, and pregnant with the promise of something very delicious.

When Cornbread came back to the cabin that evening, a wide smile spread across his face. "Is this old nose a' playin' tricks on me?" he asked. "Could that be apple pie I'm smellin'?"

"It is," Janelle said. "I hope you don't mind that I used some of your supplies for the ingredients."

"Mind? Darlin', I'm happier than a pig in mud. Why, I ain't had me no apple pie since Marthy Lou passed on."

That night they had a supper of cured ham and potatoes, followed by apple pie and coffee.

"I don't mean no disrespect to Marthy Lou, but this here may be about the best apple pie I ever et," Cornbread said.

Janelle laughed. "Or it could be that it has been so long since you had any apple pie that you have forgotten how good Martha Lou's pie was."

"Yeah, it could be that, I reckon," Cornbread said as he licked a little piece of apple from his finger. "But this here is awful good."

"Well, I thank you."

"No, ma'am, I thank you for makin' it."

As Janelle watched Cornbread enjoy his pie, she thought of the map. Should she trust him with it? Deciding that she could, she said, "Cornbread, I want to show you something, get your opinion.

"Darlin', the opinion of an old man can't be worth much, but if you want it, I'm willin' to give it."

Janelle reached under the mattress of the bed

and pulled out the map. "What do you make of this?" she asked.

"Ha," Cornbread said. "Looks to me like this is supposed to be a map of the Peralta Vein. 'Course there's dozens of 'em for sale. Who'd you buy this one from?"

"I didn't buy it," Janelle said. "I found it. What is the Peralta Vein?"

"You ain't never heer'd of the Peralta gold mine?"

"No," Janelle said.

"Sometime's it's called the Lost Dutchman mine, because a feller by the name of Jacob Waltz is supposed to have found it. Anyways, there was this here feller by the name of Carlos Peralta, Mexican he was, who had him a gold mine here 'bouts on Superstition Mountain that is s'posed to be the biggest gold vein ever discovered. For a while he was takin' gold out of the mine back to Mexico. But along about the time this here country transferred from Mexico to the U.S. ol' Carlos brought in a large group of miners to take out as much gold as they could before the mine got took away from him. So what they done is, they started back to Mexico with a mule train loaded down with gold, but they was attacked by Apache Indians. And, at least accordin' to the story, the Apache kilt all the miners, then took the mules but left the saddlebags loaded with gold ore behind."

"Is that true?" Janelle asked.

"Well ma'am, I do know that Waltz showed up with a lot of gold."

"Then it is true."

Cornbread shrugged. "Who knows?" He reached for the map. "Let me look at it again."

Janelle handed the map to him and Cornbread looked at it again, then squinted as he tried to read the bottom line.

"What's this here say?" he asked. "My eyes ain't all that good no more and this here is writ too little for me to read."

"It says that the map was drawn by Ben Hanlon," Janelle said.

"Ben Hanlon, you say?" Cornbread replied, looking up in interest.

"Yes. Is that significant?"

Cornbread rubbed his chin, then he nodded. "It could be," he said. "I know Ben Hanlon. He's been prospectin' around here for years. He's spent some time with me in this very cabin. He ain't the kind to make somethin' up. If it was him what drawed the map, I don't know. Could be somethin' to it. Why you so interested? You goin' to go look for the gold?"

Janelle laughed. "I'm a city girl from New York," she said. "Could you really see me poking around out in the desert, looking for gold?"

Cornbread laughed as well. "No, I don't reckon I could," he said. "But if you was to take a notion to do it, I would use this map."

Chapter Twenty

The next day, while Cornbread rode out on his track surveillance, Janelle found a trunk of clothes. Since they were mostly pants and shirts, she assumed they were old clothes of Cornbread's, but she also found a couple dresses. As she examined the clothes more closely, she saw that the pants and shirts were all too small for Cornbread. On impulse, she took off her torn and stained dress, and put on the pants and shirt.

They were a perfect fit.

"I see you found Marthy Lou's clothes," Cornbread said when he returned that night.

"Yes, I thought they might be hers," Janelle said, "but being as they were pants and shirts, rather than dresses, I wasn't sure."

"Dresses ain't always the handiest things to wear out here," Cornbread said.

"Now that I have spent a few days here, I think I can understand why. I hope you don't mind that I'm wearing your late wife's clothes."

"Nope, I don't mind a'tall," Cornbread said.

"Truth is, it pleasures me to see you a' wearin' 'em. It puts me in mind of Marthy Lou, and I know she would be real happy to see that the clothes was bein' worn."

By the start of the fourth day Janelle felt she had recovered all her strength and when Cornbread returned after a day of riding the track, she announced that it was time for her to leave.

"Ain't no need for you to be rushin' off," Cornbread said.

"I'd hardly say I was rushing off. I've imposed upon you for much too long now."

"You ain't done no such a thing. I was a' likin' havin' your company around."

"I have enjoyed your company as well," Janelle said. "But I really do have to leave. Besides, this country is too wild and untamed for me," Janelle said. "I think I'm going back to New York."

"Are you sure you want to do that? Whatever it is that made you leave New York is still there," Cornbread said.

"What? What do you mean whatever it is that made me leave New York? I haven't said anything to give you that idea."

"You don't need to say nothin'," Cornbread said. "I can read folks' eyes, same as I can read a critter's eyes. You have run away from someone or something that put a deep hurt on you. All I'm sayin' is, like as not when you go back that someone or something will still be there."

"You are a wise man, Cornbread."

"But you are still plannin' on leavin'." It was a comment, not a question.

"Yes."

"That means you'll be takin' the train."

"Yes. That is, as soon as I can find a nearby depot."

"You don't need a depot," Cornbread said. "I can get you on the train. You don't need no ticket, neither. That is, you don't need none betwixt here and Phoenix."

"Phoenix?"

"Yes, that's near 'bout the closest place whereat there's a depot."

"Oh, I-I don't know that I want to go to Phoenix."

"Well, I reckon I could get you on a train to Tucson 'bout as easy as I can for Phoenix. Onliest thing is, if you're aimin' to go on to Superstition Mountain lookin' for gold, you'll need to do that from Phoenix."

"Who said I was going to look for the gold?"

"Well, ain't you? I would if I was you."

"I don't know. I hadn't really thought of it before."

"But you're thinkin' of it now, ain't you?"

"Cornbread, do you really think there is anything to this map?"

"Could be. Like I said, I know Ben Hanlon, and he ain't one that goes around lyin'. If he drawed this map, then I'd say yeah, there is something to it. Before you go back to New York, you ought to at least look around for a bit."

"I wouldn't even know where to start," Janelle said.

Cornbread held up his finger as if asking for a moment's pause in the conversation, then he went to the trunk that contained Martha Lou's clothes. He pulled out four pairs of pants and four shirts, all clean and neatly folded. He handed them over to Janelle."

"You could start by takin' these clothes."

"Oh, Cornbread, I couldn't do that," Janelle said.

"Why not?"

"Because they belonged to your wife."

"Darlin', she sure won't be a' usin' 'em now, will she?"

"No, I suppose not."

"And like I told you, dresses ain't exactly the kind of clothes you want to be wearin' while pokin' around out here."

"Cornbread, I don't know what to say," Janelle said, touched by his offer. "Other than thank you."

"They ain't nothin' wrong with thank you," Cornbread said. "As far as I'm concerned, them's always been a couple of pretty good words."

Janelle smiled broadly, then put her hand out to touch Cornbread's hand.

"Thank you, my friend. From the bottom of my heart, I thank you."

"First thing tomorrow, we'll go to the track and I'll flag down the train. I'll speak to the conductor and tell him you're my kin. They'll let you on for free."

"Why, thank you, Cornbread. I appreciate that. You have been a godsend to me."

Flagstaff, Arizona Territory

It was late afternoon. Returning from New York Falcon had stopped in MacCallister to repack his luggage—from city clothes to clothes in which he would be more comfortable and that were more appropriate for mountain and desert. He also picked up his guns, and made arrangements to take his horse with him to Phoenix.

He would have to change trains to continue on to Phoenix, so he checked on the status of Lightning to make certain that he had gotten off the train, too.

"Yes, sir, we've got your horse right here, Mr. MacCallister. We have him checked on through to Albuquerque."

"No, not Albuquerque, Phoenix," Falcon corrected.

"Ah, Phoenix, is it? Well, then it's a good thing you did check on him, isn't it? Do you want him fed?"

"Yes, feed him, then give him a good rubdown. The train for Phoenix leaves when? Ten o'clock tonight?"

"I'd say it will be a little closer to eleven," the station master said.

"I'll be back by ten-thirty, just to make certain."

The station master nodded. "Probably not a bad idea."

"Where is the best place to eat?"

"We have a restaurant in the depot," the station master said. "'Bout all you can get there is fried ham and fried potatoes, but folks tend to like it."

"These would be folks who have only a few minutes between trains?"

"Yes, generally," the depot manager replied.

"I'll look for a place downtown.

Falcon gave his horse a few pats on the neck, turned to leave, and spotted a poster.

WANTED FOR MURDER

– a comely woman –

JANELLE WELLINGTON

$1,000.00 REWARD

DEAD OR ALIVE !

Contact Marshal Cairns, Phoenix, Arizona Territory

Could this be the same Janelle Wellington he was looking for? It would have to be, surely there would not be two Janelle Wellington's in a town no bigger than Phoenix. He had plenty of time before the train to Phoenix, so he decided to walk over to the sheriff's office.

The sheriff was the only one in the building, and he was sitting behind the desk, peeling an apple. His eyes were focused on the apple, and he was being extremely careful. From his dedication to the task at hand, it was obvious he was trying to pare the apple in one long, unbroken peel. So far he was having good luck. The long, thin strand of apple peel was coiling upon the desk beneath his knife. "I'll be right with you," he said without looking up.

"Troy Calhoun," Falcon said. "I haven't seen you since that little ruckus back in Higbee."

The sheriff looked up, then smiled broadly. "Well, as I live and breathe, Falcon MacCallister!" he said. He reached up to shake Falcon's hand and as he did, the long, thin apple peel broke apart.

"Your apple peel broke."

"Ahh, I wasn't going to make it to the end, anyway," Troy said with a dismissive wave.

"After what happened with your brothers Titus and Travis back in Higbee, I didn't think you would ever have anything to do with the law business again."

"After what happened to them, I had to," Calhoun said. "I'm doing this out of respect and honor for them."

Falcon nodded. "I can understand that," he said. "But the question is how does Lucy feel about it?"

"She's all right with it," Calhoun said. He smiled. "'Course it helps that nothing ever happens in this town. What brings you to Flagstaff?"

"I'm on my way to Phoenix," Falcon said.

"Yeah, Phoenix is a bustling city. Near three thousand people I hear. That's where near 'bout ever'one is goin' these days. What are you goin' for, if you don't mind my askin'?"

"I don't mind at all, because it ties in with something I want to ask you." Falcon walked over to the wall and perused a few of the wanted posters until he found the one he was looking for. Pulling it down, he took it over to Calhoun and showed it to him. "You know anything about this?"

Calhoun nodded. "Yeah, a little. According to the warrant out on her, she supposedly killed a banker down in Phoenix."

"Supposedly?"

Calhoun stroked his chin for a moment. "Falcon, why are you interested in this?"

"I'm looking for this woman," he said.

"You mean she's wanted someplace other than down in Maricopa County? What did she do?"

Falcon shook his head. "It's not like that," he said. "She's the daughter of some friends of my brother and sister back in New York. The parents are quite wealthy, and they have asked me to find her and take her back to New York."

"She comes from a wealthy family, you say?"

"Yes."

"Then, if you was just guessin', you wouldn't guess someone like her would get mixed up in shootin' a banker, would you?"

"I've not met her yet, but I have met her parents, and from what I know of them I would say no—she is not someone I would expect to find in a predicament like this."

"Uh-huh, that's sort of what I thought," Troy said.

"Why? Have you heard something about this case?"

Troy shook his head. "No, not directly. But the sheriff that got the warrant put out on her is Jimmy Cairns. From what I know of Jimmy Cairns, he's just the kind of lowlife bastard that would do somethin' like that."

"Jimmy Cairns? Wait a minute, are you talking about the Jimmy Cairns who was once a deputy for Wyatt Earp?"

"So I hear," Troy said.

"And you say he is a lowlife?"

"I guess one law officer shouldn't talk about another one this way, but in my book he is about as low as they come," Troy said.

"Is that just from what people say? Or have you ever had a run-in with him."

Troy nodded. "Oh, yeah, you might say I had a run-in with him."

"What happened?"

"Last year I had the occasion to deliver a prisoner to him. All the way down to Phoenix, the prisoner kept tellin' me that if I turned him over to Marshal Cairns, I was signin' his death warrant. I figured he was just talkin', but before I left town to come back up here, that prisoner was already dead. He 'tried to escape' Marshal Cairns said."

"Maybe he did try to escape."

"No, I don't think so. In fact, Muley, that was the prisoner's name, Muley Carson. Muley told me that Cairns would kill him, then claim that he tried to escape, and that's exactly what happened."

"Why would Cairns do that?"

"Muley said he had somethin' on Cairns, somethin' that if it got out, it would cause him a lot of trouble."

"Did Carson tell you what it was?"

"No. All he said was that his only chance of stayin' alive was to not tell anyone about whatever it is he knew about Cairns. But as it turns out, that didn't help him a-tall. Cairns kilt him anyway, and I'm the one that delivered Muley to him. That's been stickin' in my craw ever since."

"Wasn't your fault, Troy. You were only doing your job."

"Yeah, that's what I tell myself. I'm having a hard time making myself believe that, though."

"I'm not doubting your word any, Troy. But you

have to admit, that doesn't sound like the kind of person Wyatt would have working for him."

"I know," Troy said. "It puzzled me some at first too, but I have to tell you, Falcon, it ain't just what happened to Muley. I've heard a few other stories about him as well. I don't know, I can't explain it, but maybe he went bad after he left Earp. Or maybe gettin' hisself elected sheriff just went to his head. Gettin' into a position of power like that sometimes causes folks to do that. But I tell you true, Falcon, there ain't nobody I know who has ever met him that likes him. That's why I'm sayin' if he's the one who took out the warrant on this woman, there could be some reason for it, other than the woman actually bein' guilty."

"Like what?"

"Hell, Falcon, for all I know the son of a bitch could have killed the banker his ownself and is just doin' this to cover up. I'm thinkin' that if you want to get that woman back to her folks alive, you'd better find her before Cairns does. Because whatever happened down there, I wouldn't be surprised if she didn't wind up just like Muley did."

"Thanks for the warning."

Troy looked at the wanted poster in his hand then, with a shrug, he wadded it up and threw it in the trash basket. "Well, if it does happen, I don't aim to help him this time. Not even by keeping the poster up."

"There is another one down at the depot."

"Yeah, I know, but it won't be up for long. If you don't mind, I think I'll just take a walk down there with you and get that one too," Troy said.

"I don't mind at all," Falcon said. "In fact, my train doesn't leave until ten-thirty tonight, so I was about to go have some supper. How would you like to come with me?"

"I'd love to come," Troy said. "Say, Falcon, you wouldn't mind if we stopped by the house and picked up the missus, would you? I know Lucy would love to see you again."

Falcon chuckled. "Troy, I know it's been a while since we saw each other, but do you think I've changed so much that I would pass up the opportunity to have supper with a pretty woman? By all means, let's invite her. Only thing is, I hope you have a place in mind as to where to go. I don't know Flagstaff that well."

"I know exactly where to go, and it will be my treat."

"Nonsense, it'll my treat," Falcon said.

Troy smiled sheepishly. "Well, it won't exactly be my treat. There is a restaurant in town where I can eat anytime I want, and the city picks up the tab. It's part of my pay."

Falcon laughed out loud. "All right. In that case, I would be happy to let the city buy my supper."

Chapter Twenty-one

Phoenix

Behind Janelle, the train popped, snapped, and gurgled as the boiler kept up the steam pressure. Cornbread had managed to get her a ride on a train that took her right back to the place she had fled. As he explained, if she really did intend to look for the gold on Ben Hanlon's map, she would need to start from Phoenix. She didn't protest, because she didn't want him to know she had run away from there.

But was it safe for her?

The first thing Janelle saw when she walked across the depot platform was a wanted poster, offering a one thousand dollar reward for her, DEAD OR ALIVE.

She had seen other wanted posters since coming out West, and remembered thinking how quaint—and a little frightening—they were. But this dodger was about her! That made it even more frightening.

The wanted poster was nailed to the outside wall

of the depot so that every arriving and departing train passenger could see it, and Janelle stepped up closer to examine it a bit more carefully.

Seeing the words *Dead or Alive* gave her a chill. One thousand dollars was a lot of money, and it could tempt almost anyone to collect it. The fact that the reward would be paid, dead or alive, meant that, for all intents and purposes, she had already been found guilty.

At least there was no picture of her, nor was there any description beyond "a comely woman." And that, Janelle knew, could fit many women.

She wasn't sure what she should do next. She wanted, desperately, to go back to her room at Mrs. Poindexter's Boarding House, if for no other reason than to get her clothes, and the little amount of money she had there. But she was afraid to. She didn't think she had any fear from Mrs. Poindexter. She was sure her host didn't believe she was really guilty of murder. At the very least, she would be willing to listen to Janelle's side of the story. So would Mr. and Mrs. Buckner, she believed.

But to see either of them could put them in danger, and Janelle didn't want to do that.

"Excuse me, sonny," a man said. The man was pushing a handcart, loaded with luggage, and Janelle stepped out of the way for him.

Excuse me sonny? Is that what he said?

Janelle looked over at the window opening into the waiting room of the depot, and saw her reflection. She was wearing the shirt and pants she had gotten from Cornbread, and her hair was piled up under an old slouch hat. She looked nothing at all like the beautiful, sophisticated woman who once graced the most elegant salons of New York. She also didn't look like the young woman who, for the last couple months, had worked in Buckner's Ladies' Emporium, nor even like the woman who had ridden Vexation in the Independence Day race. And she certainly didn't look like someone who could be described as a "comely woman."

In fact, she didn't look like a woman at all. She looked for all the world like a young man.

Sonny! The man had called her sonny, because he thought she was a man!

Janelle smiled, broadly. That was it! That was how she could avoid the sheriff, or anyone else who might be looking for her. From now on her name was Joe—she stopped to think for a moment, trying to come up with a last name.

"Henry, you are standing too close to the track. What if you fell, and the train ran over you? Get away from there, now," a woman's shrill voice yelled.

"Oh, Mama, I'm not standing too close. And I want to see the train," a young boy replied.

"Henry Taylor, you do what I said! Get away from that railroad track!"

"Yes, Mama."

Henry, Janelle thought. *That will be my last name. Joe Henry.*

All right, she had a disguise and a name. But where was she going to stay, and how was she going to live? She couldn't take a chance on going back to the boardinghouse. Even in the camouflage, she was certain that Mrs. Poindexter would recognize her.

She had no doubt the hosteler would do nothing to betray her, but there was still the possibility of putting Mrs. Poindexter in a compromising position, which Janelle did not want to do.

As she was contemplating what she should do next, she saw a possible solution on the same wall where her wanted poster was being displayed. Not too far away was another poster. Instead of frightening her, it offered opportunity.

HELP WANTED

God-fearing Boy

To work at Housewright's Livery Stable.

Must be good with horses.

Good wages and room furnished for honest work.

"I don't know," Murray Housewright said when Janelle applied for the job. "I have to tell you, you look a might puny to me."

Janelle swallowed a chuckle, because Murray Housewright was at least an inch shorter than she was, and couldn't have weighed much over 140 pounds. But, tactfully, she withheld comment.

"What would I have to be handling that is any heavier than a pitchfork for mucking out stalls, a saddle, or a bale of hay?" Janelle asked, establishing as low a register as she could with her voice. "I can muck out shit with the best of them."

She purposely used that word to make herself

seem more masculine, though in truth, the word almost hung up in her throat.

"Well, maybe you can and maybe you can't. The real question is, can you handle horses? You see, we not only board horses, we rent 'em, too."

"I can handle horses."

"You can ride?"

"Yes sir."

"I don't mean can you just seat a horse that's been broke to ride gentle. I mean can you ride a horse that sometimes has a mean streak?"

"I am quite good with horses," Janelle said.

"I don't know. You don't look all that much like someone who can ride."

"What is your most difficult horse?" Janelle asked.

"That would be Prince John, I reckon," Housewright said. "He don't buck, or nothin' like that. But he likes to run and jump. That horse would rather jump over somethin' than go around it, and sometimes folks who are just rentin' a horse ain't quite ready to deal with somethin' like that."

"If I can ride that horse, will it prove to you I can handle horses?"

"You're wantin' to ride Prince John?" Housewright asked with a knowing grin.

"Yes."

Housewright chuckled. "You don't have no idea what you are gettin' yourself into," he said. "But if you're wantin' to ride Prince John, be my guest." He made a sweeping gesture with his right arm toward one of the filled stalls.

Looking across the stall door at her was a very

handsome chestnut horse, standing just over sixteen hands high. Janelle thought she saw a lot of intelligence and a bit of whimsy in the horse's steady gaze. She walked over to the horse and stroked him on the face. "Hello, Prince John, How would you like to go for a nice ride?"

"There are the saddles," Housewright said, pointing to a rack. "Go pick you one out."

Janelle knew the test had already started, for there were several saddles, and she had to pick the one that was best suited for Prince John, not only according to the condition of the saddle, but also because of Prince John's conformity.

She ran her hands over several saddles before picking one and, as she started toward Prince John's stall, she saw by the expression on Housewright's face that she had chosen well.

Janelle put on a blanket, then the saddle. She tightened the cinch, then slapping Prince John on the side, got him to relax so she could tighten it again.

Housewright chuckled. "I wasn't goin' to tell you 'bout that," he said. "But ol' Prince John, he likes to swell up like a toad first time you try 'n saddle him. That way the saddle sometimes slips off. But you done it just right."

Once Prince John was saddled, Janelle mounted him, then rode into the paddock. She slapped her legs against his side and Prince John reared up. Janelle hung on easily, and when he came back down on all fours, he bolted forward. Seeing a watering trough that protruded out from a windmill she headed directly for it, as the horse gathered himself for the jump. He sailed easily over the watering trough, then continued on the other side.

As she had with Vexation, she gave Prince John his head, allowing him to race all the way around the paddock, staying close to the fence. Finally she trotted back to where Housewright was standing, brought him to a halt, then slid gracefully down from the saddle.

"What do you think?" she asked.

"Do I know you, boy?" Housewright asked.

Suddenly Janelle realized she had almost exactly duplicated the ride she had done with Vexation, and she felt a quick twinge of fear that she might be recognized.

"No, I don't think so," Janelle replied. "I just arrived on the train, today."

"You just arrived today, did you?"

"Yes, sir."

"Well, that's funny, 'cause it sure seems to me like I've seen you before."

"What about the job, Mr. Housewright? Am I hired?"

"What? Oh, yes, yes indeed. I need another person to work here, and there ain't no doubt as to whether or not you can ride. If you want the job, it's your'n."

"Yes, I very much want the job. Thanks."

For the next few days, Janelle's job consisted of feeding, watering, and rubbing down the horses. She also had to muck out a few stalls, but at least it was a paying job, and it gave her a place to stay. Her plan was to make enough money to outfit herself, then see if she really could use the map to locate the mine.

She learned very quickly that Ben Hanlon, the man who had drawn the map, was dead. The story was he had died while in the jail, as a result of being beaten and robbed. But Janelle was convinced that Cairns had killed him. She had no proof of course, and not even any evidence to suggest such a thing. But she had seen him kill Mr. Montgomery over the map, so it was not hard for her to believe that he killed Hanlon as well.

She knew, also, that if he discovered she was the "boy" working at Housewright's stable, he would kill her and get away with it, since she was wanted, dead or alive.

A couple times she saw Nellie Buckner, and once she saw Mrs. Poindexter. She wanted desperately to go to them, to tell them who she was, but she bit her lip, continued her work, and watched them from afar.

"Joe?" Housewright called.

"Yes, sir?"

"Somebody just told me that Corey Minner is down at the depot. He rented a horse from me last week, and he ain't never brought it back. I want you to go get the horse from him."

"How do I do that?" Janelle asked.

"Well hell, boy, you just go up to him and ask for it," Housewright said.

"All right."

Janelle started to leave, but Housewright called out to her. "Boy?"

She didn't respond to the call.

"Joe?"

She gasped then, realizing she had not responded when called boy. She would have to watch that. She turned back toward him.

"Yes, sir?"

"Listen, Minner is, well, he ain't that friendly of a man. So if he gives you any gruff about givin' the horse back to you, don't you go pushin' him, if you know what I mean."

Janelle knew about Corey Minner. Though she had never met him in person, she had heard about his run-in with Ken Buckner. Anyone who couldn't get along with Ken Buckner, or who would purposely pick on him, couldn't be that good of a man.

"If Minner says no, just walk on down to the marshal's office and tell him. Let the marshal get the horse back."

"The marshal?" Janelle replied with a catch in her voice. She knew Minner was an unpleasant person, but no matter how unpleasant he might be, there was no chance he would recognize her. On the other hand, there was a very good chance the marshal would. She had no intention of going to the marshal. "I don't think we'll need him," she said.

"Yeah, well, if you do need him, go get him. After all, that's what we pay him for. We don't pay him to go huntin' some woman who the whole town don't believe kilt Montgomery anyway."

That was the first time Janelle had ever heard

mention of her situation, and the fact that Housewright said nobody believed she was guilty was encouraging. But she still felt it was probably better to keep her identity a secret.

As Falcon stepped down from the train in Phoenix, there were several men, women, and children present on the depot platform. To a casual observer it might look as if they were all there to board the train, or, at least to meet someone on the train. But in fact they were present for no more reason than the novelty of a train's arrival and departure. In Phoenix, as in most other towns in the West, the arrival and departure of the daily trains were people's links to the rest of the country; each train was a real and kinetic connection to civilization.

Two people on the platform were playing out their own drama, independent of the arrival and departure of the train. One was a smallish young man who was being accosted by a much larger man.

"Please, Mr. Minner," the young man said. "I don't want any trouble."

The bully laughed out loud. "Well, sonny, you got yourself a pile of trouble whether you want it or not. Most especial if you try and get on my horse."

"That isn't your horse. You rented that horse from the Housewright stable. You did not bring him back and your contract has terminated."

Minner laughed, in loud, boisterous guffaws. "My contract has terminated? That's pretty high falutin' talk from a still wet behind the ears pipsqueak like you, ain't it?"

"Please, Mr. Minner, all I am doing is picking up Mr. Housewright's horse." The young man showed the roughneck a piece of paper. "This is my authorization."

"Yeah? Well that authorization don't mean shit to me. As long as I have the horse, it's the same as my horse. Do you understand that?"

"If you pay the money you owe Mr. Housewright, I'm sure it can be worked out," the young man said.

"I ain't payin' nothin' to Housewright and you ain't takin' my horse."

"That's just it, Mr. Minner, it isn't your horse," the young man said resolutely. He started toward the horse and as he did so, the bully pulled his pistol.

"Boy, if you touch that horse, I'm goin' to put a bullet in your back."

Although there were several people standing around watching the interplay between the two, Falcon noticed that not one person was making any sign of interfering. Despite the threat, and the drawn pistol, the young man walked without hesitation to the horse in question.

Minner pulled the hammer back and raised his pistol.

"Mister, I don't think you want to do that," Falcon called out loudly. He had not drawn his own gun, expecting that, once called upon, the man would come to his senses. He was surprised, therefore, when Minner swung his gun toward him and fired, all in one fluid motion. The bullet hit the crown of Falcon's hat, knocking it off his head.

He crouched as Minner fired a second time, the

bullet frying the air but an inch away from Falcon's ear. He drew his own pistol then and fired. Falcon's shot found its mark, striking Minner in the neck. With his eyes open wide in shock, he dropped his pistol and slapped both hands to the wound in his neck. Even as the blood was spilling between his fingers, he went down.

Janelle jumped at the sound of the gunshot behind her, thinking for a moment it was directed at her. She turned as she heard a second and then a third shot.

With the smoke still curling up from the end of his gun barrel, the man walked over to look down at Minner, who was lying on his back with his eyes wide open but sightless, and clouding over with death. The hole in his neck was filled with dark red, almost black, blood, though as his heart was no longer beating, no blood was pumping from the wound.

Suddenly Janelle gasped as she recognized the shooter. It was the man she had met on the train several weeks ago! It was Falcon MacCallister!

"Are you all right, boy?" MacCallister asked.

Janelle continued to stare at MacCallister, so shocked by what had just happened that she didn't answer his question.

"Are you all right?" Falcon asked again.

"You killed him," Janelle said.

"I reckon I did," Falcon replied.

"Why did you kill him? I mean, over a horse?"

"Boy, if you had been paying attention, you would have seen that he was about to kill you over a horse. But I didn't kill him because of the horse, or you,"

Falcon said. "I killed him because he was trying to kill me."

Getting over her initial shock, Janelle began to think more reasonably. "Yes," she said. "All things considered, I suppose I owe you a debt of gratitude for saving my life."

"What's your name, mister?"

"Ja—" she almost said *Janelle*, but managed to hold her tongue, then, coughing to cover up her mistake, she spoke again. "My name is Joe. Joe Henry."

"Joe, I'm Falcon MacCallister." He put his pistol back in the holster, then stuck out his hand.

Shaking hands was something men did, and for just a moment, Janelle hesitated. Then, realizing that his hand was still hanging there, she reached out to grab it.

"Yes, I know who you are," she said.

Falcon looked surprised, and she could have bitten her tongue for having said that.

"Do I know you?" Falcon asked.

"No, sir. We've not exactly met, but I saw you once before and I remember you."

Falcon smiled. "Yes, that happens a lot to me. I don't know if that is a curse or a blessing."

"I owe you my thanks, Mr. MacCallister," Janelle said. "You probably saved my life."

"I'll accept your thanks, but what I am really going to need is your statement."

"My statement? I don't understand. My statement about what?"

"I imagine that the sheriff, or the city marshal, or someone will be here soon."

"The marshal? Why would the marshal come?"

"I just killed a man," Falcon said. "Don't you think the marshal might be interested in that?"

"Oh. Yes, I suppose so," Janelle said. She sighed. "Let me deliver this horse to Mr. Housewright. Then I'll go down to the marshal's office to tell him what happened."

"Shouldn't we see the marshal first?"

"No, I—that is, Mr. Housewright wants his horse right away," Janelle said. She swung into the saddle of the horse. "I have to get it to him."

Slapping her heel against the side of the horse, she urged the animal into a gallop and rode quickly away from the depot.

Falcon watched the young man ride off, wondering at his strange behavior. Could it be that he actually was stealing the horse? Had Falcon made a big mistake?"

"That's him, Marshal. That's the man that shot Corey Minner," someone said.

Looking toward the sound of the voice, Falcon saw an older, white-haired man pointing at him. Beside him was a broad shouldered man with a bushy moustache, who was also wearing a star on his vest.

"Is that true, mister? Did you shoot Minner?" the marshal asked Falcon.

"If that is this man's name, yes, I shot him," Falcon answered easily.

"You're kind of pompous about that little matter,

ain't you?" The sheriff drew his pistol and pointed it at Falcon. "I'll thank you to drop your gun belt."

"Marshal, if you ask anyone around here, they will tell you it was self-defense. He shot at me first."

"That's true, Marshal," one of the others on the platform said.

"Yeah, I seen it. Minner shot first. Fact is, Minner shot two times before this feller shot back. This feller here didn't have no choice."

"I knew Corey Minner," the marshal said. "He was a bully, but I've never known him to just start shooting at someone for no reason."

"I didn't say it was for no reason. All I said was that he started shooting at me. He had a reason."

"What was that reason?"

"He was bullying a young man, not much more than a boy, actually. The boy was trying to take back a horse that belonged to his employer. When the young man started toward the horse, Minner pulled his gun and threatened to shoot him in the back. I called him on it, and that's when he turned and started shooting at me."

"So, when he turned you were pointing your gun at him? Mister, I would call that a hostile act. No wonder he shot at you."

"My gun was in the holster."

"Your gun was in the holster, he started shooting at you, but you killed him. Is that right?" the marshal asked incredulously. "Is that what you are trying to tell me?"

"That is right."

"Mister, if someone else has his gun out, pointing

it at you, and your gun is in the holster, you ain't goin' to get your gun out in time to shoot him."

"You have your gun out and pointed at me," Falcon said.

"Yeah, I do, don't I?"

In a draw that was so fast those watching saw only a slight twitch of his shoulder, Falcon suddenly had his pistol in his hand.

"And now, I have my gun out as well," Falcon said easily.

"What the hell?" The marshal asked, shocked by the sudden, and totally unexpected turn of events. "How did you do that?"

"It doesn't matter how I did it," Falcon answered. "The point is, I did it. I hope it convinces you I am telling the truth."

"He *is* tellin' it true, Marshal," the man who had spoken up said. "I saw the whole thing."

"I seen it too," another man said. "Corey Minner was about to shoot the boy in the back and this here feller called him on it. Minner turned around shootin' and the next thing you know, this feller drilled him dead center with one shot."

Marshal Cairns held the gun in his hand for a moment longer, then with a sigh, put the pistol back in his holster.

"All right," he said. "If these folks are talkin' for you, I reckon you're tellin' the truth. But I'd like you to come on down to my office and sign a statement."

"I'll be glad to, Marshal," Falcon said.

"I'll be wantin' a statement from you two as well," the marshal said to the two men who had spoken up.

"What about the young man who works for the livery?" Falcon asked. "I believe he said his name was Joe Henry."

"Joe Henry?" The marshal shook his head. "I know ever'one in this town, and I don't know nobody named Joe Henry," he replied.

"He's new, Marshal," one of the two witnesses said. "He only started workin' for Housewright last week."

"All right, I'll take care of him later," the marshal said. "Come along, Mister—what is your name?"

"MacCallister. Falcon MacCallister."

"MacCallister? You are Falcon MacCallister?"

"Yes."

"What are you doing in my town, MacCallister?"

"I didn't know it was your town. I thought this was all free country."

"Yeah, yeah, it is," the marshal said. "I didn't mean it like that, I was just curious is all. Come on down to my office and make a statement for me."

Chapter Twenty-two

As Janelle rode the horse back to Housewright's Livery Stable, she was having to fight down the panic. MacCallister hadn't recognized her, but their encounter had been several weeks ago, very brief, and several hundred miles from there. MacCallister had asked her to give the marshal a statement on his behalf, and she owed such a statement to him. But she wasn't all that confident her disguise would fool the marshal.

She was not going to chance it. She had no intention of giving a statement to the marshal. She hated doing it, hating abandoning the man who had, without question, saved her life. But she knew there were many other witnesses who would testify for him. In fact, the others would be able to give even stronger statements because they had actually seen the event, whereas she had not. It had taken place behind her back.

Janelle had to get out of town, and she knew exactly how to do it.

* * *

"Any trouble?" Housewright asked when Janelle returned to the livery with the horse.

"Sort of."

"Sort of? What do you mean, sort of?"

"I didn't see it because my back was turned, but evidently Mr. Minner was going to shoot me in the back. A man named MacCallister called out to him. Mr. Minner turned and shot at MacCallister, but missed. MacCallister shot back and didn't miss."

"Damn!" Housewright said. "You mean Corey Minner is dead?"

"Yes, sir."

"I'm sorry to hear that. Not that he is dead, if there was any son of a bitch in this town that needed killin', it was Corey Minner. But he owed me a week's rent money on the horse and now I won't be able to collect."

"How much did he owe you?"

"Fifty cents a day for seven days, that's—uh—,"

"Three dollars and fifty cents," Janelle said.

"Yes. Say, you're pretty quick with figures."

"I know how you can recover that money, and a lot more."

"How?"

"By making a small investment."

"An investment with who, and for how much?"

"With me, and not too much. Just the extended loan of a horse, some bacon, beans, and salt."

"What is this about, Joe?"

"You know the young woman who the marshal says killed Mr. Montgomery?

"Yeah, I know her. She's the one that won the horse race on the Fourth of July. What about her?"

"She's a friend of mine."

"A friend of yours?" Housewright said. Then he broke into a big smile. "Damn boy, you mean she's your girlfriend?"

"Yes, she's my girlfriend," Janelle said.

Housewright laughed, and slapped himself on the knee. "Well, boy, you got more sand in you than I thought. I mean a little old pipsqueak of a man like you, with a girlfriend like that. Who would have thought it?"

"Yeah, who would have thought it?" Janelle replied.

"What's that got to do with me investin' in you?"

"Janelle told me what happened between her and the banker."

"Really? What did she say happened?"

"She had gone to the bank to apply for a job when she saw Marshal Cairns and Mr. Montgomery arguing over a map. Marshal Cairns killed Mr. Montgomery."

"I knew it," Housewright said, hitting his fist into his hand. "I never did believe that pretty girl could do anything like murder. But Cairns, I think that son of a bitch would just as soon shoot you as speak to you. You say they were arguing over a map?"

"Yes, sir."

"What kind of map?"

"A map to a gold mine."

"And you say that Cairns kilt Montgomery over the map?"

"That's right, he did. Only Montgomery had

hidden the map, so Cairns didn't get it. Then, just before he died, he told Janelle where he hid the map."

"Where is the woman now?"

"I can't tell you that."

"You can't? Or you won't?"

"I won't."

"Do you know where the map is?"

"Yes. I have it."

"Can I see it?"

"I don't have it on me. I've hidden it. But I know where it is."

"Where is this gold?"

Janelle laughed. "Why should I tell you where it is? If I did that, you wouldn't need me."

"In general, where is it? White Tank Mountains? Mazatzals? McDowel Mountains?"

"It's at Superstition Mountain, near Weaver's Needle."

Housewright laughed out loud. "That's what I was afraid of."

Janelle was surprised by his laughter. "What do you mean, that's what you were afraid of? What's so funny?"

"Hell, boy, you are talkin' about the Lost Dutchman, aren't you? Ever'body and his brother has gone out to Superstition, lookin' for that old Dutchman's gold mine."

"Yes, but this map tells exactly where to look once you get to Weaver's Needle."

"And you believe the map?"

"Evidently Mr. Montgomery did. He loaned the old prospector money just on the strength of the map. And the marshal believed it enough to kill the banker for it."

"Well somebody killed him, anyway," Housewright said. "And there had to be a reason. I guess a map to a gold mine is as good as any other reason."

"What do you say, Mr. Housewright? Will you back me?"

"Let me get this straight. All you want is the loan of a horse and some food. Is that right? And if you find this gold, you will split it with me?"

"Yes."

"How long do you plan to be out looking for it?"

"A week. Two at the most."

"All right. I may be crazy, boy, but you've got yourself a deal," Housewright said.

Terry Cooper, one of Housewright's hands, overheard the entire conversation. Telling Housewright he had to go to the hardware store to get a ring for the harness he was working on, he headed instead for a shack he owned about two miles south of town. He was renting that shack to a man who had worked at the livery for a while under the name Jesse Jones. Shortly after he rented the shack, Cooper found out the man's real name was Luke Mueller. Cooper had heard of him and felt honored that such a famous man would actually stay in his shack.

Mueller told Cooper he was only going to hang around for another few weeks, then he was going to go out on the outlaw trail again. He invited Cooper to ride with him, and Cooper fully intended to do so.

But he had something else on his mind. He was sure the information he had about the map to the gold mine was valuable, and he was equally sure Mueller would know better than he how to utilize that information.

Deputy John Forbis was sweeping the floor of the marshal's office when Falcon and the marshal stepped inside. There was no one in any of the cells.

"What was the shootin' about?" Forbis asked.

"This man killed Cory Minner," Cairns replied, nodding toward Falcon.

"Good for you," Forbis said to Falcon. "Minner was a no good son of a bitch."

"Did you hear what I said? I said this man just killed Cory Minner," the marshal said.

"I heard you say that, Marshal, but it must have been a fair fight. Otherwise the two of you wouldn't have come just walkin' in like that. You'd have him in shackles or something. Also," Forbis pointed to Falcon's belt, "he wouldn't still be wearin' his gun. So I figure the killin' must have been legal."

"It was legal, all right," the marshal growled. "But that don't mean I gotta like it." Cairns sat down at his desk, then opened a ledger book and picked up a pen and quill. "All right, for the record, tell me what happened."

"I saw a man threaten to shoot a boy in the back. I called out to him, and he turned his gun on me, fired at me, and I shot back."

"And killed Corey Minner."

"That was the whole idea of shooting at him, Marshal."

"Well, you needn't be so haughty about it, mister. Shootin' out there on the depot platform like you done, you could'a hit anybody."

Falcon shook his head. "I wasn't aiming at anybody. I was aiming at Corey Minner."

"Hell, Marshal Cairns, what are you ragging him for? In my book, anybody that killed Corey Minner ought to get a medal. He was the biggest no-count in Maricopa County, and you know it," the deputy said.

"Well, it ain't your book we're concerned about, is it, Deputy?" Cairns replied. "When you get right down to it, it's the judge's book, and I'm just tryin' to get the story straight so as to satisfy the judge, that's all." Continuing his questioning, Cairns turned his attention back to Falcon. "When you called out to him, was you holdin' a gun?"

"My gun was in the holster. I think the witnesses will verify that."

"You are talking about the feller Joe Henry that no one has ever heard of?"

"He was one of the witnesses, yes. In fact, he was the one that Minner was about to shoot, before I butted in."

"Butted in, yes, that's a good way to put it. You butted in where you had no business buttin' in."

"If I hadn't butted in, he would have shot the boy. You heard the others testify to that."

Cairns sighed, made the entry, then put the pen down. "Yeah, I heard 'em," he said. "Let me ask you this, MacCallister. How come I haven't met you before? How long you been in town?"

"I just arrived on the train."

"Damn. You just arrived and you kill somebody the first minute you are in town. I sure as hell hope you don't plan to stay long."

"Only long enough to find a young woman and take her back to her parents."

"Oh? And what young woman would that be?"

"It's someone you know, I believe. Her name is Janelle Wellington."

"Janelle Wellington?" the marshal said with a harsh, barking laugh. "Ha! I know her all right. But if you do find her, you won't be takin' her back to her parents. You'll be turnin' her over to me."

"Yes, I saw that you have paper on her, alleging that she murdered someone."

"Alleging? I ain't alleging a damn thing. She shot down Mr. Montgomery in cold blood," Cairns said.

"I have to say from everything I have heard about her, it really doesn't seem possible she would be the kind to shoot someone," Falcon said.

Cairn's eyes narrowed. "You callin' me a liar, MacCallister?"

"I'm just suggesting your information might be wrong."

"It ain't wrong, because I seen her do it my ownself. She was trying to rob the bank, and she killed the banker, C. D. Montgomery."

"You're sure we're talking about the same woman? I mean with her background, it seems unlikely she would be robbing a bank. Her father is a very wealthy man. If she needed money all she would have to do is ask. The thought of her murdering anyone is even more unlikely."

"Is the Janelle Wellington you are looking for a pretty woman? And is she from New York?" the marshal asked.

"I've never seen her, but they say she is pretty. And yes, she is from New York."

"Then we are talking about the same woman. So if you find her, you have to turn her over to me. That's the law."

"And you know all about the law, don't you?"

"Yeah, I'm the city marshal here."

"And before you became city marshal, you were a deputy to Wyatt Earp?"

"That's right," Cairns said. He squinted at Falcon. "How did you know that?"

"It's just something I heard."

"Have you ever met Wyatt Earp?"

"I've heard a lot about him," Falcon said, purposely making his answer nonspecific.

"What have you heard?"

"I've heard he likes to play cards, has a lot of loyalty to his brothers and friends, and that he is a very good lawman."

Cairns nodded. "Yep. Ever'thing you just said about him is true, all right. I know, 'cause, like you say, I oncet deputied for him."

"Where was that?"

"Beg pardon?

"Where did you deputy for Wyatt Earp?"

"It was in Wichita," Cairns replied. "Why is it you are askin' me all these here questions? What difference does it make to you?"

"No particular reason. It's just that I heard a story once, about something that happened in Wichita. You being Wyatt's deputy, I thought maybe you would know a little something about it."

"What's the story?"

"It seems that a fellow was about to repossess an unpaid for piano from a whorehouse," Falcon said. "But a lot of drovers got angry about it, so in order to keep the peace, Wyatt Earp paid for the piano himself."

Cairns chuckled. "Yep, that's true all right. I was standin' right there by his side when it happened."

Falcon stared at Cairns for a long moment. "Of course, I've also heard another story about that same event," he said.

"What story is that?"

"Well, the other story I heard was that Wyatt Earp was the one who was going to repossess the piano. The drovers had to put up the money to keep it from being taken away and that made them mad. A group of almost fifty armed cowboys gathered across the river from Wichita, planning to come into town and raise hell. But Wyatt Earp stood right in the middle of the bridge and single handedly talked those cowboys into withdrawing, without so much as one shot being fired."

"Yeah," Cairns said. "That's the way it was."

"Which is the way it was, Marshal? I've told you two different stories, and you have agreed with both of them."

"I don't know," Cairns said, clearly agitated. "That was a long time ago. How am I expected to remember ever'thing that happened that long ago?"

"Oh, I'm sure it's quite hard to remember, so much has happened since then."

"Yeah, a lot has happened," Cairns said. He closed the ledger. "I've got ever'thing I need from you now. You're free to go."

"Do I need to stay around town for an inquest?"

"Ain't goin' to be no inquest," Cairns said. "I'm through with you now."

"Thanks, I'll be on my way then."

Falcon started toward the door but before he reached it, Cairns called out to him. "MacCallister?"

Falcon turned back. "Yeah?"

"About you lookin' for that woman, Janelle Wellington? You are free to look for her but like I said, if you find her, you bring her back to me. You got that? She's a wanted murderer, and I intend to see that she hangs for it."

Falcon nodded, but said nothing as he stepped onto the boardwalk that passed by the front of the marshall's office. He'd had his suspicions about the man who was calling himself Jimmy Cairns, ever since he had spoken with Troy Calhoun, back in Flagstaff. That was why he set the trap with the story about the piano in the whorehouse. It was the second story that was true, not the first. Falcon had not been there, but his brother Matthew had, and told him all about it.

Falcon did not know who the man claiming to be Jimmy Cairns was, but he knew who he was not. He was not Jimmy Cairns, and Falcon planned to keep his eye on him. Leaving the marhsal's office, he walked down Central toward to the railroad depot to claim his horse. Then, he rode to the livery stable, not only to board his horse, but also to see why the young man Joe Henry had not come to give a statement for him.

Janelle, riding Prince John and carrying a few bags of food furnished by Housewright, rode away from town. She headed toward Superstition Mountain. Once beyond the last structure, she leaned over and patted the horse's neck a few times.

"Prince John, I'm sorry I had to lie to Mr. Housewright like that, but I couldn't very well tell him who I really am, could I? When you think about it, I didn't really lie. I said I knew Janelle Wellington, and I do." She chuckled at the private joke.

"It's just that I had to get away from town before I had an encounter with the marshal. While the disguise is working pretty well, I wouldn't want to give that evil man the opportunity to get close enough to see through it. Now, what do you say we have us a little run?"

Janelle slapped her legs against Prince John's sides and let him gallop for at least a mile. The further away from town she got, the safer she felt. Her only regret was that she had not been able to testify for the man who had saved her life. From the immediate reaction of the other witnesses, she was certain Falcon MacCallister would get all the exculpatory testimony he might need to stay out of trouble.

Chapter Twenty-three

When Falcon stepped into the livery, he saw a short, slender man rubbing down a horse. "Would you be Mr. Housewright?"

"That's right. What can I do for you?"

"A couple of things," Falcon replied. "For one, I would like to board my horse with you."

"That'll be twenty cents a day. Thirty cents a day if I have to feed him."

"By all means, feed him," Falcon said, handing the reins over.

"Good lookin' horse," Housewright said, patting the horse's neck. "He don't look like he's been rode hard."

"Hasn't been ridden at all. We just arrived on the train."

"Did you now? I heard there was a shootin' down there shortly after the train arrived. Did you happen to see it?"

"I saw it."

"The feller that got hisself kilt—a real lowlife he was. Don't know nothin' 'bout the feller that kilt him, but if it was up to me, he'd get a medal. Oh, you said there was a couple of things you wanted. Besides the horse, what else was it?"

"I'm looking for a young man, not much more than a boy really, who works here. At least, I think he works here."

"You'd be talkin' about Joe Henry, I reckon."

"Yes. I'd like to see him, if you don't mind."

"I don't mind a'tall, but he don't work here no more," Housewright said.

"But I just saw him. He said he was picking up a horse for you."

"Yes, sir, he done that all right. Fact is, he picked it up from Corey Minner, the feller that got hisself kilt. But, it's like I said, mister, Joe don't work here no more. He quit, no more'n fifteen minutes ago. Why are you so interested in him?"

"He was a witness to the shooting," Falcon said. "He said he would make a statement to the marshal for me."

"What do you mean, make a statement to the marshal for you?" Housewright asked. "Why would you be needin' a statement?"

"I'm the one that shot Corey Minner."

A broad smile spread across Housewright's face. "You would be Falcon MacCallster, wouldn't you?"

"Yes."

Housewright stuck his hand out, then pulled it back and wiped it off before sticking it out again. "Mr. MacCallister, I would like to shake your hand."

Falcon accepted the proffered handshake.

"Sorry the boy didn't come sign a statement

for you," Housewright said. "I don't know why he didn't."

"Well, as it turned out I didn't need him. There were some other witnesses who spoke up for me. I was just curious as to why the boy didn't come, is all."

"Oh, I know why."

"You do? Why?"

"You just gettin' into town and all, you might not know nothin' about it, but the marshal's done put paper out on a woman by the name of Janelle Wellington. She worked down at the Buckner Emporium, she did. 'Near 'bout the prettiest woman I done ever seen."

"Yes, I saw the wanted posters on her," Falcon said. "But what does that have to do with the boy that works, or did work for you?"

"Just about ever'thing," Housewright replied. "Joe says that Miss Wellington is his girlfriend. He also says she ain't the one who killed Mr. Montgomery, that the marshal hisself is the one who done the killin'. Joe claims the girl seen it all."

"Does he know where she is?"

"Well, he"—Housewright started, then stopped—"look here, you ain't a' lookin' to find the woman and claim that reward for your ownself, are you? 'Cause if you are, I ain't plannin' on helpin' you none a'tall. Me 'n Joe Henry's in cahoots on this. I loaned him the horse and give him some food, and soon as he finds the gold, well we're goin' to split it."

"Finds the gold? What gold?" Falcon asked, confused by the sudden turn the conversation had taken.

"I don't know as I should tell you anythin' else,"

Housewright said. "I got nothin' agin' you, you understand. But I got me an investment to protect."

"Very well, Mr. Housewright, I won't bother you any more. Please just see to my horse."

"You ain't got nothin' to worry 'bout there. I'll take real good care of your horse."

Leaving the livery, Falcon considered his next move. Where was it Housewright said Janelle had worked? Buckley's?

Falcon walked Central from one end to the other but saw nothing that looked like Buckley. Then, on Adams, he saw Buckner's Ladies' Emporium and knew at once that it was the place he was looking for.

The bell on the door jingled as he pushed it open, and he was greeted by an attractive woman in her late thirties or early forties.

"Yes, sir, something I can do for you?" she asked with a broad smile. "You have a wife, or maybe a lady friend you want to buy for?"

"No, ma'am," Falcon replied. "Actually I'm here to ask you a few questions, if you don't mind."

"Questions about what?"

"About Janelle Wellington."

The smile left the woman's face. "Mister, if you are a lawman or a bounty hunter out to collect the reward, then I don't have a thing to say to you."

Falcon shook his head. "No, it's nothing like that," he said. "I came here to take her back to New York. Her parents sent me."

"You expect me to believe that?"

"What's going on, Nellie?" a man asked, coming up to the front of the store."

"Ken, this man says he is looking for Janelle. And

get this, he says he isn't a bounty hunter. He says he was sent by her parents to find her and take her back home."

"Is that true, mister?"

"Yes," Falcon answered.

"Are you willing to put that story to a test?"

"What sort of test?"

"You say you have been sent by her parents. What are their names?"

"Their names are Joel and Emma Wellington," Falcon said.

"That's right."

"Ken, I don't know."

"Nellie, I don't think a bounty hunter would have the slightest idea as to what her parents' names are. He gave me the right names, because that's what is on the letters they sent her, Joel and Emma Wellington. You've seen them yourself. Those are the letters she never opened."

"Do you still have those letters?" Falcon asked.

"Maybe I do, and maybe I don't. Why do you ask?"

"Because I, too, have a letter from her parents," Falcon said. "When I find Janelle, I am supposed to try and persuade her to read it. I thought if we compared the handwriting between the letter I have, and the ones you have, it would further ease Mrs. Buckner's concern."

"What do you think, Nellie?" Ken asked.

"I'll get one of the letters," Nellie replied. She disappeared for a moment, then returned carrying just one of the letters.

"Let me see your letter," Ken asked of Falcon.

Reaching into the inside pocket of his jacket, he produced the letter and handed it to Ken.

"Nellie, I believe the man is genuine," he said after examining both letters, side by side. "Look at these. It's clear they were both written by the same person."

"You're right," Nellie said. The expression on her face softened considerably as she looked back at Falcon. "I'm sorry I doubted you, Mister . . . uh, I didn't get your name."

"It's MacCallister. Falcon MacCallister," Falcon replied. "And please, don't apologize. I'm glad Miss Wellington was able to make some friends out here."

"Falcon MacCallister!" Nellie said. She gasped, and put her hand to her mouth. "You are the one!"

Falcon found Nellie's reaction puzzling and the expression on his face reflected that. "I beg your pardon? I am the one what?"

"On the train," Nellie said. "Janelle told me all about you. You came to her rescue on the train." Nellie then related the story as told to her by Janelle, about the young man, dressed all in black. "She was particularly amused as to how when the young man tried to draw his pistol, it was already in your hand."

"That was Janelle Wellington?" Falcon asked.

"Yes. Then you do remember," Nellie said.

"I certainly remember the incident," Falcon said. "But I never got the young lady's name. I had no idea it was Janelle Wellington."

"How odd life can be," Nellie said. "Here you are

looking for her and she was right there but you didn't know it."

"I wasn't looking for her then," Falcon said. "That didn't come until later, when I went to New York to meet her parents. Her parents are very good friends of my brother and sister, Andrew and Rosanna—"

"MacCallister, yes of course!" Nellie said, interrupting him excitedly. "Oh, Janelle spoke of them often. She was very fond of them both. They are famous actors."

"Yes, and they are the ones who asked me to come to New York to meet with Miss Wellington's parents. I did so, and I agreed to come here to search for their daughter."

"Oh, I do hope you find her. I am so worried about her. You obviously know about the trouble she is in. She has been accused of killing poor Mr. Montgomery."

"Yes," Falcon said. "I have heard."

"Of course, I don't believe for one minute that she actually did it. And neither does anyone else who knows her."

Falcon considered telling the Buckners what Housewright told him—what Joe Henry said about the marshal being the actual murderer. He decided it would only complicate matters, so he said nothing about it.

"Could you tell me about some of Janelle's friends?"

"Friends? Well, I considered her a very close friend of course. I still do. And so does Ken."

"Anyone else?"

"There's Mrs. Poindexter over at the boarding-house," Ken said.

"What about Joe Henry?"

Both Ken and Nellie looked confused.

"Joe Henry," Falcon repeated. "Miss Wellington's boyfriend."

Both Ken and Nellie laughed.

"What's wrong?"

"Heavens, I don't see how she could have had a boyfriend. She did nothing but work all the time, often volunteering to stay late. Of course, as beautiful as she is, I can certainly see how some young man would wish to be referred to as her boyfriend."

"Joe Henry never came here, to the store, to visit her?"

"No. She never had any young men visitors."

"Was she in the bank on the day Montgomery was killed?"

"Yes, she was."

"Why was she there?"

"Mr. Montgomery had offered her employment in his bank, and she had gone over there to take him up on the offer of a job. Oh, she was so excited that morning," Nellie said.

"And you say that, as far as you know, she was not friends with Joe Henry?"

"I'm almost certain that if she were friends with this—Mr. Henry, that I would have met him. To tell you the truth, Mr. MacCallister, I have never even heard of him."

"He told Mr. Housewright that Janelle had gone to the bank to speak with Montgomery about a job. How do you think he knew that, if he didn't know her?"

Ken shook his head. "I'm afraid I don't know, Mr. MacCallister, but I am telling you neither one of us have ever even heard of this fellow, Joe Henry."

"Won't you have a piece of pie with your coffee?" Mrs. Poindexter offered.

"No, I shouldn't, really. I'm sure you made the pie for your guests and—"

All the while Falcon was saying no to Mrs. Poindexter, she was carving out a generous piece of apple pie, onto which she put a slice of cheese. Then she put the piece of pie, with cheese, in the oven.

"I'll leave it in there just for a minute or so, just long enough for the cheese to melt," she said.

"Well, I have to confess, that looks very good," Falcon said.

A moment later the pie came out of the oven and Falcon took a bite, then closed his eyes and shook his head slowly in appreciation.

"So, Janelle's mother and father sent you out here to look for her, did they?" Mrs. Poindexter said as she watched Falcon enjoy the repast.

"Yes, ma'am, they did."

"It's too bad they didn't send you out here sooner. She would have never gotten into trouble."

"Tell me, Mrs. Poindexter, do you believe Janelle is guilty?"

"Oh, heaven's no," she replied. "I have no idea what would make the marshal lie like that."

Falcon looked up at her, but had to chew quickly to get rid of the bite he had just taken. "Interesting, that you would call it a lie, rather than a mistake," he said.

"Well, a lie is what it was," Mrs. Poindexter said. "The marshal claims to have actually seen Janelle kill poor Mr. Montgomery, and I know for a fact that Janelle did not do it."

"How do you know?"

"Because I just know she wouldn't do such a thing," Mrs. Poindexter insisted.

"Do you know a man named Joe Henry?"

"Joe Henry? No, I can't say that I do. Why do you ask?"

"He claims to be Janelle's boyfriend."

Mrs. Poindexter laughed out loud. "I would say that is just a case of wishful thinking. Janelle didn't have a boyfriend, though heaven knows she could have. She is an absolutely beautiful girl, inside and out."

Falcon finished his pie then slid the plate aside.

"Would you like another piece of pie?"

"No, thank you. It was delicious, but I need to be going. Thank you for the pie, and for the information."

"Please find her, Mr. MacCallister," Mrs. Poindexter said. "Find her and get her out of here. I don't know why the marshal claims he saw her shoot Mr. Montgomery, but I know as sure as I am sitting here that she didn't do it.

"I will do what I can," Falcon promised.

Chapter Twenty-four

Falcon's next stop was the Boar's Head Saloon. He wanted a beer, but he had also learned a long time ago that casual conversation in a saloon was often the best way to find out information.

Buying a beer, he walked over to an empty table and when one of the bar girls approached him with an inviting smile, he smiled back at her. "Join me for a drink," he invited.

"Thank you, I will," the girl answered. She called over to the bar. "Wally, my special when you get a chance."

"Your special?" Falcon asked. "Don't you mean tea?"

"Whoa now, you want to ruin a girl's reputation? What would all my customers think if they knew I drank only tea? How did you know, by the way?"

"If you drank whiskey every time a man offered to buy you a drink, you'd be so drunk by the end of the day you couldn't stand."

The girl laughed. "You're pretty smart, mister. My name is Maxine."

"I'm Falcon," he replied.

"Falcon? That's a strange name. How did you come by a name like that?"

"My pa gave it to me," Falcon said.

"Was your pa into strange names?"

"No. All my other brothers and sisters have ordinary names, like Jamie, Morgan, Andrew, Rosanna, Joleen. . ."

"Whoa," Maxine said, laughing and holding our her hand. How many brothers and sisters do you have?"

"There are nine of us," Falcon said.

Wally brought the drink over and put it in front of Maxine. "You want another beer, mister?"

"Don't mind if I do," Falcon replied.

"You're not from here, are you, Falcon?" Maxine asked.

"No, I'm not."

When Wally brought the beer back, Falcon gave him a dollar and said, "Why don't the two of you divide the change?"

"Really? Well, that's very generous of you, Falcon," Maxine said.

"I like to consider myself a generous man," Falcon said.

"Wait a minute," Maxine said. "You are the man who killed Corey Minner, aren't you?"

"Yes," Falcon said easily. "If he was a friend of yours, I'm sorry. I had no choice."

"Ha," Maxine said the word, but didn't actually laugh. "That son of a bitch was a long way from being a friend of mine. You did the whole city a favor when you killed him. It's just too bad it wasn't the marshal or his deputy instead."

"Maxine," Wally cautioned. "I've warned you about talking like that. You never know who your friends really are."

Maxine smiled at Falcon. "Well, you are my friend, aren't you, Falcon?"

"I'm trying to be," Falcon said, returning the smile.

"What are you doing in Phoenix?"

Falcon paused for a moment before he answered. He had to give it just the right inflection to keep the conversation open, and not make it appear as if he were looking for information.

"I came here to find a woman," he said.

Maxine smiled broadly. "Really? Well, cowboy, I'm available," she said, then she laughed out loud.

"I wish you were the one I was looking for," Falcon said. "Then my job would be over."

"Oh. You mean you are looking for a very specific woman?"

"Yes. She's a young woman who came here a few months ago. But I haven't had much luck."

"What's her name?"

Falcon held up his hand as if asking for a moment, then reached into his pocket and pulled out a piece of paper.

"Her name is . . . Janelle Wellington," he said.

"Janelle Wellington?" Maxine said. "Are you serious? You are looking for Janelle Wellington?"

"Yes," Falcon said. "Oh, maybe my luck is about to improve. It sounds like you know her. Does she work here?"

"Ha, a beautiful classy woman like that would never work in a place like this," Maxine said.

"Why not? You are beautiful and classy," Falcon said.

"Woo hoo! Did you hear that, Wally?" Maxine whooped loudly.

"I heard it. Evidently this cowboy hasn't gotten used to our heat yet. It's cooked his brains," Wally teased, then he ducked a swing from Maxine.

"Are you a bounty hunter, Falcon?" Maxine asked. "Because if you are, and you are looking for Janelle Wellington, I say shame on you."

"Well, I am looking for Miss Wellington," Falcon said. "But I'm not a bounty hunter, and I'm not looking for her for the law. Her parents sent me out here to look for her."

"Her parents, you say?"

"Yes."

"In that case, I wish you good luck, and hope you can find her before the marshal does."

"From your comment a few moments ago, I take it you don't like the marshal," Falcon said.

"What is there that anyone can like about him? I think he is a liar and a thief," she replied.

"Maxine," Wally cautioned again. "I'd be careful if I were you. It wouldn't be too smart for the marshal to know how you feel."

"I don't care," Maxine said. "There's no doubt in my mind but that he stole the gold from poor old Ben. And probably his map, too."

"Map?" Falcon asked, picking up on the reference.

"We don't even know that there was a map," Wally said.

"Oh, there was a map all right," Maxine said. "I

believe Ben found the Lost Dutchman. Where else would he have gotten all that gold?"

"Who are you talking about?"

"Ben Hanlon," Maxine said. "He was a delightful old man who—"

Wally interrupted her with a laugh. "Delightful? Come on, Maxine, if he hadn't had all that gold and money, you wouldn't have had anything to do with him."

"I suppose that is true," Maxine said. "But that's only because if he hadn't had all that gold and money he would have never come in here in the first place."

"What happened to him?"

"He left to—uh—use the privy, and he never came back in," Maxine said.

"We thought he had gone out somewhere and passed out. But we learned the next day that Deputies Forbis and Appleby found him out back. They took him to jail."

"Why?"

"I think they just thought he was some old bum, passed out drunk in the alley. Most of the time when they find someone like that, they just take him into the jail to let him sleep it off."

"He didn't sleep it off?"

"Deputy Forbis found him dead the next morning," Wally said.

"I wouldn't be surprised if Cairns didn't kill him for his map."

"Careful, Maxine," Wally said.

"Why do I need to be careful? There's nobody here who is going to say anything to Cairns."

"What map?" Falcon asked. The conversation was beginning to get productive for him, but he didn't want to push it too far, too fast.

"It is supposed to be a map to the location of the Lost Dutchman mine. Only Ben didn't have the map, because he told us he left it with Mr. Montgomery and—oh my!" she suddenly said. "Wally, I just figured this out! Miss Wellington didn't kill Mr. Montgomery. Marshal Cairns did! He killed Montgomery to get old Ben's map."

"You don't know that, Maxine. You are just speculating, and it is dangerous speculation," Wally said sharply. "I don't want you saying any such thing in here about it. I don't know about you, but I don't think I would like having Cairns mad at me. Especially if what you are saying is true. He would not be the kind of man you want against you."

"It may not be any of my business, especially seeing as I am such a recent arrival," Falcon said, "but if nobody likes this marshal—and nobody I have spoken to so far does like him—why don't you take the next logical step and get rid of him?"

"How? He wasn't voted into office, he was appointed by the city council. They are the only ones who can hire a city marshal, and they are the only ones who can fire him."

"Then why don't you go to the city council?" Falcon asked.

"Ha!" Wally said. "Cairns has the city council so afraid they ain't goin' to do a damn thing."

* * *

Drumm was leaning back in his chair with his feet up on his desk when Luke Mueller came in.

"Is it true?" Mueller asked.

"What the hell are you doing here?" Drumm asked. "I thought you were gone."

"Is it true that the old coot had a map to a gold mine?" Mueller asked. "I mean a real map."

"I don't know. Why are you asking?"

"Because if the map is real, I know where it is."

Drumm took his feet down from the desk, then sat up straight. "Where is it?"

Mueller grinned. "I'll be damned. It is real, isn't it?"

"Where is it?" Drumm repeated.

"A man named Joe Henry has it."

"Joe Henry?"

"Yeah, do you know him?"

"No, I don't know him," Drumm said.

"Terry Cooper told me that this feller, Joe Henry, has the map.

"Terry Cooper? Are you talking about the Cooper who works for Housewright?"

"Yeah, that Cooper. Me'n him become pards when I was workin' down at the livery. Before you run me out of town."

"I did that for your own good," Drumm said. "Remember, you killed the old prospector."

Mueller shook his head. "No, I hit him over the head and I robbed him, all right. But I didn't kill him. I think you killed him after you learned about the map."

"Are you going to tell me where the map is, or not?"

"That depends on whether or not I decide to let you in on my deal," Mueller said.

"What do you mean, let me in on your deal?" Drumm replied sharply. "This is my deal, not yours."

"All right, you find the map yourself," Mueller said. Turning, he started to walk out of the office.

"Wait," Drumm called. "Okay, what is the deal?"

"First, let me ask you something. Did you kill Montgomery for the gold map?"

"Why do you need to know that?"

"Because if you did, it will prove that the person who claims to have the map, really does. Cooper said Joe Henry is a friend of the woman you are looking for. According to him, the woman watched you shoot Montgomery. Only you and the woman know the real truth. If you really did shoot him, that means Joe Henry knows what he's talkin' about, which means he really does have the map.

"Yes, I shot the son of a bitch for the map, but he didn't have it."

"Ha! I thought so. He did have it, you just didn't know where it was. Cooper told me Joe Henry said Montgomery had taped it behind a picture, and he told the woman where to find it, just before he died."

"I *knew* it was in back of that picture," Drumm said, hitting the palm of his hand with his fist. "I checked and saw a little piece of paper still sticking there. Damn it, I knew it. Now the woman really does have it."

"No, she don't," Mueller replied.

"What do you mean, she don't?"

"Like I told you, she give it to this feller, Joe Henry."

"Where is Joe Henry now?"

"According to Cooper, he's out looking for the gold."

"Then we have to get the map from him, don't we?"

"We?"

"You and me. Partners again."

"No. We are going to need Cooper to lead us to Joe Henry."

"If we take Cooper, we're going to take Bert Appleby."

"Appleby? Why do we need him? I never did like that son of a bitch and you know it."

"Yeah, I know it. That's why I want him with me. You've got Cooper with you, I want Appleby with me, to keep it even," Drumm replied.

"All right, get your deputy and let's go," Mueller said.

"Now?"

"If you want to be a part of it, yes, we leave now. Cooper is waiting for us, just outside of town."

"You go on. I'll have to find Appleby."

"Don't wait too long, or we'll leave without you," Mueller said.

Deputy Forbis walked into the Boar's Head Saloon.

"Watch what you're sayin'," Wally said to Maxine. "Deputy Forbis is here."

"Heck, I'm not worried about Deputy Forbis," Maxine said. "He's the only decent one of the bunch. I don't think he cares any more for Marshal Cairns than we do." Maxine waved at Forbis and motioned for him to come over.

"Mr. MacCallister," Forbis said as he joined them at the table. "We meet again."

"You two know each other?" Maxine asked, surprised by Forbis's words.

"No, we met for the first time this morning, when Mr. MacCallister killed Corey Minner," Forbis said.

"MacCallister is not in any trouble is he, John?"

"No. Half a dozen witnesses gave statements saying it was self-defense." He laughed. "Hell, I told Cairns he should give Mr. MacCallister a medal. I don't think there is anyone in Maricopa County who is sorry to see the son of a bitch dead."

"I think you are right," Maxine said. "Wally barred him from going upstairs with any of the girls a long time ago. He used to beat on the girls sometimes." She shuddered. "Thank goodness, I never had anything to do with him."

"Listen, have you seen either Marshal Cairns or Deputy Appleby lately?" Deputy Forbis asked.

"No, why? What are they doing now?"

"That's just it. I don't have any idea what they are doing. Or where they are. They seem to have disappeared."

"Having the two biggest bastards in Phoenix out of town is a problem because?" Maxine asked, with a laugh.

Forbis laughed as well. "I guess it's not really a problem. It's just curious, though. They don't normally wander off like that, at least not both of them at the same time."

"Maxine tells me you are the one who found the old prospector," Falcon said.

"Yes, sir, I found him."

"And he died the next morning?"

"Yeah. Cairns told me to wake him up and let him go, but when I went over to him, I found him dead, with blood all over the bed."

"Was he bleeding badly when you first found him?" Falcon asked.

"No, he wasn't. I guess the wound must have opened up again during the night. What I'm upset about now is his mule."

"His mule? What about his mule?"

"We've been keeping his mule in the stable behind the jail, but Cairns says he doesn't want to be out the money it takes to feed it. He wants me to put her down. I hate to do that. I mean she's a gentle natured soul. It just doesn't seem right to shoot her. That's the reason I'm looking for Cairns. I'm going to try and talk him out of it."

"You think you'll have any luck in talking him out of it?" Falcon asked.

"The truth?" Forbis shook his head. "I doubt it."

"What if I took the mule off your hands?"

"Took her off my hands for what reason?"

"To keep her alive."

"You'd do that?"

"Yes, I'll take her."

"Her name is Rhoda. I know that, because when we picked the old man up, he kept asking about Rhoda." Forbis laughed. "At first, I thought he was talking about a woman, but it was his mule. So, you would take her, huh?"

"Yes."

"What do you plan to do with her? I know you said keep her alive, but how?"

"I have a ranch up in Colorado. I would probably just turn her out to pasture and let her live out the rest of her life in peace."

"Mr. MacCallister, that is a very noble thing for you to do," Forbis said.

"How soon can I pick her up?"

"You can have her as soon as you want. Now, if you'd like."

Falcon stood, then nodded his head toward Maxine. "Maxine, it has been a delight meeting you," he said.

"Same here, cowboy," Maxine replied. "You are welcome back, anytime."

As Falcon left the saloon with Deputy Forbis, a plan began forming in his mind, and the old prospector's mule was part of it.

Chapter Twenty-five

Just as he thought she would, Rhoda led Falcon straight to the area where the old prospector had been camping. The first thing Falcon found was Hanlon's quick claim.

> This heer claim is made by me, Ben Hanlon. I found, and heerby clame all the gold that is within five hunnert yards of this spot.

> This quick clame will be leegle until I can make a clame at the rekorders office.

There were few people anywhere who could read sign as well as Falcon, and within half an hour he could have written a report about Hanlon's time there. He found depressions in the ground where Hanlon had thrown out his bedroll, he found bones and seeds from his meals, and feces from his toilet. He also found areas where Ben Hanlon had been using his shovel and pickax in his quest for gold.

Falcon saw indications that Hanlon had climbed up the side of the mountain and was about to explore there when he heard sharp, flat, echoless reports of gunfire. Without an echo, he was able to determine the direction from which the gunfire was coming, and did something he had been doing from the time he was a very young man.

Swinging into the saddle and drawing his pistol, he rode to the sound of battle. When he reached the top of a small rise, he saw a single rider being chased and shot at by four others. The single rider was making no effort to return fire.

The situation would have been dire except the person being chased was an excellent rider. He was riding the horse at a full gallop, expertly maneuvering around the mesquite, cholla, and saguaro, as well as the occasional boulders and rifts that cut across the desert floor. At one point the horse seemed to take wings as it cleared a wide draw, providing the rider with a brief advantage. None of the pursuing horses were able to make the jump. The riders had to pull them to a halt, navigate down one side, across, and up the other side.

Falcon took the opportunity to show himself, and as he did, he recognized the fleeing rider. He shouted, "Joe! Joe Henry! Come this way!"

For a moment, Janelle didn't react to the call. She didn't know whether or not it was a trap. Once she recognized the one who had called, she guided Prince John toward him, with a huge sense of relief.

"This way!" Falcon hollered. "There is a natural fortress of rocks where we can hold them off!"

As the two rode toward the rock formation Falcon had chosen, he was once again impressed with the skill of the young rider. Lightning and the other horse matched each other stride for stride, until Falcon signaled for them to stop.

"Do you have a gun?" he shouted.

"No!"

"Get over behind those rocks!"

Janelle dismounted and ran in the direction Falcon pointed.

Sliding down from his horse, he snaked his rifle from its saddle sheath, then slapped both horses on their rumps, sending them out of harm's way. He darted to the rocks where Janelle was sitting with her arms wrapped around her knees. The pursuers were still shooting, the bullets whistling through the air. Falcon handed over his pistol.

"Shoot back!" he shouted. "Give them something to worry about!"

"I don't know how."

"What do you mean you don't know how?"

"I've never shot a gun before."

"All right. Just keep your head down," Falcon said. "It's too bad you can't shoot as well as you can ride." Rising up above the rocks he fired, and one of the pursuers tumbled from the saddle.

* * *

Drumm held up his hand to bring the others to a stop behind some boulders. "Hold it! Hold it! We can't ride up on 'em like this," he said. "We're goin' to have to move up on 'em slow."

"Son of a bitch!" Mueller shouted. "Did you see who that was? That was Falcon MacCallister!"

"Yeah," Drumm said. He looked back toward the place where the rider had fallen. "Looks like Appleby is done for."

"Yeah, well, I never liked the son of a bitch anyway," Mueller said. "I'm just wondering what MacCallister is doing out here."

"Looks to me like he's going after the gold," Drumm said.

"So, what do we do now?" Mueller asked.

"What do you mean what do we do now? This was your deal, remember?"

"Cooper, get over there behind that rock. See if you can get a shot at him," Mueller said.

Cooper dismounted and started toward the rock, but a single shot brought him down.

"Damn, Appleby and Cooper are both gone. We'd better get out of here," Drumm said.

"And leave the gold?"

"What gold?" Drumm replied. "We don't even know for sure if this Joe Henry has the map. I don't intend to get myself killed trying to find out."

"I want MacCallister dead," Mueller said.

"Good for you. I want me alive more than I

want MacCallister dead. I'm leaving. If you want to stay and face MacCallister, you go ahead."

"All right, all right, I'm comin' with you," Mueller said.

"Maybe you aren't as dumb as I thought."

Half an hour later, Falcon and Joe Henry were still well covered behind the rocks. No shots had been fired in a while. Falcon raised up a bit to look in the direction from which the fire had been coming.

"I think they are gone," he said.

"What if they aren't?"

"I'm pretty sure they are," Falcon said. "There are only two of them left, there are two of us, and we are well positioned. They no longer have the advantage."

"How can you be sure? They may just be waiting for us to show ourselves."

"I'll go down and look."

"No! Don't leave me up here by myself!"

MacCallister chuckled. "All right, then you come with me."

"You-you want me to come with you?"

"If you don't want to stay here by yourself, you have no choice. You have to come with me," Falcon said.

"Couldn't we both just stay here for a while longer?"

"Look, Joe, you got yourself into this mess, I didn't. They were already shooting at you when I came along, remember?"

"Yes. Yes, you are right. All right, I'll come with you."

"First give me the pistol," Falcon said, holding out his hand.

"Why?"

"The way you are holding it, you are going to wind up shooting yourself with it. Or me."

Falcon retrieved the pistol then, holding it in his right hand and his rifle in his left, moved out from behind the rocks. "Stay behind me."

"Don't worry about that. I'll be right behind you."

Five minutes later they were standing in the exact spot where their pursuers had been positioned during the gun fight.

"Yeah, it's just as I thought. They're gone," Falcon said, putting his pistol back in its holster.

"Thank you for coming along when you did. I guess this is the second time you've saved my life."

"I guess it is," Falcon said. "So I would say that you owe me now. Wouldn't you?"

"Owe you? Owe you what? I've given you my thanks."

"That's not enough."

"What else do you want?"

"I'm told you are Janelle Wellington's friend. Is that true?"

"Yes, that's true."

"Where is she?"

"Mr. MacCallister, surely you aren't looking for her for the reward money, are you?"

"No, I'm looking for her for her parents."

"Her parents? What about her parents? Has something happened to them?"

"No. But they want me to find Miss Wellington and bring her back."

"How do I know you are telling the truth? How do I know you aren't just trying to find her for the reward?"

Falcon sighed, then pulled a letter from his pocket. "I have this letter for her," he said.

Joe reached for it. "Let me see it."

"I'll let you see the envelope, but not the letter. The letter is for Miss Wellington. Now, if you know where she is, I want you to tell me."

"I'll tell you on one condition," Joe said, and pulled out the map, showing it to Falcon. "I want you to help me find the gold."

"Joe, do you really know Janelle Wellington?"

"Yes, of course I know her. I know her very well. Why would you think otherwise?"

"I have spoken with Mr. and Mrs. Buckner, and they have never heard of you. I spoke with Mrs. Poindexter, and she has never heard of you. They all know Miss Wellington very well. Why is it they have never heard of you?"

"I don't know."

"So I ask you again. Do you really know Janelle Wellington?"

"All right, I'll tell you something she told me, that she has told no one since she arrived. If you know her parents, then you will know that what I am telling you is true. Janelle told me the story of her shame in having a child without being married. She left New York so as not to be an embarrassment to her family."

"That is true. How do you know that?"

"I know it because she told me."

"All right, if she told you that, then I am convinced you do know her. Will you take me to her?"

"I will take you to her, if you will stay with me until I check out this map. Then Janelle and I will split the fortune with you. That way, Janelle will have enough money to go back home."

"She has enough money now," Falcon said. "Her parents gave me enough money to take her back home."

"That may be so, but if you want to find her, you are going to have to stay with me."

Drumm and Mueller had gone about two miles, with Drumm riding in the lead.

"Drumm?" Mueller called.

"Yeah?"

"Turn around. I want you lookin' at me when I kill you," Mueller said.

"What?" Drumm responded, the inflection of his voice rising in fear. When he turned, he saw Mueller pointing his pistol at him.

"I just don't need you no more," Mueller said.

"Mueller, what the hell are you—"

That was as far as Drumm got before the pistol shot cut him off. He fell from the saddle and lay on the desert floor without moving. Mueller rode up to Drumm's horse and took the canteen. Then he turned around, and started back. He was going to kill MacCallister, and he was going to find the gold.

Damn, it was going to be a good day.

Chapter Twenty-six

Falcon and Joe were at least three miles away from the drama that had taken place between Mueller and Drumm, but Falcon heard the shot—flat, and far away.

"Did you hear that?" Falcon asked.

"Did I hear what?"

"That sound just now. It sounded like a gunshot."

"I didn't hear a thing," Joe said.

"Maybe I just imagined it," Falcon said. He knew he had not imagined it, and he knew it was a gunshot, but he didn't press the issue. He sensed that Joe was very nervous, and he needed to keep him as calm as possible.

"Is it always this windy out here?" Joe asked.

"It pretty much is," Falcon said. "I think it has something to do with the heat. It's like the hot air in a balloon that makes it go up. There's no balloon here, but the hot air still goes up, and pulls more air in to replace it."

Joe laughed. "I've never thought of it like that,

but I guess it makes as much sense as anything else."

Falcon and Joe were standing at the foot of Weaver's Needle, looking up at the steep and craggy side of Superstition Mountain. Rhoda the mule stood nearby.

"Let me look at the map again," Falcon said.

Joe handed it to him, and Falcon began studying it.

Map to gold Mine

Follow the salt river til you reech superstishen montan. Find Weevers Nedel, then look at the montan bhind the nedel.

You haf to clum up the side of the montan to find it cuz the hol that gos into the mine can only be seed for a cupel minits in the aftrnun, and only for a cupel days in the erly sumer but evn if you caint see it, dont meen it aint ther caus tis. This heer X is the hol that gos into the mine. You haf to git down on yur belly and skiny thru to git inside wherats the gold.

This heer map was drawd by Ben Hanlon

He looked at the side of the mountain for a long moment, then he smiled. "There it is." He pointed to a spot about four hundred feet up.

"There what is?"

"The opening."

Joe looked where Falcon pointed, then shook his head in confusion. "Either I'm blind, or you are seeing things, because I don't see anything that looks like an opening up there."

"You have to know what to look for," Falcon explained. "Look, see the color of the side of the mountain?"

"Yes, it's red. Well, mostly red. Some of it is brown or yellow."

"Right. Now, do you see how it gradually goes from yellow to red, and how the red deepens as you go up?"

"Yes."

"Except right there—he pointed again—right there is a tiny spot that is a deeper red than the rest of the mountain. Do you see it?"

"Yes, I do!"

"That's where the opening is."

"There's no opening there. Do you see a hole?"

"No. The actual opening is hidden by shadows. But there is a very slight difference in the shadows and color right there, and that is where Hanlon said the opening is."

"Hanlon also said you can only see it at certain times."

"You can only see the actual opening at certain times, but if you know how to look, you can see where it is, all the time."

"And you know how to look?"

"Yes."

"All right, I'll take your word for it."

"Are you ready for a climb? Or do you want to stay down here?"

"No, I'm ready to climb," Joe said.

Falcon walked over to Lightning and retrieved his lariat. Making a double tie around his waist, he laid out about ten feet of rope, then double tied it around Joe's waist.

"What's that for?" Joe asked.

"As we go up, I will be going up first, finding the best way to climb. You'll be coming up right behind me, so pay close attention. If you fall, this rope will allow me to stop your fall. It will either save you— or it will pull both of us down."

"That's a pleasant thought," Joe said.

"Yes, well, if you fall, give out a yell so I can brace myself," Falcon said.

"What if you fall?" Joe asked. "If you fall, you are just out of luck, because there is no way I can stop you."

Falcon chuckled. "If I fall, we are both out of luck. So maybe I should just be very careful."

"Good idea," Joe agreed.

Falcon started up the mount, then looked back at Joe. "Are you ready?" he asked.

Joe gave a resolute nod. "I'm ready."

The mountain was very steep. The climb was slow and hard. Falcon's cowboy boots slid in the dry, rocky dirt. It was an intricate task to find secure spots to place his feet, keeping in mind the person behind him was not nearly as strong, and had a much shorter stride. At one point he came to a particularly precipitous section and he knew Joe would not be able to negotiate that stretch on his own.

"Joe!" he called down.

"Yes?"

"Stay where you are, and give me as much rope as possible."

"All right," Joe answered in a voice that reflected fear and uncertainty.

Falcon walked around until he found solid footing, then he called back down to Joe. "Grab hold of the rope and hold on. I'm going to help you by pulling you up."

Setting his feet firmly he dug in his heels and began hauling Joe up, pulling on the rope hand over hand. It was easier to pull him up than he anticipated. Falcon doubted that Joe weighed much over 115 pounds.

He pulled him all the way up, then pointed to a place where Joe could plant his feet securely.

"All right, just stay right there until I call back for you," Falcon said.

Joe nodded, but said nothing.

From that point it got considerably easier up to a wide ledge that ran along the wall of the mountain, gradually elevating toward the place where Falcon was sure the opening would be. Once he was secure on the ledge, he backed up against the wall and, as he had before, pulled Joe up to him.

"I could have climbed the last part of it alone," Joe said when Falcon pulled him onto the ledge.

"I know," Falcon said. "But this was a lot faster. It took us less than an hour to get this far. Besides, you don't weigh much more than a half-starved dog. Don't you ever eat?"

"I eat," Joe said defensively.

"Stay as close to the wall as you can," Falcon instructed. "It looks like this ledge will take us all the way to the mouth opening. Remember, if you fall, let me know so I can brace myself."

Joe laughed.

"What is it?"

"Believe me, Mr. MacCallister, if I fall, I will let you know. I will let the whole world know."

Falcon laughed as well. "Yeah, I guess you will at that, won't you?"

"What if you fall?" Joe asked.

"If I fall, it won't matter, will it?" Falcon replied.

With their backs pressed against the wall they continued on until Falcon called to Joe. "There it is," he said. "Hanlon was right, the opening is pretty narrow."

When they reached the opening, Falcon stuck his head and shoulders through and looked around. He was surprised at the amount of light. In addition to the mouth opening, there were three or four smaller openings at the top that let in light. And, once inside, there would be plenty of room to stand.

Falcon rolled over the lip of the opening, then standing inside, he called back to Joe. "Come on in."

Joe appeared in the opening, then rolled through.

They looked around for a moment.

"Where is this big vein of gold that is supposed to be in here?" Joe asked.

"There," Falcon said, pointing to a couple canvas bags. "It's not a vein of gold, but it is gold. It looks like Mr. Hanlon already gathered it up." Both bags were filled with gold-bearing rocks or, in some cases, almost solid gold nuggets.

"Did he dig them out of this cave?" Joe asked. "Where did they come from?"

Falcon shook his head. "Not here," he said. "They were mined somewhere else and moved here."

"Hanlon brought them here?"

"No. I'm sure he found them here. If the story is true, Peralta's mining party probably moved them here for safe keeping until they could get back to retrieve them."

"Yes, I've heard that story," Joe said. "How the Apache attacked the mule train, killed all the Mexican miners, and left the gold."

"It would appear the story is true, and this is some of that gold," Falcon said.

"Not exactly the millions of dollars everyone has been looking for, is it?" Joe asked.

Falcon walked over and hefted the two bags. "No, but I would say there are at least ten or fifteen thousand dollars here," he said. "Certainly enough that you can call yourself a rich man."

"It's not all mine," Joe said. "I promised to split it with Mr. Housewright."

"And Janelle Wellington, I would hope."

"What? Oh, yes, of course. And Janelle Wellington."

"All right, Joe, I've carried out my end of the bargain. It's your turn. Tell me where I can find Janelle Wellington."

"I—" Joe's response was interrupted by the sound of a bullet hitting flesh. His eyes grew wide in shock, fear, and pain, and Falcon saw a shoulder wound begin to gush blood.

"Get down!" Falcon yelled. Tearing off a piece of his own shirt, he stuck it over the wound, then put Joe's hand on it. "Hold it there, tight," he said.

"MacCallister, how does it feel to know you are about to die?" a voice called from outside the cavern.

"Mueller?" Falcon called back.

"Yeah, I'm Mueller. I'll just bet you thought we'd never meet again, didn't you?"

"Where is Marshal Cairns?"

"Cairns?" Mueller replied. He laughed. "His name ain't Cairns, it's Drumm. Egan Drumm. I mean, it *was* Egan Drumm. It ain't nothin' now, 'cause I kilt him. Just like I'm about to kill you."

Mueller fired again, three quick shots, and in so doing made the walls of the cave work for him. The bullets hit the wall, then ricocheted around so each bullet did the work of three.

Falcon knew Mueller had a significant advantage over him. He and Joe Henry were literally trapped inside the small cave, unable to improve their position. Mueller was outside, well covered, armed with a rifle, and with an excellent field of fire.

He fired three more quick shots, the bullets ricocheting from wall to wall. Joe cried out as one more bullet found its mark. Falcon was hit twice, though by the time he was hit, the bullets were nearly spent. He fired back, but it was just to let Mueller know he couldn't come into the cave at will. Falcon knew he had no shot.

"You got yourself in quite a spot, ain't you, MacCallister?" Mueller shouted. "You know the only thing that bothers me? Here I am, about to kill the great Falcon MacCallister, and there ain't no one around to see me do it, so as to tell the story."

Mueller fired four more shots.

"That was just to let you know I got me a whole pocket of bullets," Mueller called out. "And I got me two canteens. I seen that you left your canteens down below. Too bad."

Muller fired three more times, nicking Falcon a little worse than before, bringing blood.

"Mr. MacCallister, if we are going to die in here, there's something I want to tell you," Joe said.

"We're not going to die in here," Falcon said resolutely.

Although the situation was looking bad, Falcon saw what might be a way out. A huge boulder, precariously placed, sat just outside the mouth of the cave. If he could get to it, he might be able to push it far enough and force Mueller to give up his position.

Falcon ran to the boulder, chased by another shot from Mueller.

"Ha!" Mueller called out to him. "You ain't goin' to have any better shot at me from there than you did before."

Falcon began pushing on the boulder.

"Where did you go?" Mueller asked. "You think hidin' behind that big rock is goin' to help you? You can't shoot at me without lookin' around it. That gives me a lot better shot at you, than it does you at me.

Falcon continued to push, and after a gut-busting strain he felt the rock move slightly. He figured the rock weighed at least four or five hundred pounds. If he could get it dislodged, the leverage would be in his favor.

"Ha! You're trapped back there, ain't you MacCallister?" Mueller called. You come out, then get behind that rock, only there ain't no shot, and now you can't get back." Mueller cackled in glee. "Oh, Lord, I'm enjoyin' this!"

With one final heave, Falcon felt the leverage suddenly shift in his favor. The boulder started down so quickly he had to reach back and grab the edge of the opening in order to keep from tumbling with the boulder.

He pulled his pistol and waited to see if the falling boulder would expose Mueller's position. To his surprise it had results beyond his best expectations. The rock knocked into Mueller, pushing him over the edge of the high cliff. As he fell over four hundred feet, his terrified death scream echoed and re-echoed throughout the canyon.

"Mr. MacCallister!" Joe called out. "Mr. MacCallister, are you all right?"

"Yeah, I'm fine!" Falcon replied and he hurried back in to attend to Joe. Like his own nicks, Joe's subsequent wounds were minor, but Falcon was concerned about the first hit—the wound in the shoulder. He ripped open Joe's shirt to get to the bullet. Seeing a woman's perfectly formed breast, he gasped. "Damn!"

"I'm sorry about keeping the secret from you," Joe said. "*I* am Janelle Wellington."

"Why didn't you tell me?"

"I never seemed to find the right time." Janelle replied. She chuckled, even as she winced with pain. "Now seems to be a good time."

New York

The Wellingtons had reserved the entire upper floor of Shoemaker's Dining Salon and were throwing a huge dinner celebration for the family. The event was to welcome back Janelle who was safely at home, and on the mend. Falcon and his brother and sister were there as well.

Janelle, over her original embarrassment and shame, had reclaimed her son and was proudly showing him off to all. At the moment, Rosanna was bouncing him on her knee, and the baby was grinning broadly at her, as a little string of drool escaped from his lips.

Andrew had bought the latest issue of the *New York Times* before coming into the restaurant, and, somewhat detached from the rest of the party, was reading the Entertainment and Amusements page.

"Ah ha!" he suddenly shouted, his outburst interrupting all other conversations and drawing attention to him.

"What is it, Andrew?" Rosanna asked.

"Listen to this. It's the play review from the *New York Times*. "'No stars in the firmament could possibly shine more brightly than the luminance Andrew and Rosanna MacCallister bring to the stage. Long after the nineteenth century has slipped into history, the accolades of these two wondrous players will ring down through the ages.' What do you think of that?" he asked, flipping his hand against the paper.

"Andrew, that is awful!" Rosanna said.

"Awful? What do you mean awful? No stars in the

firmament could possibly shine brighter than us? What is awful about that?"

"Janelle is the guest of honor at this party, and here you are calling attention to yourself. I mean it is awful that you would brag so about it."

"Wait a minute!" Andrew said. "I'm not bragging! I'm merely reading what the *New York Times* reported!"

The others laughed, then Joel tapped on his glass to get everyone's attention. "Ladies and gentlemen, there is another MacCallister I wish to laud tonight. I offer a toast to the man who not only found our daughter, but saved her life, and delivered her safely home to us." Joel held his wineglass out. "To Mr. Falcon MacCallister!"

"Here, here!" Andrew shouted enthusiastically, and everyone around the table lifted their goblets toward Falcon, who responded with a slight nod.

"Janelle, tell us again how much gold you and Mr. MacCallister found." Sue said.

"It came out to a total of eleven thousand, three hundred and twenty-seven dollars and fifty-three cents," Janelle said.

"You should have given it all to Mr. MacCallister," Joel said.

Janelle shook her head. "I couldn't. I had promised half of it to Mr. Housewright. I tried to give half of what was left to Mr. MacCallister, but he wouldn't take it. So I gave the rest of it to Mrs. Montgomery."

"I'm so glad she didn't blame you for her husband's death," Emma Wellington said.

"As it turns out, I wasn't the only one who saw Marshal Cairns, I mean, Egan Drumm, kill Mr.

Montgomery," Janelle said. "Mr. Depro, who worked in the bank, also saw it, but he was too afraid of the marshal to say anything until after the marshal was killed. Then he went to Mr. Forbis, who became the new marshal, and told him everything. By the time I left Phoenix, I was completely cleared."

"Well, I don't understand how anyone could have ever believed such a thing about you, anyway," Emma said pointedly.

"Nobody did believe it, Mrs. Wellington," Falcon said. "I found that out very quickly when I was looking for your daughter. Everyone I talked to, everyone who knew her, or had anything to do with her, was absolutely convinced of her innocence, from Maxine Butrum to Mayor Alsop."

Janelle took a swallow of her wine, but she laughed and sprayed some of it out of her mouth at the mention of the bar girl's name. "Maxine," she repeated.

"Who is Maxine, dear?" Emma asked.

"She is"—Janelle started, then stopped and smiled—"she is a Western lady with a heart of gold. Wouldn't you say so, Mr. MacCallister?"

"Yes," Falcon replied. "I would definitely say so."

"Speaking of gold, Falcon, do you think there really is a lost gold mine on Superstition Mountain?" Andrew asked.

"That gold had to come from somewhere, so yes, I do."

"Do you think it will ever be found?"

"If I find it, I'll let you know," Falcon replied, as he lifted his own glass of wine.

Turn the page for an exciting preview of

SAVAGE GUNS
A Cotton Pickens Novel

By William W. Johnstone, with J. A. Johnstone

Coming in October 2010

Wherever Pinnacle Books are sold

Chapter One

I was mindin' my daily business in the two-holer when I got rudely interrupted. Now I like a little privacy, but I got me a bullet instead. There I was, peacefully studying the female undies in the Montgomery Ward catalog, when this here slug slammed through the door and exited through the rear, above my head.

"Hey!" I yelled, but no one said nothing.

"You out there. Don't you try nothing. This here's the law talking. I'm coming after you."

But I sure didn't know who or what was in the yard behind Belle's roomin' house. I thought maybe a horse was snorting or pawing clay, but I couldn't be sure of it. I wanted to see what was what, but the half-moon that let in fresh air was high up above me, and I had my business to look after just then. You can't do nothing in the middle of business.

I don't know about you, but I wear my hat when I'm in the two-holer, just on general principles. A man should wear a hat in the crapper. That's my motto. It was a peaceful enough morning in the town of Doubtful, in Puma County, Wyoming, where I was sheriff, more or less. So that riled me some—the bullet that slapped through there. It knocked down my good Five-X gray felt beaver Stetson topper, which teetered on the other hole but did not drop. If it had dropped down there, I'd have been plumb peeved.

I thought for a moment I oughta follow that hat through the hole and get my bare bottom down there in the perfumed vault, but that was plum sickening. Besides, how could I slide a hundred fifty pounds of rank male through that little round hole? I don't need no more smell than I've already got. When I pull my boots off, people head for the doors holding their noses. It just wouldn't work. If someone was gonna kill me, they held all the aces.

The truth of it was that I wasn't finished with my business. All I could do was sit there and finish up my private duties, rip a page out of the Monkey Ward catalog, and get it over with. Like the rest of us who used the two-holer behind Belle's boarding-house, I was inclined to study ladies' corsets and bloomers and garters for entertainment, saving the wipe-off for the pages brimming with one-bottom plows, buggy whips, and bedpans. Them others in Belle's boardinghouse, they felt like I did, and no female undie pages ever got torn out of the catalog. That sure beat corncobs, I'll tell you.

"Sheriff, you come outa there with your hands up and your pants down," someone yelled. I thought maybe I knew the feller doin' all that yelling but it was hard to tell, sitting there with pages of chemises and petticoats on my lap.

"Hold your horses," I said. "I ain't done, and the longer it takes, the better for you, because I'm likely to bust out of here with lead flying in all directions."

That fetched me a nasty laugh. I knew that laugh and thought maybe I was in more of a jam than I'd imagined.

But no more bullets came sailing through. I finished up, ripped out a page of men's union suits and another page of hay rakes and spades, and got it over with. I wasn't gonna bust out of there with my pants down, no matter what, so I stood, got myself arranged and buttoned up. I drew out my service revolver, and with a violent shove, threw myself out the door and dodged to the left to avoid any incoming lead.

It sure didn't do me no good. As my mama used to tell me, don't do nothing foolish.

Sure enough, there before me were eight or nine ratty-assed cowboys on horses, all of the lot waving black revolvers in my direction, just in case I got notions. And a dude with a buckboard, holding some reins.

"I shoulda known," I said to the boss, who was the man I figgered it was.

"I told you to come out with your pants down,

and you didn't. That's a hanging offense," the man said. "You do what I say, and when I say it."

"My pants is staying put, dammit," I replied.

I knew the joker, all right. I'd put his renegade boy in my jail a few months earlier, and the punk was peering at the blue skies through iron bars. This feller on a shiny red horse waving nickel-plated Smith and Wesson at me was none other than Admiral Bragg. The boy I was boardin' in my lockup, he was King Bragg, and his sister, she was Queen Bragg. Mighty strange names bloomed in that family, but who was I to howl? I sure didn't ask to have Cotton hung on me, and Pickens neither, but that's how I got stuck, and there wasn't nothing I could do about it except maybe move to Argentina or Bulgaria.

Them names weren't titles, neither. Bragg's ma and pa, they stuck him with the name of Admiral. If he'd have been in the navy he might have ended up Admiral Admiral Bragg. But the family stuck to its notions, and old Bragg, he named one child King and the other child Queen. It was King Bragg that got himself into big trouble, perforating a few fellers with his six-gun, so I caught him and he would soon pay for his killin' spree. I think the family was all cheaters. Name a boy King, and the boy's got a head start, even if he ain't even close to being an admiral. Name a girl Queen, and she's got the world bowin' and scrapin' even if she ain't one.

I was a little nervous, standing there in front of his pa with a bunch of Bragg cowboys pointing their artillery at my chest. Makes a man cautious, I'd say.

"Drop the pea-shooter, Sheriff," Admiral Bragg ordered.

I thought maybe to lift it up and blow him away, which would have been my last earthy deed. It sure was temptin' and my old pa, he might've approved even as he lowered the coffin. Nothing like goin' out in style.

But there was about a thousand grains of lead pointing straight at me, and I chickened out. I set her down real slow, itching to pull a trick or two on those rannies. I sure was mad at myself for not spitting a few lead pills before I got turned into Swiss cheese. It just put me out of sorts, but I figured at least I was alive to get my revenge another day. So I set her down slow.

"Now you get into the buckboard, Sheriff," said Admiral Bragg. "We're taking you for a little ride."

I got in, sat next to the old fart who held the reins. I knew the feller, old and daft, with a left-crick in his neck that some said was from a botched hanging. He spat, which I took for a welcome, so I settled in beside him. There was still about a thousand grains of lead aimed at me, so I sat there and smiled at those gents.

The old feller slapped rein over the croup of the dray horse, and we clopped away from there, heading down the two-rut road out of Doubtful in the general direction of the Bragg ranch. I sort of had a hunch what it was about and wasn't too comfortable thinkin' about it.

Bragg was one of the biggest stockmen around Doubtful. He had a spread up in the hills north of town that just didn't quit, and took a week with a couple of spare Sundays to ride across. He called it the Anchor Ranch, and it sure did anchor a lot of turf. He controlled as much public land as anyone in the West, and had an army of gunslicks to pin it all down, given that it wasn't his turf but belonged to Uncle Sam.

I guess that wasn't so bad; he raised a lot of beef and his men kept the saloons going in Doubtful. Admiral was a tough bird, all right, but I didn't have no occasion to throw him into the iron-barred cage in the sheriff's office, so I pretty much ignored him and he ignored me.

I didn't like the way that buckboard was surrounded by his gunslicks and we was headin' out of town, me a little bit against my will. But the bores of all them pieces aimed my way kept me from doing much complainin' about all that.

Old Admiral, perched on that shiny red horse, he ignored me, so I didn't have a notion what this was all about or how it would end. Or maybe I did. All this here stuff had to do with that scummy son of his, King Bragg, who grew up twisted and bad, and got himself into big trouble. From the moment King was big enough to wave a Colt six-gun around, he was doing it, shooting songbirds and bumblebees and gophers and snakes. It must have been a trial for old Admiral to keep that boy in cartridges, because that's about all that King did. He got mighty fine at it, too, and could shoot better and faster than anyone, myself included. He could put a bullet through the edge of the ace of spades and cut that card in two.

Well, that kid, soon as he was big enough to ride

into town on his own, without his ma or pa, was
bent on showing the good citizens of Doubtful who
was who. It wasn't lost on that boy that his pa was
the biggest rancher in those parts, and maybe the
biggest cattleman in the Territory, if not the whole
bloomin' West.

He was also fast. Throw a bottle or a can or a
silver dollar into the skies, and King would perfo-
rate it. He could pretty near sign his name with
bullet holes in a tomato can. I had to chase the kid
out of a few saloons because he was only fifteen or
so, and he didn't take kindly to it, but that was all
the trouble I had, until the day he turned eighteen.

He come into Doubtful that day, few months ago,
on his shiny black stallion, wearing a brace of
double-action Colts, a birthday gift from his old
man. I didn't pay no attention, but maybe I should
have. I was busy with all that paperwork the Territory wants all the time, full of words I never heard
tell of. I don't lay any claim to being more than
fifth-grade schooled, so sometimes I got to get
someone who's got more smarts to tell me what's
what. But I make up for it by being friendly and en-
forcing the law pretty good.

Anyway, King Bragg tied his horse up on saloon
row—five drinkin' parlors side by side on the east
end of town, catering to the cowboys, ranchers, and
wanderers coming in on the pike heading toward
Laramie—and wandered into the Last Chance
wearing his new artillery. I wasn't aware of it, or I'd
have kicked his ass out. He's too young to hoist a
few shots of redeye, and I'd have turned the brat

over my knee and paddled his butt for pretendin' to be all growed up.

Well, next I knew, there was a ruckus, a bunch of shots to be exact, and I popped out of my office and hustled over to saloon row. There's a mess of shouting from the Last Chance, so I hurry over there and it was plain awful. There were three dead cowboys sprawled on the sawdust, leakin' blood. A few fellers were trying to stanch the flow some, but it was hopeless. That threesome finished up their dying while I watched, and then people were just staring at one another. King Bragg was sitting in the sawdust, his emptied revolver in his hand. The barkeep, he was starin' over the bar, and them cowboys in there, they were staring at the dead ones, and there's me, law and order, staring at the whole lot, wondering who did what to who, and why. It wasn't a very fine moment.

Well, I asked them cowboys a few questions and then pinched the kid, took him in and locked him up. Got him tried by Judge Nippers, who told the jury the kid was guilty as hell, and sentenced him to hang by the neck until dead. Doubtful, Wyoming, was going to see a hanging in just two weeks. In fact, I'd just hired Lemuel Clegg and his boys to build me a gallows and charge it to Puma County. Meanwhile, the Bragg family lawyer was screechin' and hollerin', but it didn't do no good. That punk killer, King Bragg, was going to swing in a few days and there was nothing I could do about it. Me, I'm all for justice, and with all them dead cowboys lying around, I'm thinkin' it ought to be sooner, but all that was up to Judge Nippers.

I sorta thought maybe the ride with Admiral Bragg was connected to that, but I don't take no credit for smart thinking. Whatever the case, I was being transported by a rattling old buckboard out of town by some pretty mean-lookin' fellers with a lot of .45 caliber barrels poking straight at me, so I didn't feel none too comfortable.

"What's this here all about, Admiral?" I asked.

But that wax-haired, comb-bearded blue-eyed snake wasn't talking. He was just leading that there procession out of Doubtful, with me in the middle. I sure was getting curious. But I didn't have to wait too long. About two miles out of Doubtful, right where a bunch of cottonwoods crowded the creek, they were steering toward a big old tree, with a mighty thick limb pokin' straight out. Hanging from that limb was a noose.

Chapter Two

I sure didn't like the looks of that noose. That thing was just danglin' there, swaying in the breeze. That rope, it was thick as a hawser, and coiled around the way them hangmen do it. Like some one done it that had done it a few times and knew what to do.

Them cowboys and gunslicks was uncommon quiet as we rode toward that big cottonwood, which was in spring leaf and real pretty for May. But I wasn't paying attention to that. All I was seein' was that damned noose waiting there for some neck. I was starting to have a notion of whose neck it was waiting for, and that didn't sit well with my belly. I sure wasn't a happy sheriff, I'll tell you.

It got worse. That old goat driving the buck board headed straight to that noose, and when it was plain dangling in my face, he whoaed the nag and there it was, that big hemp noose right there in front of me. None of them slicks was saying a word, and none of them had put away their ar tillery, neither. I knew a few of them. There was

Big Nose George, and Alvin Ream, and Smiley
Thistlethwaite, and Spitting Sam. They didn't
think twice about putting a little lead into anything
alive. You had to wonder why Bragg kept those
bozos around. Times were peaceful enough.

"Admiral, this ain't a good idea," I said.

He laughed softly. You ever hear a man laugh
like that, like he was enjoying your fate? Well, it's
not something a person forgets, a laugh like that.

"I'm the law, Admiral, and you'd better think
twice."

I was thinkin' maybe I'd go down fighting, but
before I could think longer, that old boy beside me
wrapped his knobby old arm around me, and one
of them slicks grabbed my hands, yanked them
behind me, and wrapped them in thong until my
arms were trussed up tighter than a fat lady's
corset. Me, I'm not even thirty and had a lot of
juice in me still. I wrestled with them fellers but it
was like kicking a cast-iron stove. They knew what
they was up to, and had me cold.

I began thinking them spring leaves coming out
on the cottonwood would be about the last pretty
thing I'd ever see. I don't rightly know why I kept
that sheriff job but I had. I sorta liked the fun of it,
and I was never one to dodge a little trouble. I
kinda thought one of my deputies might be hunting for me, but I was just being foolish. Them
fellers slept late and played cribbage or euchre half
the night in the jailhouse.

I didn't need any explanations. Admiral Bragg,
he was getting even with me. Hang that boy, hang
me. There wasn't no point in asking a bunch of

questions, and no point in trying to talk him out of it. The hard, belly-grabbing truth was that this thing was gonna happen and there wasn't no way I could jabber and slobber my way out of it.

But I wasn't dwelling on it. I was eying the bright blue sky, and hearing some red-winged blackbirds making a racket down on the creek, feeling good mountain air filling my lungs, thinkin' of my ma and pa, and how they brought me into the world and raised me up.

I writhed some, but there was a passel of them around me in the buckboard. Strong hands pinned me while one of them slicks pulled off my Five-X gray beaver hat and dropped that big, scratchy noose right over my neck. It was the first time I ever felt a noose and it wasn't a very good feeling. It was just a big, cold, scratchy twisted rope, and it rested on my shoulders. One of them slicks tugged it pretty tight, and tipped it off to the side a little so as to break my neck.

I was standin' there in that buckboard with a noose drawn tight on my young neck, and all trussed up. They backed off and left me standing there, my knees knockin' and waiting for the final, entire, no-return end. I wondered if Admiral Bragg was gonna preach at me some, tell me it was his brand of justice, or whatnot, but he didn't. He just nodded.

That old knobby-armed geezer, he settled down in the wooden seat of the buckboard, me standing in the bed, and then he let loose with his whip. He smacked the dray right across the croup, and away it went, jerking me plumb off my pins as the wagon got yanked out from under me. I tumbled past the wagon and started down, feelin' that hemp yank hard at my neck and jerk my head back. Then I felt myself topple to the ground, and couldn't figure what happened. I wasn't dead yet. Maybe it was just the last gasp. I banged myself up some, hitting that dirt so hard, landing on a cottonwood root. I was really hurtin' and that noose was as tight as a neck-tie at a funeral. Pretty quick I was starin' up at the sky, seein' lots of blue and the pale green of them cottonwood leaves.

"Now you know what a hanging is," Admiral said.

That was the dumbest thing ever got said to me.

They rolled me over and cut that thong that had me tied up like some beef basting on a spit. I felt some blood return to my wrists and hands, and I flexed my fingers, discovering they was alive, all ten, or eleven, or whatever I got. They loosened that scratchy hemp and pulled that thing loose and tossed it aside. One of them slicks even slapped my Five-X gray beaver Stetson down on my head. Then they let me stand up, even if my legs was trembling like a virgin in a cathouse.

I couldn't think of nothing to do, so I slugged Admiral—one gut-punch and a roundhouse to his jaw. He staggered back as my boot landed on his shin.

That might not have been too smart, but it sure was satisfying. He let out a yelp and in about two seconds half of them slicks was pulling me off and holding me down. I figured they'd just string me up for certain, and make no mistakes, but Admiral, he got up, dusted off his hat, wiped some blood off his lip, and smiled.

It sure was getting strange.

All them slicks let go of me. I was of a mind to arrest the bunch for manhandling a lawman, but the odds weren't good. I never got a handle on arithmetic, and took long division over a few times, but I know bad odds when I see them.

Admiral Bragg, he spat a little more blood, and nodded.

That old knobby-armed geezer, he fetched that hemp rope and brought her over to me, but he wasn't showing me the noose end. I was more familiar with that end than I even wanted to be. No, he showed me the other end, which had been razored across, clean as can be, save for one little strand that sort of wobbled in the morning breeze. I hated that strand; it pretty near did me in.

They'd cut that rope, and I sure wondered why. The whole deal was to scare the bejabbers out of me, and it sure as hell did.

"King won't be so lucky," Admiral Bragg said.

"No, but neither was them three he killed."

"He didn't kill them."

"I saw them three lying in the sawdust. Every last one a cowboy with the T-Bar Ranch."

"You jumped to conclusions."

"There was the barkeep and two others, saying King Bragg done it. They testified in court to it."

"You've got two weeks to prove that he didn't do it. Next time, the rope won't be cut."

"You tellin' me to undo justice?"

"I'm telling you, my boy didn't do it, and you're going to spring him."

"That boy's guilty as hell, and he's gonna pay for it."

Admiral Bragg, he scowled. "I'm not going to argue with you. If you're too dumb to see it, then you'll hang."

Me, I just stared at the man. There was no talkin' to him.

"Get in the wagon, or walk," Bragg said. "I'm done talking."

I favored the ride. I still was a little weak on my pins. I climbed aboard next to the geezer, and the buckboard rattled back to town, surrounded by Bragg and his gunslicks and cowboys. They took me straight to Belle's rooming house. I got out and they rode off.

The morning was still young. I'd already been hanged and told I'd be hanged again. It sure was a tough start on a nice spring day.

I looked at them cottonwoods around town and saw that they were budding out. The town of Doubtful was about as quiet as little towns get. I didn't feel like doing nothing except go lie down, but instead, I made myself hike to Courthouse Square, where the sheriff's office was, along with the local lockup.

Bragg made me mad, tellin' me I was too dumb to see what was what.

Doubtful was doing its usual trade. There was a few ranch wagons parked at George Waller's emporium, and a few saddle horses tied to hitch rails. A playful little spring breeze, with an edge of cold on it, seemed to coil through town. It sure was nicer than the hot summers that sometimes roasted northern Wyoming. I was uncommonly glad to be alive, even if my knees wobbled a little. I smiled at folks and they smiled at me.

At the courthouse, which baked in the sun, I made my way into the sheriff's office. Sure enough, my undersheriff, Dusty, was parked there, his boots up on a desk.

"Where you been?" he asked.

"Getting myself hanged," I said.

Dusty, he smiled crookedly. "That's rich."

I didn't argue. Dusty wouldn't believe it even if I swore to it on a stack of King James bibles.

"You fed the prisoner?"

"Yeah, I picked up some flapjacks at Ma Ginger's. He complained some, but I suppose someone with two weeks on his string got a right to."

"What did he complain about?"

"The flapjacks wasn't cooked through, all dough."

"He's probably right," I said. "Ma Ginger gets it wrong most of the time."

"Serves him right," Dusty said.

"You empty his bucket?"

"You sure stick it to me, don't ya?"

"Somebody's got to do it. I'll do it."

Dusty smiled. "Knew you would if you got pushed into it."

I grabbed the big iron key off the peg and hung my gunbelt on the same peg. It wasn't bright to go back there armed. King Bragg was the only prisoner we had at the moment, but I wasn't one to take chances. I opened up on the gloomy jail, lit only by a small barred window at the end of the front

corridor. Three cells opened onto the corridor.
King was kept in the farthest one.

He was lyin' on his bunk, which was a metal shelf
with a blanket on it. The Puma County lockup
wasn't no comfort palace. King's bucket stank.

"You want to push that through the food gate
there?" I asked.

"Maybe I should just throw it in your face."

"I imagine you could do that."

He sprang off the metal bunk, grabbed the bucket,
and eased it through the porthole, no trouble.

"I'll be back. I want to talk," I said.

"Sure, ease your conscience, hanging an innocent man."

I ignored him. He'd been saying that from the
moment I nabbed him. I took his stinking bucket
out to the crapper behind the jail, emptied it,
pumped some well water into it and tossed that,
and brought it back. It still stank; even the metal
stinks after a while. That's how it is in a jailhouse.

I opened the food gate and passed it through.

"Tell me again what happened," I said.

"Why bother?"

"Because your old man hanged me this morning.
And it set me to wondering."

King Bragg wheezed, and then cackled. I sure
didn't like him. He was a muscular punk, young
and full of beans, deep-set eyes that seemed to
mock. He was born to privilege, and he wore it in
his manners, his face, his attitude, and his smirk.

"You don't look hanged," he said, getting smart-
alecky.

I wanted to pulverize his smart-ass lips, but I didn't.

"Guess I'm lying to you about being hanged," I said. "So, go ahead and lie back. Start at the beginning."

The beginning was the middle of February, when King Bragg rode into Doubtful for some serious boozing, and alighted at saloon row.

"You parked that black horse in front of the Last Chance and wandered in," I said, trying to get him started.

"No, I went to the Stockman, then the Sampling Room, and then the Last Chance. Only I don't remember any of that. Last I knew, I took a sip of redeye at the Last Chance. Sammy the barkeep handed it to me, and I don't remember anything else. I couldn't even remember my own name when I came to."

Chapter Three

There's some folks you just don't like. It don't matter how they treat you. It don't matter if they tip their hat to you. If you don't like 'em, that's it. There's no sense gnawing on it. There was no sense dodging my dislike for King Bragg. I don't know where it come from. Maybe it was the way he kept himself groomed. Most fellers, they got two weeks to live, they don't care how they look. But King Bragg, he trimmed up his beard each morning, washed himself right smart, and even washed his duds and hung them to dry. That sure was a puzzle. The young man was keeping up appearances and it didn't make no sense. Not with the hourglass dribbling sand.

He stood quietly on the other side of them iron bars, telling me the same story I'd heard twenty times, and it didn't make any more sense than the first time he spun it. It was just another yarn, maybe concocted with a little help from that lawyer, and it was his official alibi. Actually, it was more a crock than an alibi.

What King Bragg kept sayin' was that he had dozed through the killings, and when he woke up, he was holding his revolver and every shell had been fired. So he'd come awake after his siesta and got told he'd killed three men. And that was all he knew.

Well, that was bull if ever I heard it.

"Maybe you got yourself liquored up real good, got crazy, picked a fight with them T-Bar cowboys, spilled a lot of blood, and got yourself charged with some killings."

That was the official version, the one that had convicted King Bragg of a triple murder. The one that was gonna pop his neck in a few days.

He stared. "I have nothing more to say about it."

"Well I got nothing more to ask you," I said.

"Why are you asking? I've been sentenced, I'm going to hang. Why do you care?"

"Your pa, he asked me to look into it."

"Admiral Bragg doesn't ask anyone for anything. He orders."

"Well, now that's the truth. He sort of ordered me to."

"What did he say?"

"He didn't. He just hauled me out of Belle's crapper and hanged me."

"Now let me get this straight. My father—hanged you?"

"Noose and drop and all."

"I don't suppose you want to explain."

"It sure wasn't the way to make friends with the sheriff, boy."

"You calling me boy? You're hardly older than I am."

"I got the badge. I get to call old men boy if I feel like it."

"So my father, he hanged you?"

"Complete and total. And when I'm done here, I'll going to haul his ass to this here jail and throw away the key."

King Bragg laughed. "Good luck, pal."

He headed over to his sheet metal bunk, flopped down on it, and drew up that raggedy blanket. Me, I was satisfied. That feller wasn't gonna weasel out of a hanging with that cock and bull story. As for me, I was ready to hang him whether I liked him or not, because that was justice. A man shoots three fellers for no good reason, and he pays the price. I'd just have to deal with Admiral Bragg one way or the other. Now I'd talked with the boy to check his story and nothing had changed.

I didn't much like the thought of pulling the lever, but it would be my job to do it. They made me sheriff, and I was stuck with it. I could quit and let someone else pull the lever that would drop King Bragg from this life. But I figure if a man's gonna be a man, he's got to do the hard things and not run away. So when the time comes, I'll pull the lever and watch King drop. Still, it sure made me wonder whether I wanted to be a lawman. It was more fun being young and getting into trouble. I was still young, but this wasn't the kind of trouble I was itching for. My ma used to warn me I had the trouble itch. If there was trouble somewhere, I'd be in the middle of it. Pa, he just said keep your head down. Heads is what get shot.

I thought I'd ask a few more questions, just to satisfy myself that King Bragg done it, and his ol' man was being pigheaded, more than usual. Admiral Bragg was born pigheaded, and sometime it would do him in.

Sheriff business wasn't really up my alley. It took someone with more upstairs than I ever had to ask the right questions. I could shoot fast and true, but that didn't mean my thinkin' was all that fast. There was a feller I wanted to jabber with about it, the barkeep over to the Last Chance Saloon, Sammy Upward. That was his sworn-out legal monicker. Upward. It sure beat Downward.

The Last Chance was actually the first bar you hit coming into town, or the last one if you were ridin' out. That made it a little wilder than them other watering places. The rannies riding in, they headed for the first oasis they could find. It didn't matter none that it charged a nickel more for redeye, fifteen cents instead of a dime, and two cents more, twelve in all, for a glass of Kessler's ale. It didn't matter none that some of them other joints had serving girls, some of them almost not bad lookin', if you didn't look too close. And it didn't matter none that the other joints were safer, because the managers made customers hang up their gun belts before they could get themselves served. No, the Last Chance was famous for rowdy, for rough, and for mean, and that's why young studs like King Bragg headed there itching for some kind of trouble to find him.

It wasn't yet noon, but maybe Upward would be polishin' the spittoons or something so I rattled the double door, found it unlocked, and found Upward sleeping on the bar. He lay there like a dead fish, but finally come around.

"We ain't open yet, Sheriff," he said.

"I ain't ordering a drink; I'm here for a visit."

"Visits cost same as a drink. Fifteen cents."

He hadn't yet stirred, and was peerin' up at me from atop the bar. That bar was sorta narrow, and he could fall off onto the brass rail in front, or off the back, where he usually worked, and where he had easy access to his sawed-off Greener.

"We're gonna visit, and maybe some day I'll buy one," I said.

"Someone get shot?"

"Not recently."

"I could arrange it if you get bored. If I say the word, someone usually gets shot in this here drinkin' parlor."

He peered up at me. He needed to trim the stubble on his chin, maybe put on a new shirt, and maybe trade in that grimy bartender's apron for something that looked halfway washed.

"Tell me again what you told the court," I said.

"How many times we been through that, Sheriff? I'm tired of talking about it to people got wax in their ears."

"All right, pour me one."

"I knew you'd see it my way, Cotton."

The keep slid off the bar, examined a glass in the dim light, decided it wasn't no dirtier than the rest, and poured some redeye in. The cheapskate poured about half a shot. I dug around in my britches for a dime and handed it to him.

"I owe you a nickel," I said. "Start with King Bragg coming in that night."

He didn't mind, or pretended he didn't.

"Oh, he come in here, and he was already loaded up. I could see by how he weaved when he walked."

"Why'd you serve him?"

"I make my living by quarters and dimes and nickels, damn you, and I'd serve a stumbling drunk if he had the right change. Hell, I'd even serve you, Cotton—even if it made my belly crawl. Just lay the change down, and I'll take it, and that's the whole story."

"You sure are touchy. How come?"

"I'll be just as touchy as I feel like. I'm tired of telling you the story over and over. I ain't gonna tell it to you no more. You heard it, you've tried to pick it apart and you can't. Now finish up and get out. I don't want you in this place. It's bad for business."

Upward was polishin' the bar so hard it was pulling the varnish off.

But I wasn't quitting. "What did King Bragg say to them T-Bar cowboys?"

"He said—oh, go to hell."

"That what he said?"

"No, that's what I'm telling you. I'm done yakking."

"How many T-Bar cowboys was in here?"

"I don't know. Just a few."

"Was Crayfish with the boys?"

"I don't remember. You want another drink? Fifteen cents on the barrelhead."

The man I was talkin' about owned the T-Bar, a few other ranches, and wanted Admiral Bragg's outfit too, just so he could piss on any tree in the county and call it his. His name was Crayfish Ruble. I don't know about that Crayfish part, but since I got Cotton hung on me, I don't ask no one about their first names. Not Crayfish, not Admiral. Crayfish Ruble had a southern name but I'd heard he was from Wisconsin. Who knows how he got a name like that. He come west with some coin in his jeans and bought a little spread, then began muscling out the small-time settlers and farmers, paying about ten cents on the dollar. Pretty soon he was the biggest outfit in Puma County, and the T-Bar kept Doubtful going. Without the T-Bar, Doubtful would be a ghost town, and no one would know Puma County from New York City.

I liked Crayfish. He was honest in his crookedness. Ask Crayfish what he wanted from life, and he'd not mince any words. He wanted all of Puma County, as well as Sage County next door, and Bighorn County up above. He also wanted half the legislature of Wyoming, along with the judges and the tax assessor. I asked him, and that's what he told me. I also asked him what else he wanted, and he said he wanted half a dozen wives, or a good cathouse would do in a pinch, his own railroad car, and a mountain lion for a house pet. He got no children, so there ain't nothing he wants but land and cows and judges and women.

You sorta had to like Crayfish. He was a plain-speaker, and he sure beat Admiral Bragg for entertainment. Crayfish tried to buy out Admiral, but

Admiral, he filed a claim on every water hole and creek in all the county, and that led to bad blood. They've been threatening to shoot the balls off each other ever since. There's no tellin' what gets into people, but I take it personal. I gotta keep order in this here Puma County, and I know from experience that when a few males got strange handles, like Admiral and Crayfish, or Cotton, there's trouble a percolatin' and no way of escaping it. The feller with the worst handle usually wins. I've always figured Admiral is a worse name than Crayfish, and even worse than Cotton, though I'm not very happy with what got hung on me.

Well, I was gonna go talk to Crayfish again, for sure.

"Sammy, I think I asked you a question. Was Crayfish Ruble in here when the shooting started?"

Upward just polished the bar, like he didn't hear me.

"Who pays your wages, Sammy?"

I knew who. It was Crayfish. He owned the Last Chance, but didn't want no one to know it, so the name on the papers was Rosie, but she didn't have a dime more than she could make on her back. Someone put up a wad to buy the place, and it was Crayfish.

"I get my pay from Rosie," he said.

I leaned across the bar, grabbed a handful of apron, and pulled him tight. I seen his hands clawing for that Greener under the bar, so I just tugged him tighter.

"Don't," I said. "Who owns this joint?"

"Never did figure that out," he replied.

"You're a card, Upward. I think I'm going to look a lot closer at this here triple murder. Somebody shot three of Ruble's hands. Maybe it was King Bragg, just like the court says it was, but maybe it was someone else. You know who and ain't saying. I'm poking around a little more until I got a better handle on it. This ain't makin' me happy."

Upward, he didn't like that none.

THE FIRST MOUNTAIN MAN SERIES BY
WILLIAM W. JOHNSTONE

THE MOUNTAIN MAN SERIES BY
WILLIAM W. JOHNSTONE